Murder in the Air

(Twin Lakes Mysteries Book Two)

Marilyn Levinson

Cover Art Design by: Kelly Moran/Rowan Prose Publishing
Photo Credit: Adobe Images/Deposit Photos
Second Edition
ISBN: 978-1-961967-67-0
Rowan Prose Publishing, LLC
www.RowanProsePublishing.com
Published in the United States of America

PRAISE for Marilyn Levinson

"A master of the mystery and suspense genre."
Midwest Book Review

"A 'spirited' start to a fun new mystery series that kept me guessing to the end."
Booklist

"Plenty of red herrings and amusing characters."
Kirkus

Dedication/Acknowledgements:

For my wonderful daughter-in-law, Amy, who is special in every way.

Chapter One

Lydia Krause covered her ears against the grunts and groans of the bulldozer as it set about demolishing the old house. Though she'd placed her folding chair under the oak tree at the far end of the property, the noise still managed to grate on her nerves and rattle her spine. And on such a lovely May afternoon, too. She'd agreed to co-chair the Twin Lakes' New Development Committee because Dr. Andrew Varig had promised to observe the demo and construction and leave decorating the new clubhouse to her and her team. And where was Andrew, now that work had begun? Off traipsing around Europe—courtesy of his kids' surprise seventieth birthday gift.

"Lyddie!"

Benny Lieberman, friend and member of the Twin Lakes' Board of Directors, came bounding toward her. Benny was tall and skinny—a long drink of water, as Lydia's mother would have described him—in his mid-seventies.

"Come and watch!" he shouted over the din, as enthusiastic as a child. "They're about to start up the backhoe to excavate the root cellar!"

What do people find so fascinating about knocking down a house? Lydia wondered as she accompanied Benny to the work site. At least thirty spectators had their eyes glued to the action. A wall crashed to the ground, setting her teeth on edge.

"I'll be glad when destruction, construction, and decoration are done."

Benny grinned. "Your granddaughters will love playing miniature golf. I can't wait to start using the putting green."

Lydia's face softened at the mention of her granddaughters. Then she glanced at her watch. "I have to leave soon. Today's my day off and I've several errands to run."

"Then quit your job," was Benny's unsympathetic answer. "Isn't that why you sold your company and retired to the good life?"

Men, Lydia thought, though Izzy had always understood her need to work.

They joined George Linnett, the board president, and a few other Twin Lakes residents.

"Too bad Andrew's missing all this!" Benny exclaimed.

George cast him a look of disbelief. "You've gotta be kidding. The guy's having the time of his life taking in the sights of Europe and staying at five-star hotels."

"Still... you have to admit, this is exciting."

There were a few minutes of blessed silence. The bulldozer drove off and the backhoe took up its position. The noise began again, and Lydia decided she'd fulfilled her obligations for the day. She'd stay a few more minutes, and then say her good-byes.

A shout caught her attention. The backhoe driver pulled the machine to a halt then jumped down to stare at the ground he'd been excavating. The foreman and the general contractor joined him, followed by George and Benny.

"What is it?" Lydia called, peering down at them.

The driver, a huge, burly man wearing a bandana around his forehead, spared her a glance then turned to his foreman.

"Take a look at that." He pointed down at the ground.

The men huddled closer, blocking Lydia's view.

"Oh, my God, that looks like a body!" Benny exclaimed. He turned away and downed deep gulps of air.

"What was a body," the foreman agreed. "Whoever it was died a long time ago."

"Well, I'll be damned. Buried in the basement all these years," George mused.

"The root cellar, not the basement," the foreman corrected him.

Lydia made her way down to the work site. "Excuse me," she said pointedly, pushing her way past the men.

She stared down at the remains, blinking fiercely at what first appeared to be a bundle of rags wrapped around long sticks. The corpse had been shrouded in a blanket or quilt, though parts of the fabric had rotted away along with the body. The face remained covered, but the bottom part of the blanket had fallen open, revealing yellowed bones encased in tatters of what must have been brown trousers.

How sad to think this relic had once been a living, breathing person.

"I'll be damned," George said. "I bet these remains were in the root cellar for forty, fifty years while people lived in the house."

"Creepy," Benny commented.

"I wonder who it was," Lydia mused. "Who hid the body and why?"

"Probably someone killed the guy, and the murderer stashed it away," the backhoe driver said.

"Right, Joe," the foreman wryly replied. "Then conveniently forgot all about it."

"You have a better explanation?"

"Not at the moment, no."

His driver looked at him. "Does this mean I'm done for the day?"

"Looks that way," his boss agreed. He turned to George and Benny. "This throws a monkey wrench into our schedule."

"I can see that," George said, moving closer to the body.

The foreman edged closer, too, with Benny right behind them.

"Don't touch anything!" Lydia instructed.

"Wasn't going to," the foreman said. "Just trying to get a better look."

"Make sure that's all you do," she called over her shoulder as she went to retrieve her cell phone from her pocketbook beside her chair. "I'm calling the police."

Lydia gripped her ringing cell phone to still the tremor in her hand.

"Homicide. Molina."

The sound of Sol's voice set off a roman candle deep inside her. She had to struggle for control. "Hello, Sol. It's Lydia. Lydia Krause. I—"

"Lydia." Warmth crept into his voice, and she knew he was smiling. *Damn him!* Those green eyes lit up, no doubt, like lanterns. "Hi there. I've been meaning to call you for some time. How have you been?"

Lydia glanced back at the spectators, their eyes riveted on the remains in the root cellar.

"I'm fine, but this isn't a social call."

"Oh?"

His ability to convey disbelief, amusement and raw sexuality in one syllable was quite a feat.

"There's a dead body."

"You mean at Twin Lakes?" Sol groaned. "Tell me you're not caught up in another murder case, Lydia Krause."

She grinned, glad to have caught him on the hop. It took a hell of a lot to surprise Lieutenant Detective Sol Molina.

"Technically it is Twin Lakes, but actually it's the new property we've acquired. The demolition crew was razing the house, and they've uncovered the remains of a body. Whoever it was died a long time ago."

"I'm coming right away. What's that noise I hear?"

Lydia glanced at the backhoe moving to where the rest of the machinery was parked. "A backhoe."

"Tell them to shut off all machinery and to keep away from the site of discovery now! Death may have occurred fifty years ago, but if it's a homicide, the case remains open until solved."

Lydia strode back to the half dozen men gathered around the remains. The foreman crouched close to the body. He stretched out his hand.

"Don't touch the remains!" she shouted.

He stared at her in disbelief, but didn't back away.

Lydia ordered, "Get away from there now! The police are coming, and they want this area cleared." She eyed the construction foreman again. "And have the backhoe driver shut off his machine."

The burly man pushed back his bandanna and scratched his head. "Aye, aye, ma'am," he said lazily, and climbed back to the surface.

Her mission accomplished, Lydia ignored the foreman as he'd ignored her earlier. *Of course. I'm a woman.* But to be fair, she'd shown little interest in the demolition all day until they'd unearthed the body.

Benny and George flanked her on either side.

"Feeling okay, Lydia?" Benny asked, his kind leathery face wrinkled in concern.

"Want some iced tea? Caroline left me with a gallon of the stuff."

Lydia was about to rebuff his attention, when she realized her knees were a bit shaky. It wasn't every day one encountered a corpse, even one that had been dead for half a century.

"Sure, Benny. Thanks. I'm kind of thirsty."

She sipped, then smiled when George retrieved her folding chair and pocketbook. "Thank you, George." She sank into her chair, surprised when the two men remained standing on either side of her like sentries.

"I'm fine," she insisted. "No need for you guys to fuss over me."

"This isn't fussing." George shook his head in dismay. "Fussing's what's going to happen when the residents hear work on our new additions has been stopped and why."

Chapter Two

Lydia made her excuses and hurried off before Sol had time to arrive on the scene. She told herself that George and Benny could fill him in with whatever information he required. Her presence wasn't necessary. They knew as much as she did about the remains unearthed in the root cellar. More, since they'd been avidly watching the demolition all morning. She'd done her part by calling in the report.

"You're a coward!" Her own words startled her, bringing her to a dead stop in the wooded area that separated Twin Lakes from the construction site.

She walked slowly along the dirt path as she faced facts: she was acting cowardly, running from the scene of the crime, because she didn't want to see Sol. Oh, she wanted to see him, all right, but she simply couldn't wait there, wondering how he'd act, how she'd act, how seeing him would make her feel. She'd go home and eventually talk to whichever of his men he sent to interview her—unless he decided to talk to her himself.

Why had she called Sol directly instead of dialing 911? Was it to take pathetic advantage of a legitimate excuse to contact him after all these months? All these months of his not calling.

Lydia passed through the opening in the fence and turned onto Lake Nissaquage Boulevard, which led to her house.

"Lydia, wait up!"

Stefano Ligoris, the handsome grounds and maintenance manager, waved to her from the Twin Lakes' white pickup truck. "Do you still want me to oil your garage door?" he asked, stroking his luxurious mustache.

"Yes, Stefano, since it still squeaks. When can you stop by?"

He flashed his seductive smile that sent the hearts of most female residents aflutter. "I will come to your house the moment I am free, Lydia," he said in his East European accent, pronouncing her name "Lee-dia."

"What time is that?"

"I'll stop by at four, if that is suitable."

"Very suitable," Lydia said, knowing he'd arrive closer to four-thirty.

Stefano gestured with his chin toward the site. "Were you there when they found the corpse under the old house?"

"Yes. How did you hear about it so soon?"

"George called the clubhouse."

Lydia tensed, expecting the usual stab at humor at how she seemed to have an affinity for dead bodies. Instead, Stefano asked, "Did the demo equipment turn up anything else?"

"Anything else? Like what?"

He shrugged. "Like—anything?"

"I don't think so. See you later." She walked on, puzzled by his comment.

Reggie, her red tomcat, greeted her as she entered the kitchen from the garage.

"Have you been a good boy while Mommy was away?"

"Meow!" Reggie answered, rubbing against her legs.

"I see you're hungry as usual."

Lydia reached into the refrigerator for cat food and scooped some into a bowl. Though still a bit shaky from the shocking discovery, she longed to hop into her car and escape from Twin Lakes—at least as far as Main Street to run her errands. But common sense won out and she stayed put, available to whichever officer the police sent to question her. The phone rang. It was Katherine Linnett.

"Hi, Lydia. George told me what happened. How awful for you."

"More awful for the poor person hidden away in the root cellar. God knows if he was murdered."

"Or she," Katherine countered. "George asked me to let you know the police will be coming by your house to take your statement."

Already? "I figured they'd send someone, though I've nothing to add to what George, Benny, and the workmen have to say."

"A formality, my dear. Maybe that cute detective who saved your life will be the one stopping by. Detective Moreno?"

"Molina," Lydia corrected. "Thanks for letting me know, Katherine."

"Try to relax. Have some tea or scotch, or whatever works for you."

Tea, Lydia settled on as she put the kettle on. Soon the calls would begin. She considered disconnecting the phone, but decided, instead, to call her daughter. She and Merry were on much better terms than they'd been in years, but all that might go down the tubes if Merry heard second-hand that Lydia had witnessed the discovery of a corpse.

Before she could press the button that fast-dialed Meredith's number, the doorbell rang. Lydia hurried to answer it. Detective Lieutenant Sol Molina stood before her, as sexy and handsome as ever.

"Hello, Lydia."

"Hello, Sol." They stared into each other's eyes. His emerald gaze seemed to pulse with deep emotion. She cleared her throat. "Come inside."

Sol strode past her, his glance darting from side to side. "You've added some nice touches since my last visit. The place looks great."

"Thank you," Lydia murmured, speaking to his back as he studied her new living room drapes and curio cabinet.

She sat on one of the facing sofas separated by a glass coffee table. He settled down across from her and leaned forward. She felt an erotic stirring, which she quickly suppressed.

"How have you been, Lydia?"

"Fine, thank you."

"You look wonderful."

She nodded, pressing her lips together to keep from thanking him for a ridiculously ludicrous third time.

Sol gave a forced laugh. She was glad to see he felt as uncomfortable as she. "Here I am, once again questioning you about a corpse."

"About which I know nothing," Lydia pointed out, a bit sharper than she'd intended. "I'm co-chair of the New Development Committee and was on the site when they unearthed the body."

"That must have been upsetting."

She shuddered. "Not a pleasant sight."

"I'm sorry you had to see it." Sol reached across the table as though to pat her hand then jerked back. "The crime team's removing the remains. I doubt they'll get much information from the site, considering the demolition and passage of time. The corpse is another story. The lab people can determine sex, age, probable time frame, and cause of death."

"You mean how he or she was murdered?"

"The forensic tests will determine if it was murder." Sol paused, then said, "Tell me exactly what you saw at the time."

Lydia told him. She ended by saying, "The corpse seemed so... slender. I got the impression it was a young person."

She took his half smile for approbation that her assumption was correct. Despite the gruesome subject under discussion and the reason for his visit, Sol's approval gave Lydia a frisson of pleasure.

"The backhoe driver said the root cellar ran the length of the house," Sol said. "The body was at the end of a long section barely two feet high—it was well hidden. Still, it's a wonder no one discovered it until now."

"Sounds very suspicious to me."

"Naturally, we'll investigate. Thanks for calling me."

Lydia nodded. Clearly, the interview was over. She stood and waited for Sol to do the same. Instead, he cleared his throat. "Would it be too much trouble to boil some water for coffee? I forgot to eat lunch."

"No trouble at all," Lydia said formally. "Let's go into the kitchen."

He followed her across the dining room. Reggie came racing from a bedroom and rubbed up against Sol's leg. Smiling, Sol bent down to pet Reggie's flank. The cat began to purr. "Good boy!" Sol grinned up at her. "Reggie remembers me."

"He's a friendly feline," Lydia said, though in truth Reggie rarely sought attention from her guests. *Damn Sol!* She smiled to herself when Reggie dashed into the kitchen ahead of them to meow beside his dish. "I just fed you! Eat what's left," Lydia told him.

For once, Reggie obeyed, eliciting a look of admiration from Sol. "You have him well trained."

"For a cat," Lydia amended, thinking cats obliged their human companions only when they chose.

She filled the kettle with water and placed it on the stove. With a sigh, Sol dropped into a chair and stretched out his legs. "It feels good to take a five-minute break."

"Make yourself at home," Lydia said sarcastically.

"Lydia...."

"Yes?"

"Please don't make this more difficult than it is."

"Me make it difficult?" She let out a humorless laugh. "You've got to be kidding."

"You knew this would be treated as a homicide, which is why you called me."

When she didn't respond, he continued. "I have to question you and everyone else who was present when they unearthed those remains."

"You or someone on your homicide team. I bet Officer McK-lusky is questioning George or Benny this very minute."

He laughed. "You're quick, Lydia. It's one of the things I like most about you."

Lydia sat down and stared him in the eye. "I never would have guessed you liked anything about me."

"Couldn't you tell the last time we were out together?"

"The last time? Let's see, that was back in February. The second Saturday in February, to be exact. If I remember correctly, you jumped up from what we were doing and said you'd be calling."

"And I never did." He sounded mournful.

A silence descended. Lydia stifled her natural inclination to encourage a reluctant speaker. She would not give Solomon Molina the satisfaction of asking why he'd never called again.

After a long minute, he asked, "Didn't you wonder why?"

Lydia glared at him. "Of course I wondered why! I ran through every stupid thing I might have said or done to chase you away."

Sol covered her hand with his. Lydia tried to pull free, but he held fast. "I was frightened, all right? Afraid I was falling for you big time. Now go ahead and laugh."

"I'm not going to laugh," she said, doing her best to absorb Sol's admission. He liked her. He really liked her. But to her great surprise, she tossed back her head and roared with laughter until tears streamed down her cheeks. His shocked expression set her off on another peal. Lydia reached for a napkin and dabbed at her eyes. "I'm sorry, but seeing those remains must have unhinged me. It's just that you're a homicide detective who deals with murderers and corpses, yet *I* scare *you* away?"

Sol leaped to his feet, his now-hazel eyes narrowed with anger, his earlobes red with humiliation. "Knock yourself out," he muttered, and strode toward the front door.

"Sol, wait!" she called after him. "I didn't mean to laugh at you."

"It doesn't matter." He reached for the doorknob.

Lydia's heart thumped as she touched his shoulder. Sol Molina was an unknown quantity. He was relationship-phobic and would break her heart. Or things between them would change for the better.

"Of course it matters. I know what you mean—about being afraid."

"Lydia, I don't want to discuss it."

"There may not be another time, so I want to discuss it." She took a deep breath. "Everyone's afraid when it comes to relationships, including me."

He gave a snort. "I doubt that sincerely."

She shrugged. "Sol, no one likes to get hurt, and you hurt me by not calling."

"I apologize. I thought it would be easier if I made the break when I did. We're too different, you and me. We live in different worlds."

"So what?" She felt the laughter rising again, along with the urge to croon "Two Different Worlds We Live In." This time she managed to control herself. "We're not getting married, lieutenant. No need to be so dramatic. Please, Sol." She gazed into his troubled face.

He rubbed her arms. "I've missed you, Lydia Krause."

"Then do something about it."

He bent to kiss her lightly on the lips. "I'll call you. This time I mean it."

<hr>

The discovery of the body put a stop to all work on the site for the rest of the week. From Tuesday afternoon until Friday noon, the site was secured and bound off by yellow tape as various crime teams investigated the root cellar and rummaged among the remains of the razed house in search of clues.

More than ever, Lydia appreciated her part-time job at Carrington House, which removed her from the hothouse community of Twin Lakes. The old mansion had been converted into a restaurant-catering house, with a world-famous chef at the helm. Though Lydia had been hired as bookkeeper, her duties now extended to interviews with prospective clients and handling bookings. Business was good, and the corporation had begun the construction of Carrington Suites—an elegant hotel for guests attending Carrington affairs. Lydia had been offered the position of managing Carrington Suites, and she still hadn't made up her mind if she'd take it or not.

"An impossible task," Sol told her late Wednesday afternoon as she poured them both a cup of coffee. "The lab estimates the body's been down there between fifty and seventy-five years, and they're leaning toward the longer time period."

"Whew!" Lydia shook her head. "For three-quarters of a century families lived in that house, along with a body in the root cellar. Any idea who it was?"

"No ID yet, except he was a young male between thirteen and seventeen years of age."

She nodded, making her calculations. "Any unusual deaths in the family who lived there seventy-five years ago?"

Sol grinned as he stretched out his legs. "We're checking on that, Miss Marple. We're following every possible lead, every which way—going through town records, old newspapers, old police files. You name it, we're working on it. It's not easy when most of the people you want to question are living in another state, dead, or too senile to remember."

"I wonder who killed him and why?"

Sol grinned. "You don't give up, do you?"

Annoyed, Lydia demanded, "What do you mean, 'give up?'"

"Playing detective is what I mean." His green eyes twinkled mischievously. "The boys at the station house can't get over how you were in on the discovery scene."

Lydia stood up. "I was not in on discovering the body. I was there because my co-chair swore he'd watch all demolition and construction then went on vacation instead."

Sol stood, also, and placed his hands on her waist. "Regardless, the fact is you were there when they made the discovery, and it stirred your curiosity." She shrugged, refusing to admit he was right.

"But you won't go poking around on your own, correct?"

"I've no intention of usurping your job, if that's what you mean!" Lydia broke free and strode out of the kitchen. "Sorry to be so abrupt, but I've been working all day and I've things to see to."

"No need to get all heated up," he said.

Lydia turned, startled to discover he was close behind her. The man moved as swiftly as a cougar.

"But I'm serious about you not getting involved." He paused. "Remember when the homeowner died last fall?"

Lydia nodded. "The old man was in his nineties and refused to go into a nursing home."

"As soon as the house became vacant, local drug dealers took it over to make sales and shoot up."

"Really!" Lydia exclaimed. "I had no idea."

Sol laughed. "Your ignorance of the matter blows me away."

Lydia wasn't amused. "I don't know everything that goes on around here, nor do I want to. You needn't fear. I've no intention of 'poking around,' as you put it."

He took her hand and raised it to his lips. "If only I could believe that were true."

Chapter Three

The following week, Lydia had to contend with a barrage of phone calls from Twin Lakes' residents, all of whom assumed she had the inside track regarding the police investigation. Neighbors stopped her in the clubhouse, as she power-walked, and as she shopped in the local supermarket to inquire about the boy: What was his name? How had he died? Who had stuck his body in the root cellar? Lydia's insistence that she knew no more than they did was waved away with fluttering hands and the blithe declaration that Detective Lieutenant Molina was sure to keep her apprised of any new developments in the case. After all, she'd taken part in the investigation of the murders that had occurred the previous autumn. And—wink, wink—didn't she and Lieutenant Molina enjoy a special friendship?

Even Meredith, her own daughter, decided that Lydia had chosen to be involved in this new Twin Lakes mystery.

"Honestly, Mother, I would think you've had enough of murder and mayhem to last you a lifetime," she'd called to tell Lydia the evening the body had been found.

"You thought correctly, Merry."

When Merry remained silent, Lydia let out a snort of indignation. "You can't imagine for one minute that I wanted to be there."

Merry paused, then said, "Of course not, but it's odd that you happened to be on the scene. Almost as though you're drawn to dead bodies, or they're drawn to you."

"Thank you, dear. I appreciate your support," she said dryly, and Meredith quickly apologized.

Relieved, Lydia sent her love to Jeff, Brittany, and little Greta, and ended the conversation. Merry seemed happier these last few months, now that she was back teaching school. Lydia was delighted Merry and Jeff had agreed to let her pay half of their new nanny's wages. Kirsten was a bright, energetic young woman who added a dimension to her charges' lives. These days, whatever time Lydia spent with her granddaughters were special occasions instead of a baby-sitting chore.

The autopsy on the remains showed that the boy had been between fourteen and sixteen years of age when he'd died, and he'd been dead for seventy-five years. But a week later, his identity still remained a mystery. Driving home from Carrington House, Lydia found herself wondering who he was. *Had he lived in the house? In the neighborhood? Why hadn't anyone reported his disappearance? But even if they had, who would have considered investigating root cellars?*

Still musing over her unanswered questions, Lydia drove into the garage and stepped out of her car. She was about to press the button that shut the automatic door, when someone called her name. She turned to find Daniel Korman, who lived across the street, standing in the entrance.

"Daniel, I didn't see you! My God, I almost closed the garage door on you!"

Daniel chuckled. "You can't imagine I'm too decrepit to move out of the way. You're speaking to last summer's winner of the over-seventy-five singles' tennis tournament."

"So I've been told." Lydia nodded approvingly at his erect six-foot frame. "Not to mention, you're the most handsome eighty-five-year-old I know."

"Much appreciated, my dear, though my birthday's not till Tuesday."

"We're all looking forward to celebrating with you tomorrow night. Evelyn stopped by before to go over some last-minute details. You're going to have the best party Carrington House has to offer. You've my word on that."

"Thanks, Lydia. I appreciate your special efforts on our behalf." Daniel's smile wreathed his face. He was handsome, with his strong chin, classical nose, and high forehead. And a full head of white hair. "I'm not one for a big fuss and dressing up, but Evelyn's insisted on the works to celebrate my birthday. And who am I to say no? She's the light of my life."

"You picked one terrific lady," Lydia agreed. "Evelyn has more energy than most women half her age."

"I don't know how I managed to live eighty-five years without her," he murmured, retrieving two candies wrapped in gold foil from his shirt pocket. Daniel's other passion—Bertran's Best—was probably the most expensive Belgian chocolate on the market.

He extended his hand. Lydia smiled and shook her head. Daniel unwrapped both dark chocolates and popped them into his mouth.

She was about to make a wisecrack about finding romantic love in one's golden years but refrained. Despite his joviality a minute ago, Daniel's expression had turned somber. His shoulders slumped as though weighed down by unseen burdens. "Is something wrong, Daniel?"

He shrugged. "Could be. If you don't mind, I'd like to run something by you—get your input, so to speak."

His manner set off warning bells in her head. "Sure. Come inside and we'll talk about it."

He refused her offer of coffee with a quick shake of his head. The gesture struck her as decisive rather than rude. It reminded her that, until a few years ago, Daniel had been a powerful corporate wheeler-dealer. He'd taken over several companies on the verge of bankruptcy, and breathed life into them via bold innovations.

She managed not to trip over a hungry Reggie weaving in and out of her legs and led Daniel into the living room. "Have a seat. I'll be with you as soon as I feed the feline."

A minute later, she perched on the sofa opposite him and offered her full attention. "What is it, Daniel?"

He studied her for a minute as though wondering how she might receive his words, then cleared his throat. "All my working life I've made important decisions—decisions affecting hundreds if not thousands of employees. But this is something else entirely." He frowned. "Normally I'd discuss it with Evelyn, but she's up to her ears in plans for my birthday festivities. Since my son, Arnold, and his crew are staying over, she insists on hosting a Sunday brunch at our place."

Seconds passed. Lydia pressed her lips together to keep from urging him to continue. Daniel would divulge what he had to say in his own good time. When she could bear it no longer and opened her mouth to encourage him, he asked, "What would you do if you learned that a crime you suspected of occurring many years ago actually had taken place? And that you knew who'd committed this crime but had no way of proving it."

Lydia immediately thought of the dead body discovered ten days before. *Surely Daniel wasn't referring to that!* It was too preposterous. The corpse had been found behind Twin Lakes.

"I'm not sure what action I'd take," she answered as calmly as she could manage. "It would depend on the severity of the crime. How certain I was of the person's guilt."

"A friend of mine disappeared, Lydia. Now I'm sure he was murdered."

"Are you talking about the body the excavators unearthed? Was that your friend?"

Instead of answering, he stared at her intently. "I've no proof, but now it all adds up. The question is, do I let sleeping dogs lie after all these years, or do I make the guilty pay for the crime?"

The guilty. "Are you saying there's more than one person responsible? I think you should tell the police."

"Tell them what exactly? They investigated years ago and came up with zilch."

"But these days the police have DNA and other tests they can use."

"It's too late for tests," he said, then added more softly, "And Evelyn invited them to my party."

Lydia stared at him. "You still talk to them?"

Daniel stood and patted her hand to soften his dismissal. "My dear, I'm not sure of what I'm saying. You've been very kind, letting an old man ramble on."

"But Daniel," she protested. "If this has something to do with the body they found, you need to tell the police what you know."

He kissed her cheek. "I'll take what you say under advisement. Meanwhile, I trust I can count on your discretion not to breathe a word of this to anyone, including your friend, Lieutenant Molina."

Dumbly she nodded, feeling she'd been sworn to a lawyer-client or doctor-patient oath of silence, and walked him to the door.

Daniel's birthday party was at seven o'clock. Lydia slipped into the simple black designer dress she knew did wonders for her figure and scrutinized herself in the mirror. Her light brown hair had been cut and blown that afternoon, so it framed her face, making her look years younger. It was a pity Sol Molina couldn't see her now. Even more of a pity that he wasn't her date for the evening. Actually, she'd considered asking him to be her escort, then immediately squelched the idea. Not only was it a bad move—such an invitation would probably send him fleeing for his life—but he'd feel ill-at-ease mingling with Twin Lakes residents, all of whom were bound to ask a barrage of questions regarding the unidentified body.

She finished applying her lipstick and shook her head. She wouldn't waste time speculating about Sol Molina. Either he'd call when the case was over, or he wouldn't.

As she lined her eyelids, she ruminated about what Daniel had told her. Clearly, he was disturbed by what he considered to be proof that someone had been murdered. Lydia had assumed this involved the recently discovered body, but now she was no longer sure—just as Daniel couldn't decide whether or not to take his suspicions to the authorities. When she'd run into him and Evelyn earlier in the day, he'd greeted her warmly then whisked Evelyn away. She'd heard Evelyn chiding him for being rude and asking where they were off to in such a hurry.

Lydia didn't hold Daniel's behavior against him. He probably regretted having shared what he'd told her, and didn't want to risk her asking questions. At any rate, he was entitled to enjoy his birthday party without worry. She'd wait a few days then bring up the subject with him in private.

Caroline and Benny came for her at a quarter to seven. She greeted them and her closest Twin Lakes friend, Barbara Taylor, already ensconced in the rear seat of the Liebermans' car.

"Don't you look stunning!" Benny commented.

"Well, thank you," Lydia said.

Slowly, Benny backed out of the driveway. "Lucky me, escorting the three loveliest ladies to Daniel's party."

"Watch that car speeding toward us!" Caroline stared at Benny. "Or none of us will get there in one piece."

"Yes, dear," Benny answered.

Caroline, a tall, lanky brunette whose tan and wrinkled face attested to her many years of playing golf, bent over to kiss his cheek. "There's only one woman you're escorting, and that's me."

"Yes, dear."

"Don't worry about us, Benny," Barbara teased. "Lydia and I are sure to hook up with some good-looking friends of Daniel's before the evening's over." Petite and slender, and a widow like Lydia, she appeared to be many years younger than a woman approaching the age of Medicare.

"Lydia, why didn't you bring Detective Molina along?" Benny asked as they exited Twin Lakes. "I noticed his car outside your house the other afternoon."

Lydia felt her face redden, but before she could answer—"Benny, watch out for that truck!" Caroline was chiding her husband again.

Benny took the hint and dropped the subject. As they turned onto the main road, he said, "The police say we can resume work on Monday. They've investigated the land around the root cellar but found nothing to give them clues about the body."

"Glad to hear it," Lydia said, though Sol had told her this the day before. Caroline turned around to stare pointedly at the Bertran's gift bag Lydia had placed on the seat between Barbara and her. "I see you've disregarded the invitation's 'no gifts, please' and bought Daniel a present."

"It's only a box of his favorite chocolates," Barbara explained.

Benny laughed. "Admit it, Caroline. We have a gag gift in the trunk."

"Much as we try, we can't break the habit of bringing a present to a birthday party."

Minutes later they drove up the winding road that led to Carrington House. The stone manor house, built by a rich entrepreneur in the early twentieth century, sat atop a crest, behind which flowed a two-tiered bluestone patio and an extensive lawn, bounded by woods on each side. They followed the road to the parking area, passing azalea and rhododendron bushes bursting with red and purple blossoms. Lydia smiled as they climbed the wide stairs rising to the front entrance. Though she worked here three days a week, she never failed to admire the graceful lines of the mansion enhanced by its perfect setting.

She winked at Thomas, the evening manager, who showed them into the small cloakroom to the left of the entrance. Lydia and Benny placed Daniel's birthday presents on a table beside other gift-wrapped boxes. Clearly, they weren't the only guests to ignore the "no gifts" request.

From there, Thomas ushered them into a high-ceilinged, tastefully decorated salon, its trio of floor-to-ceiling windows allowing the last rays of sun to filter through the sheer curtains. A harpist played softly in the corner while young servers circulated among the thirty or so guests, offering champagne and hors d'oeuvres. Lydia, finding herself separated from her friends, reached for a glass of champagne. She sipped, exchanged greetings with a Twin Lakes couple, and then went in search of her host and hostess.

Evelyn and Daniel stood welcoming their guests beside a brocade sofa in the center of the room. They made an elegant couple: Evelyn in a pale green satin gown that set off her salon-coiffed, auburn hair, Daniel, tall and dashing in a tuxedo.

Lydia kissed both on the cheek. "What a wonderful party, Evelyn. Happy birthday, Daniel. And many, many more."

They embraced her warmly. Daniel slipped an arm about her waist.

"Thank you, Lydia. You're one of our favorites, and we're delighted you're celebrating with us." He grinned and lowered his voice. "Stay tuned to the big announcement later on."

Evelyn reached inside her beaded purse and slipped a ring on her finger. She extended her left hand to show Lydia the sparkling diamond. At least three carets, Lydia surmised, in an exquisite modern platinum setting.

"It's beautiful! Congratulations, both of you. I wish the two of you every happiness."

"Thank you, my dear," Daniel said, looking past her, "but please keep it to yourself for the time being."

"Certainly," Lydia murmured, watching Evelyn return the ring to her purse. She was puzzled. Surely others must have noticed this display. But she had no time to wonder about it, because a flurry of people were descending on Daniel, hugging him and nodding to Evelyn. Lydia started to move away, when Daniel called after her.

"Lydia, come and meet my children!"

"With pleasure," she said, though she would have much preferred to leave Daniel to his family. She knew and liked his youngest daughter, but the older two—Evelyn had confided—were bad news.

Daniel made the introductions, his hand resting on the sloped shoulder of the fifty-something, balding man in glasses who stood beside him. "This is my son, Arnold and his wife,

Madge." He presented their two children and their spouses. "And my favorite great-granddaughter, Elizabeth."

"Your only great-grandchild, Poppy," the ten-year-old informed him.

Everyone laughed. Lydia, knowing Daniel's son and his offspring had rented a van so they could all travel together from New Jersey, asked about their drive to Long Island. To her dismay, Arnold told her in detail how bad the traffic had been on the Garden State Parkway and the George Washington Bridge, and of the accident on the Cross Bronx Expressway. Before he could complain about the traffic pattern on the Long Island Expressway, his daughter, Carolee, a younger, prettier version of her matronly mother, interrupted.

"We're here, Dad, that's what's important. Let's focus on the positive."

Her father scowled, but, before he could respond, Daniel declared, "Denise and Bennett have arrived!"

"Hi, everyone." Denise had a smoker's raspy voice. She was tall like her father, but gaunt enough so that her collarbone jutted out unbecomingly above her low-cut dress. The deep tan on her face and arms came from either a very long beach vacation or a tanning salon. She emitted the stale odor of tobacco. Daniel wrinkled his nose as his daughter hugged him.

"Hello, Denise. I thought you were giving up the habit."

"I'm tapering off." Her dark eyes glanced around the room until she spotted one of the servers in a far corner. "Be back as soon as I get myself a drink."

"Bring me one, Mom," Bennett said, squeezing his mother's arm in a way that made Lydia cringe—though she wasn't quite sure why. "Something strong."

Lydia was certain she'd seen Daniel's grandson before, probably when he'd come to visit his grandfather. Bennett appeared to be in his early thirties and, but for a weak chin, would have had the good looks of a dark Adonis. *She adores and spoils him*, Lydia decided, watching Denise kiss her son's cheek then dash off to do his bidding.

Bennett slapped Daniel on the back. "Hey there, Grandpa! You look great for a guy getting up there in years."

Daniel winced. "Thanks, Bennett. Did you say hello to Evelyn?"

Bennett raised a finger to Evelyn and offered her a weak smile, then turned his back to chat with his cousins.

"I see you've met the family," Barbara said when Lydia joined her at a tiny round table for four in the adjoining room.

"Mmm," Lydia answered, nibbling a buffalo chicken wing. "They're as bad as Evelyn said they were. The son's a kvetch, the daughter's the nervous type that smokes and drinks but rarely eats, and her son thinks he's God's gift to humanity."

"All that in five minutes," Barbara murmured. "You are becoming quite the sleuth."

Lydia rolled her eyes. "If running a company didn't teach me to size up people on the spot, I'd have been in deep you-know-what."

"True enough," Barbara agreed.

"Getting back on topic, I'm glad Daniel has Polly close by," Lydia said, referring to his youngest child who lived in the same development as Meredith and her family, a five-minute drive from Twin Lakes.

Barbara nodded. "They have a loving father-daughter relationship."

For the next few minutes, they concentrated on polishing off the appetizers they'd collected at the serving table. After Lydia devoured the last morsel of food on her plate, she stood and threw back her shoulders. "Be right back. I'm after sushi this time. You can take it from me—it's fresh and it's terrific."

"Everything's terrific!" Caroline said as she and Benny joined them.

The sushi bar was proving popular, but Jimmy, one of Lydia's favorite waiters, beckoned to her and handed her pincers. Lydia grinned as she filled a small plate with pieces of yellow fin tuna, salmon, eel, and slivers of ginger. *It always helps to know the staff.*

She stopped en route to her table as Polly and her husband approached, flanking one of their daughters, as though she was a bride. Not that anyone would take Gillian for a bride. Her getup was more suited for a bordello. Her hair, dyed a garish orange-red, stood up in half-inch spikes. Thigh-high black boots revealed a flash of black tights before the black Lycra dress began and soon ended in a deep v-neckline. Gillian's thick eye liner—more decoration than makeup—gave her cats' eyes, which set off her one enormous purple hoop earring and diamond nose stud. *All she needed was a whip*, Lydia thought, *and she'd make the perfect dominatrix.*

Nicole, Gillian's twin, followed the trio wrapped arm in arm with a young man. He wore a black jacket over a black polo and black jeans. His unkempt hair and three days' beard contrasted sharply with the appearance of the other guests. Nicole was dressed in a short frilly skirt and gypsy-styled satin white blouse, her long blonde mane rippling down her back. *The good twin and the bad twin*, Lydia mused, then berated herself for the unkind thought.

She walked up to Polly, who was blonde like Nicole and looked considerably younger than her forty-five years. Tonight, she wore a fitted, flower-print dress that showed off her slender figure.

"Polly, Matt, how nice to see you on this happiest of occasions. And Nicole and Gillian."

Matt, a successful real estate lawyer, bent down to kiss her cheek. His daughters greeted Lydia. Nicole introduced her boyfriend, Ringo, who offered a half-hearted smile. The three young people disappeared in the crowd.

Polly stared after them, a frown on her face, then turned back to give Lydia a quick hug. "Lydia, have you seen Dad?"

Lydia looked around for Daniel, but he was nowhere in sight. "I was speaking to your father and Evelyn in the other room—"

"Are my brother and sister here?"

"Yes, dear. Your father introduced me—"

"Thanks!" Polly took off before Lydia could finish her sentence.

"Is something wrong?" Lydia asked Matt.

He shrugged and offered an apologetic smile. "You know families. Something's always brewing."

"I hope nothing that will upset Daniel, especially tonight."

"Don't worry. Polly's an ace at making life run smoothly. I'd better go find her."

His words did nothing to reassure Lydia. She suddenly remembered that the people Daniel suspected of murder had been invited to the party.

She returned to the table and said to Barbara, "Something's wrong. I can feel it in my bones."

Her friend placed a hand on her arm. "Lydia Krause, you're letting your imagination run away with you."

Lydia forced a smile. "I sincerely hope so."

"Relax. Enjoy the party."

She tried to shrug off the feeling of unease that something heavy threatened the festive mood of Daniel's birthday celebration. She made herself listen to Benny's joke, to eat the sushi she'd desired only minutes earlier. When Thomas approached, inviting them to take their places in the dining room, she gave a sigh of relief. Maybe nothing would mar Evelyn's carefully planned party, after all.

Chapter Four

Lydia sat between Barbara and Caroline, and within chatting distance of the Linnetts. Across the table, two couples were catching up with each other's news. Lydia wondered if the men were the old friends Daniel had alluded to. She didn't think so, as both appeared to be in their seventies, about ten years younger than Daniel. Introductions were made and easy conversation followed. A server approached to take their orders for prime rib, chicken cordon bleu, or pecan-crusted salmon.

Arnold rose to toast his father and to thank Evelyn for hosting the event. *A lukewarm salute from a drip of a man*, Lydia thought as family and friends applauded.

The wait staff served cold red borscht.

"Yummy," Benny declared after he'd finished his serving and half of his wife's. "I haven't had borsch in years."

Katherine Linnett scolded him. "Benny, they'll serve you seconds if you ask. No need to take poor Caroline's food."

Caroline grinned. "Are you kidding? Benny call over a waiter when he can grab what's on my plate? But fear not—he won't be pirating any of my prime rib until I've eaten my fair share."

"Caro, dear, I have no designs on your red meat," Benny protested. "Everyone knows fish is healthier. Which is why I ordered the salmon."

Lydia joined the others in laughter, as she set aside her concerns regarding Daniel and allowed herself to enjoy the festivities. She felt as though she was sitting in the midst of long-time friends when in fact she'd met Barbara, the Liebermans, and the Linnetts a mere eight months before. But living in a gated community fostered a bond among its residents, much the way college dorms, sleep-away camp, and the armed forces did.

The three musicians ended the Mozart sonata and struck up a medley of Cole Porter songs. Benny and George led their wives to the small dance floor where Daniel and Evelyn were already doing the foxtrot. Evelyn's head was tilted back as she gazed into Daniel's eyes. He whispered into her ear, and they burst out laughing. They stopped dancing, realized they had, and then Daniel pulled Evelyn close, and she nestled against his tall frame as they moved once again to the music.

"Now that's something I'd give my eyeteeth and my front teeth to have," Barbara murmured so only Lydia could hear.

"It would be nice, wouldn't it?"

"How's our favorite detective these days?"

Lydia gave a start because she'd been imagining herself swaying to the music in Sol's arms. "Fine. He's busy with the case."

They observed the dancers in silence. George escorted Catherine to her seat and asked Lydia, "May I have the honor?"

"Of course," Lydia responded. They walked to the dance floor now filled to capacity. She was surprised when George, who was a few inches shorter than she, held her in a practiced grip and led her masterfully into a modified lindy as the musicians picked up the tempo.

"I'm glad the workers will be back on the job Monday morning," he said. "I'm hoping things will move along so residents will be able to use the putting green and miniature golf by mid-August. We'll be placing news updates of our additions in the local papers." He gave a rueful laugh. "God knows Twin Lakes can use some good PR."

"Why, George? You sound concerned."

"I am, somewhat," he admitted. "We've a few units on the market and they haven't been moving. I'm afraid the discovery of the body in the root cellar, on top of the other murders, has made us a less than desirable senior community. Two recent sales went for appreciatively less than their asking price."

"Oh," Lydia said. "That means—"

"If it continues, the value of every unit goes down."

Lydia eyed him. "Are you and Catherine thinking of moving?"

George's laughter had a guilty ring to it. "Nothing gets past you, Lydia Krause. You must have run your company like a battleship."

She giggled, warmed by his praise. "Not exactly, but I made it my business to be up on what was happening in every department." She shook her head. "Not that it matters in the long run. I understand Krause Enterprises is being sold again—this time to a big conglomerate."

George sighed. "Still, one always cares."

"Too true," Lydia agreed. "But to return to the subject of moving. Are you and Catherine considering leaving Twin Lakes?"

George shrugged his shoulders. "Could be. Our son-in-law may be taking a job in North Carolina. Catherine wants to live near the grandchildren."

"You have two grandchildren who live in Manhattan," Lydia pointed out.

"Yes, but they're older and willing to travel at the drop of a pin. My son and his wife used to send them to us in Florida when they were six and seven. They'll come visit us there."

The music stopped. George bowed over her hand. "Thank you, Miss Lydia. And please keep what you've wheedled out from me under your hat."

"Of course. I'll be sorry to see you both leave."

Nothing stays put, Lydia thought as she took her seat. A problem arises and roars for attention. We find a solution, and another matter arises in its place.

"What's wrong?" Barbara asked.

Lydia shook her head. "Nothing. Just pondering the strange phenomenon called life."

Barbara laughed. "Is that all?"

They ate their salads, which were followed by another period of dancing. Daniel and Evelyn stopped by the table to kibitz.

"We're having a wonderful time," Caroline answered in response to Daniel's question.

"We sure are! It's like a wedding!" Benny said "Ouch!" he exclaimed and tossed Caroline an aggrieved look of bewilderment. "What did you do that for?"

Everyone laughed, Daniel and Evelyn most of all. Clearly, they were hugging their secret to themselves and having the time of their lives doing it.

The musicians ended their medley of tunes. Polly approached the microphone. In a shaky voice, she thanked everyone for coming to celebrate her father's eighty-fifth birthday. Her confidence increased and her voice grew stronger as she related fond memories of growing up as Daniel's daughter. She told anecdotes illustrating what a wonderful father he'd been: how he'd taught her to ice skate at Rockefeller Center and smuggled her pet dog into camp on visiting day.

Daniel, Lydia noted, glowed under his daughter's cloak of love and praise, as happy as she'd ever seen him. Her gaze fell on Denise, whose head shook in angry denial. Clearly, Denise's memories were nothing like her sister's.

Polly ended to a hearty round of applause. Daniel came up to the microphone, gave Polly a bear hug, and she returned to her seat. Silence fell when his guests realized Daniel intended to speak.

"Thank you, Polly, for your kind words. Raising you, my youngest child, was both an honor and a joy." He went on to thank family members and friends for coming to celebrate his eighty-fifth birthday. Then he beamed at Evelyn, who smiled back with adoration in her eyes. He beckoned to her, and she came to stand beside him.

"My dear Evelyn arranged my birthday celebration tonight." He reached for her hand. "She is the woman of my heart, my life companion these last four years. And now we're making it official. By next week this time, we'll be an old married couple and away on our honeymoon."

Shouts and cheers filled the room as servers refilled champagne glasses. Daniel proposed a toast to his fiancée. Everyone cheered and sipped. Daniel's friend, Allen, rose from his seat at Lydia's table, and proposed a toast to the engaged couple.

"Now that's a surprise," Barbara commented as she finished off the last of her champagne."

"I think it's romantic," Benny said. "Evelyn and Daniel are mad about each other."

His wife sighed, exasperated. "Of course they're mad about each other, but these days couples in their late seventies and eighties usually don't bother with legalities like marriage. It avoids complications."

"You're referring to inheritances," Benny said. "I'm sure Daniel has seen to that. And Evelyn's not a pauper, you know."

Catherine nodded and, in a lowered voice, added, "She certainly isn't. And her daughter's husband has big bucks. But Daniel has a rocky relationship with his two older kids. I'm glad they came tonight."

"I sensed strained relationships when I met them earlier this evening," Lydia said.

"I don't know Daniel's kids," Barbara said, "but I've always found him to be warm and generous."

"He certainly has a good relationship with Polly," Lydia said. "She and her family adore him."

Catherine grimaced. "The other two are examples of 'small children, small problems, big children, big problems.' Daniel's fed up with bailing Arnold out of one business failure after another. And Denise goes into drug rehab like other women go to a spa."

"Poor Daniel," Lydia murmured. Their food appeared and conversation died away as they concentrated on their meal.

Lydia finished most of her salmon, then got up to go to the ladies' room. There was one close by, opposite the kitchen, which she used during the week. She tried to open the door, but found it was locked. *Damn Len, the general manager of Carrington House, and his overdeveloped sense of security!* She'd have to trek down to the ladies' room near the front entrance of the mansion.

She passed the room where they'd had the cocktail hour earlier. This section of the mansion was dimly lit. Another one of Len's economical ideas! She'd give him a piece of her mind on Monday morning, reminding him that a lawsuit brought on by a broken leg or a dislocated hip was costlier than a few dozen light bulbs.

Lydia walked slowly down the corridor, keeping close to the wall so she wouldn't trip. She was about to turn into the narrow passageway that led to the ladies' room when angry voices spilled across the front entrance hall. She paused before peering into the cloakroom, where earlier Daniel's guests had left their presents on a table. Arnold was speaking at what appeared to be a family conclave.

"…we made a point of arriving early enough to stop by the house and talk to Dad. This stationery store is a moneymaker. It's in an excellent location, and the only reason the guy's selling is his wife's sick, and they have to move to Arizona. But did Dad listen? I barely got three words out, when he said he didn't have the money to subsidize another business venture!"

Denise chortled as she pointed her cigarette at her brother. "What do you expect? This is the third handout you're asking for this year."

"Thanks, Denise. I can always count on you for support. The one member of this family who's never earned a cent in her life."

Madge, Arnold's wife, said softly, "We needed the money to pay my medical bills. And to help Robert and Andrea with a down payment on their new home."

"Don't waste your breath explaining, Madge," Arnold told his wife. "We all know Dad never spent two minutes with Denise or me when we were growing up. He was too busy making his millions. And why shouldn't I ask him for a loan? I'm his only son, for God's sake. He should have faith in me!"

"Arnold, stop whining," Polly said. "This is Dad's birthday party, not group therapy."

Denise let out a derisive laugh. "You've nothing to complain about because you've always been Daddy's little girl. Lucky Polly! He discovered the joy of fatherhood when you were born."

Arnold said, "Let's not dwell on the past, Denise. We're here to talk about the way Dad's changed. How he's suddenly gone cheap. All because he's marrying that gold digger, Evelyn."

"When you're right, you're right," Denise said. "And we can thank Madge for introducing them."

Lydia refused to listen to another word of this dreadful conversation. In the ladies' room, she shut the door behind her and welcomed the silence. When she walked back to the dining room a few minutes later, the cloakroom was empty.

Curious now about Daniel's older children, she decided to find out what she could from Daniel's friends. Her chance came just before dessert was being served when she found herself alone at the table with Allen, who had toasted Daniel earlier, and his wife, Rosalie. She scooted over to the seat next to Rosalie, a pleasant, plump woman in her mid-seventies.

"You've both known Daniel for many years now," she said to open the conversation.

Allen needed no prompting. He rested his hand on the back of his wife's chair and leaned toward Lydia so she could hear him over the cha-cha music.

"Rosalie and I've known him for half a century now."

Rosalie smiled, revealing a dimple in her cheek. "Al and Danny met working in a shoe store in Queens. Al and I were newlyweds. Freda and Danny had been married for five years and were considering having kids." She laughed. "None of us made much money in those days, so our idea of a good time was to see a movie then stop for an ice cream sundae."

Lydia nodded. "Sounds like good memories to me. And you've been friends ever since?"

Rosalie glanced at her husband, as though seeking his approval to continue. When he shrugged, she said, "Then Danny got his big break, and we lost track of them for ten years or so."

Lydia's pulse raced. "What kind of break? Did someone leave him money?"

Allen laughed. "It might as well have been an inheritance. An old friend included Danny in a business deal. One thing led to another, and a few years later he was taking over failing businesses and turning them around."

"For their new owners, that is," Rosalie said with some asperity.

"Come on, Rosalie, that's business," Allen said.

A longstanding argument between them, Lydia thought. "What was Freda like?"

"Nice. A homebody," Rosalie answered. "Al and I moved out to Long Island, and I ran into her in the supermarket. Turned out she and Danny had moved, too, but into a home in Brookville twice the size of our small ranch. But they stayed the same down-to-earth people."

"It sounds like you resumed your friendship with them," Lydia said.

She'd made her comment without giving it much thought and was surprised by the quick exchange of guilty glances between husband and wife.

"We sure did!" Allen said, a bit too loudly. "Especially since we lived in the same school district. Our kids are a year or so younger than Arnold and Denise. They were friendly with them in elementary school, but afterward they grew apart."

Lydia could easily see why. Neither Arnold nor Denise was appealing. She lowered her voice. "I got the impression they're not very close to Daniel."

"No surprise there," Rosalie said. "Daniel was hardly home when they were growing up. He left all the child rearing to Freda."

Allen eyed his wife meaningfully. "Be fair, Rosalie. She did her share of turning them against him."

"That was after...that incident."

Read "affair." Aloud, Lydia said, "But he seems to have a wonderful relationship with Polly."

"Yes, Polly." Rosalie smiled. "She was the only child living at home when Daniel and Freda made a concerted effort to strengthen their marriage. It seemed to have worked. Daniel made it his business to spend more time with his wife and daughter. Things were going well until Freda, poor thing, was diagnosed with breast cancer. She died two years later. She never had much luck."

Allen leaned back in his chair as he considered his thoughts. "Danny hasn't had it easy, either, and I'm damn glad he met Evelyn." When he saw his wife about to protest, he held up a palm. "I know, I know. He's an ace at making money, still plays a mean game of tennis, and his health was excellent until that bout of congestive heart failure last year. But he's prone to depression. Something from his childhood always bothered him."

Lydia's pulse quickened. "Did he ever say what it was?"

Allen shook his head. "Nope. Never did."

The music had stopped, and the others were returning to the table. Lydia said it was nice chatting and moved back to her seat.

The party broke up shortly after. Lydia and her friends joined the group milling around Evelyn and Daniel to say their good-byes.

"Great party," she said, hugging each of them in turn.

"That's my girl!" Daniel enthused, kissing his fiancée's cheek.

While Evelyn related an anecdote to Barbara and the Liebermans, Lydia grabbed her chance to have a word alone with Daniel. She moved closer to him so no one could hear them.

"Did you resolve your moral dilemma—the one you talked to me about?"

His eyes took on a steely expression in a face set in stone. When he answered, his tone was icy. "I've put it out of my mind, and fervently wish you'd do the same."

She'd succeeded in angering him, which wasn't her intent. Chastened, she followed Barbara into the cloakroom and slipped into her jacket. Tonight had not been the time or place to bring up an unpleasant topic. Still, Lydia thought, if that was an indication of how Daniel could react to someone who had his best interests at heart, maybe it wasn't surprising that two of his children had issues with their father.

Chapter Five

S unday morning, Lydia walked over to the clubhouse to swim laps. Home again, she treated herself to a brunch of blueberry pancakes and yogurt, then decided to pay some bills before picking up Barbara and heading for a library book sale in a nearby town. Afterward, if they felt like it, they'd take in a foreign film and have a light dinner out. This was what widows did—planned excursions with their single friends. There was nothing wrong with it. She enjoyed Barbara's company, her humorous comments and witty observations. She simply missed being with a man.

Reggie jumped onto the desk. She stroked his red flank absently as she wrote out a check for her electric bill. How could one person—okay, one person and a cat—run up such a large bill? She'd call PSEG Monday morning and have them explain exactly how they'd arrived at this inflated figure.

The sound of a siren sent Lydia leaping to her feet. *Now what?* She rushed to the front door and looked about, hoping another of her neighbors wasn't being rushed off to the emergency room. Her heart gave a jolt when she spotted an ambulance double-parked in front of Evelyn and Daniel's house. The van and car in the driveway prevented it from getting any closer. She stepped outside in time to see two EMTs bringing a patient out through the front door. Lydia gasped. It was Daniel, his eyes closed, his skin pale and moist with sweat.

Polly dashed out of the house, followed by her husband and daughters.

"What happened?" Lydia asked as she caught up with Polly climbing into a car.

Polly shook her head. "We don't know. Dad said he was in pain. He suddenly collapsed."

Car doors slammed and they drove off. Arnold and his family piled into the van and followed after them. Denise and Bennett paused to light cigarettes then walked toward the red Corvette taking up two spots in front of the house. *It figures*, Lydia thought—both the make of the car and the way it was parked. Denise said something to her son then stepped into the street to speak to a man at the wheel of a black Honda. When he stuck his head out of the window, Lydia caught sight of his impressive mustache. It had to be Stefano. What was he doing here on a Sunday?

One of the EMTs helped Evelyn into the back of the ambulance and closed the doors. A moment later they were gone, the sound of the siren fading as the ambulance raced to the hospital.

Lydia forced herself to wait half an hour to allow for traveling time and the admissions procedure, and then she called the ER at Brookhaven, the hospital closest to Twin Lakes. The first few calls got her nowhere. On the third try, she said she was a relative and was told to wait a minute. There were various sounds—calls over the PA system, nurses chatting. Then someone answered the phone and, in a pleasant male voice, asked who she was. Lydia lied and said she was Daniel's niece, and very concerned about his condition. The young man, no doubt a doctor, told her, his tone kind and respectful, that he was very sorry but the patient, Mr. Korman, had expired.

"You mean he's dead?" Lydia shouted, incredulous. "What happened?"

"We're not certain. Most likely a coronary, from the way his family members described his pains."

"Will there be an autopsy?" Lydia demanded. "Daniel, I mean Uncle Daniel, was a robust man for his age."

"A coronary can strike anyone at any age," the doctor replied. "And who is this I'm speaking to?"

Lydia hung up, trembling with sorrow and rage and a sense of dread that made her want to crawl into bed and pull the covers over her head.

Daniel was buried on Monday afternoon. Lydia drove Barbara and two other women to the funeral home for the service, and then joined the caravan of cars to the cemetery. Lydia's heart went out Evelyn, who, beset by grief and exhaustion, looked even more petite buoyed up by her daughter and son-in-law. Gayle and Roger had flown up from Atlanta to offer their support. They stood on either side of Evelyn as she waited her turn, behind Daniel's family members, to cast a shovelful of dirt onto the coffin.

Lydia, worried that Evelyn might not be up to the task, moved closer in case her assistance might be needed. She watched nervously as Bennett handed Evelyn the shovel. Just then, Arnold strode over to the small group gathered on the verge of the grave and thrust an angry red face close to Evelyn's.

"My father would still be alive if not for your damn party!"

Evelyn moaned and would have crumpled to the ground if her children and Lydia hadn't broken her fall. The two women led her to a nearby bench while Evelyn's son-in-law went after Arnold, who had walked off, oblivious to the effects of his words.

Roger spun the older man around. "How dare you insult Evelyn like that, after all she's gone through?"

"All she's gone through!" Arnold echoed in disbelief. "It's my father who's dead, remember?"

"Such filial devotion," Roger said sarcastically. "The way I heard it, you only came around to beg for money. And now you'll have some, won't you?"

Arnold let out a roar and threw himself onto Roger. Roger punched him in the stomach, and he sank to the ground, looking as if he was about to cry. Arnold's son and son-in-law led him away.

A hush fell over the mourners.

"I see it's true when they say funerals bring out the worst in some people," Barbara murmured.

"That was Danny—a life filled with saps and beautiful women," a male voice behind them commented.

His companion laughed maliciously. "It must have killed him to have a loser like Arnold for a son. If Danny ever heard the kid talk to Evelyn that way, he'd have wrung his neck."

Lydia turned around. Ron Morganstern, an elderly Twin Lakes resident, was speaking to a short, barrel-chested man of his vintage with a drinker's ruddy complexion. Both had been guests at Daniel's party. At the moment, she was too upset by Arnold's outrageous behavior to be concerned that she was intruding on a private conversation.

"Ron, I didn't realize you knew Daniel from years ago."

Ron nodded. "Sure did. So did Mick, here. Mick Diminio, Lydia Krause and Barbara Taylor. Two fellow Twin Lakes residents."

"A pleasure, ladies." Mick Diminio flashed a practiced smile, then muttered an excuse about having to get home and wandered off.

"Diminio," Barbara mused. "That name sounds familiar."

"Mick used to be a big political wheel in the county. His son, Michael, is a state representative and moving up."

"Of course!" Lydia remembered. "I've read articles about him in the newspaper. But tell me, where did you live when you knew Daniel?"

"Around the corner from Twin Lakes, so to speak. We were friends when we were kids, then we drifted apart. Frankly, I was kind of surprised Evelyn invited us to Daniel's shindig. So was Mick."

Before she could ask another question, Andrew Varig joined them. The retired physician looked fit and tan after his European trip. Lydia decided he'd be downright handsome if only he'd lose his habitual somber expression.

"I got back last night and heard the news. Awful about Daniel."

"We're all upset," Barbara said, "especially with it happening right after his party."

"All the excitement could have brought on a coronary. Any word regarding the body they unearthed?" Andrew asked. "I find it astounding that someone hid a corpse, and it lay rotting in a cellar until now."

"Nothing yet," Lydia said, "but the police are working on the boy's identification and cause of death."

Ron groaned. Lydia turned to him. "Are you all right?"

"It's the sun," he answered. Sweat was beading along his forehead. "It makes me dizzy when I stay outside too long."

Andrew reached for Ron's wrist to take his pulse, but Ron waved him off. He offered them a wan smile. "I'm all right, thanks. See you back at the ranch."

They watched him extricate his wife from a group of women and head for his car. Lydia said, "If I were a suspicious person, I'd say your comment about the body they unearthed upset Mr. Ron Morganstern."

"Precisely what I was thinking," Andrew agreed. "But that's neither here nor there. Goodbye, ladies. I'll see you both soon." He winked at them and went on his way.

"There's something different about Andrew," Barbara mused. "He looks absolutely... sexy."

"Sexy? Andrew?" Lydia threw her friend a look of disbelief. "Let's see how Evelyn's bearing up."

They found Evelyn weeping on a bench in the protective care of her daughter and son-in-law. As Lydia and Barbara approached, she stretched out her arms and they hugged her.

"My poor Daniel," she moaned. "Polly adored him, but the others couldn't care less that he's gone. I'll be glad when they go home and leave me in peace."

"I'm so sorry, Evelyn. You'll miss him more than anyone," Lydia said, her eyes tearing up. The funeral brought back the pain of Izzy's death more than a year before.

Evelyn sniffed. "Who's going to brew my coffee every morning? Daniel made the best coffee in the world."

Lydia and Barbara sat on either side of Evelyn as she sobbed quietly. After a few minutes, they nodded to Gayle to reclaim her mother and joined the mourners moving toward their cars, either to go home or to the shiva at Polly's.

"I've had enough for one day," Barbara said as they passed headstone after headstone on the way to the exit.

"Me, too," Lydia agreed. "We've all week to pay a shiva call."

It was with a sense of relief that she drove past the gatehouse and entered Twin Lakes. She declined Barbara's offer to come in for coffee and drove slowly home. She was emotionally drained from seeing Daniel laid to his rest. Plus, she felt a pang of guilt for not having done more to help him resolve his problem. What if he'd been dwelling on it, and stress from that had brought on the coronary? She thought about Ron Morganstern and Mick Diminio, who had known Daniel when they were young, though Ron made it sound as though they were no longer friends.

If they were no longer friends, why had Evelyn invited them to Daniel's party? Had Ron and Mick taken part in a crime when they were young? Ron had reacted when Andrew mentioned the body unearthed by the excavators. His reaction had nothing to do with the sun.

Daniel and Evelyn's house looked abandoned—no lights were on, no cars in sight. Would Evelyn ever be able to step foot inside without being reminded of Daniel's unexpected death?

As soon as she pulled into her driveway, Lydia was overcome by a state of restlessness. Though she had chores to see to, she was too agitated to focus on getting them done. She found herself backing out and exiting Twin Lakes. She'd go and pay a shiva call that day, after all.

The street where Polly lived was already lined with cars on both sides of the road, and Lydia had to park her Lexus at the end of the long block. She walked back, a five-pound box of cookies in hand. She entered the colonial-style house, which was the mirror image of Meredith's, and went in search of Polly.

The downstairs rooms were filled with people eating from paper plates laden with food amid the din of several conversations going at once. Huge platters of delicatessen and accompanying salads covered the dining room table. Lydia left her box of cookies on the kitchen counter, which was crowded with cake and cookie platters, a coffee urn, and sodas. She extended her sympathy to Polly's daughters and waved to Matt, engaged in conversation with an elderly woman. She saw no sign of Polly.

She finally caught sight of her hostess entering the maid's room at the far end of the narrow hallway. Believing Polly had gone to get more paper cups or some such item, Lydia strode toward her, glad for the opportunity to catch her on her own. The sounds of contention, however, made her halt outside the room where Polly faced her siblings, Arnold's wife, and Bennett.

"You're letting your grief and hysteria override the obvious," Arnold was saying.

"Arnold's right," Denise chimed in. "Dad was old. He had a heart attack. End of story."

Bennett let out a bray of laughter.

Polly spoke so softly, Lydia couldn't make out what she said. But it must have offended the others because all four stomped from the room, down the hallway, and out through the front door.

Polly came to stand beside Lydia and watched their departure.

"I'm sorry," Lydia said, referring to both Daniel's death and the quarrel she couldn't pretend not to have witnessed.

Polly shook her head. "My brother and sister refuse to listen to me. They still treat me like the baby sister they used to pretend was a doll." Her eyes welled up with tears.

Lydia led her back inside the room where seconds earlier she'd been arguing with her siblings. It was made up as a guest room, with two double beds. Polly sank onto one bed and Lydia sat beside her. Today seemed to be her day for comforting the bereaved.

"I didn't know your father very well or for very long, but we were friends. I always felt we understood one another." *Except for our last conversation.*

"Dad told me he thought the same of you." Polly seemed to be debating something in her mind. She came to a decision and rose to close the door so no one could overhear them.

"Lydia, I want to tell you something."

Lydia wondered if Polly knew what had been troubling Daniel.

"My father didn't have a coronary. He died because someone killed him."

Lydia sighed. "Polly, dear, it's very difficult to accept the death of someone we love. An unexpected death is even harder."

Polly shook her head and laughed. It wasn't a pretty sound. "Do you think I'm imagining things? Looking for some explanation because I can't accept losing my father to natural causes?"

"Regardless of the circumstances, losing a loved one as you have is a shock to the system. I know I had dreary thoughts for several months after my husband died."

Polly turned to Lydia. "Please listen to me, or I think I'll go out of my mind. My father was worried someone had it in for him. He'd received strange phone calls and…" she faltered, "this past week a car followed him when he was driving alone."

"Did he call the police?"

Tears streamed down Polly's cheeks, making her look like a little girl. "Get help from the police? Are you kidding? He said he knew who was harassing him, and he'd put a stop to it."

"Did he say whom he suspected?"

Polly shook his head. "He only told me that much because I happened to be at his house when he got one of the calls. I'd picked up the phone to hand it to him. I made him tell me about it after I saw how upset and angry it left him."

Lydia thought a minute. "Does Evelyn know any of this?"

"Dad didn't tell her, but she knows something was troubling him this past week."

"Something was. Your father was trying to decide what to do about a crime he believed was committed many years ago. He refused to tell me who or what it involved."

Polly gave a wry little smile. "Of course he didn't. Dad's modus operandi was to keep everything to himself. It used to infuriate my mother. He claimed every problem had a solution and he considered himself the best problem solver around."

"Putting together what we both know, Daniel suspected a person or persons had committed a crime. He intended to investigate on his own. Let's assume he started asking questions, got someone's back up, then someone took to following him." Lydia shuddered.

"And now he's dead. Murdered." Polly rubbed furiously at her wet cheeks. "I called his doctor this morning and explained why I believe someone killed my father. The old goat stands by his conclusion. He offered to give me a prescription for a sedative. Can you believe that?" She drew a deep breath and continued.

"I told Arnie and Denise everything I told you. I explained why Dad's body has to be exhumed, and I got nowhere with either of them." Polly made a face. "My brother's the biggest hypocrite. He says an autopsy is disrespectful of my father and it's against Jewish law. Hah! As if he gives a hoot for my father or Jewish law. He thinks my imagination's gone wild because—well, because...

"And Denise says there's no point in an exhumation," she hurried on. "It's over and done with. Dad's dead and buried and we'd best get on with our lives. That's Denise, all right. She only cares about her next drink or fix, and that miserable spoiled son she dotes on. Actually, she's glad because now she'll have some money. So is Arnie. Neither of them gives a damn."

Polly pressed a hand to her mouth. "Please forget what I've just said about my sibs. It's been a grueling day, and their lack of grief or caring if Dad was murdered makes me want to scream."

Lydia was beginning to wonder where all of this was leading. "Will you tell the police?"

She nodded. "I have to, for Dad's sake. I'd like you to go with me to speak to the homicide detective Merry says you know. I want you to tell him what Dad told you."

"Of course, I will."

"After the shiva's over would be best," Polly said. "Will you go with me to see him next Monday or Tuesday?"

"Whenever you're ready," Lydia said soothingly, though she intended to speak to Sol immediately. If Daniel had indeed been murdered, the investigation had to begin ASAP. She stood. "I'll say goodbye. I only came to see you."

"Thank you, Lydia." Polly hugged her. "I wish you'd stop by Evelyn's. She refused to come here today because of my stupid brother. I've no idea what got into him. Thank God he and his brood are going home tonight."

Chapter Six

Lydia called the station and was told Sol wasn't expected in until the following morning. Since she didn't want to disclose information to another officer, she asked that the lieutenant call her back.

"Is this concerning an ongoing case?" he asked her.

Lydia hesitated. Daniel's death was not a case—yet—but his death might be connected to the body the backhoe had unearthed. "It might be. I'm not sure," she finally said. "Please tell Lieutenant Molina I've information to share with him."

"And what is the nature of this information, Miss? Mrs.?"

Lydia hung up. It was a foolish gesture since the police telephone system revealed the number she was calling from. But she didn't feel like answering questions right now. And by the time Sol contacted her, the issue would be cleared up. She decided not to call him on his cell phone. He'd get the message soon enough.

She fed Reggie and went into the den to watch the news, but she couldn't concentrate. Polly's insistence that her father had been murdered preyed on her mind. If this were so, it undoubtedly was connected to the old matter Daniel had alluded to when he'd stopped by.

Idiot! Lydia berated herself. Daniel had come to ask her advice and had chickened out in the end. She should have drawn him out, coaxed him to spill the entire story instead of settling for generalizations and innuendos. What had happened to her probing skills? Her intuition that something was amiss? She'd taken the easy way out, "respecting" Daniel's wish not to reveal the issue weighing on his mind. As a result, the poor man was now dead instead of about to marry Evelyn and enjoy his newly wedded bliss.

She wondered how Evelyn was coping. After being humiliated by Arnold in that appalling, public way, she'd refused to go to Polly's house. Lydia's heart went out to her. Though everyone at Twin Lakes considered them a couple, Evelyn wasn't Daniel's widow. No doubt she was feeling lonely and abandoned.

Lydia walked over to see how she was faring. She arrived as Evelyn's daughter and son-in-law were leaving.

"Call me, Mom," Gayle was saying. "If you change your mind and want to stay with us, either Roger or I will fly up to get you."

"Thank you, dear, but this is my home. I intend to sit shiva for Daniel right here."

Gayle and Roger kissed Evelyn good-bye, then climbed into the waiting taxi that would take them to the airport.

"They're wonderful kids," Evelyn told Lydia, her voice hoarse from crying. "I couldn't ask for better."

"Not like Daniel's, you mean?"

Evelyn gave her a tear-stained smile as she closed the door behind them. "Polly's sweet. She's often told me she was glad Daniel and I had each other—but the other two are horrors."

"I'm sorry for the way Arnold treated you at the cemetery."

"Oh, that?" Evelyn's laughter held no humor. "He was furious at his father and couldn't very well say so at his funeral, so he picked on me."

"You mean because you and Daniel were getting married?"

"More to the point, because Daniel changed his will. Last week, as a matter of fact. He bequeathed fifty thousand dollars to Arnold and to Denise, and twenty-five thousand to each grandchild. After that, a quarter of his estate goes to Polly, three-quarters to me—that is, the money's to remain in trust for me as long as I live." She frowned. "Upon my demise, the money's to be divided between Arnold, Denise, and Polly."

"Did Arnold and Denise know about the new will?"

"Not exactly, although Daniel dropped hints that we'd be getting married and there would be changes."

"They must have resented that."

Evelyn sighed. "Daniel was fed up with them both. He said they were leeches and didn't deserve another penny from him. I urged him to change his mind. He finally gave in and said they'd share what he left me after I no longer needed it."

"The trust," Lydia murmured.

Evelyn nodded. "But let's talk about more pleasant matters."

Lydia, socially adept as she was, had no idea what a pleasant topic might be under the circumstances. Besides, she had her own news to deliver. She followed Evelyn into her comfortable yet elegant living room and refused her offer of refreshment.

"Evelyn, I feel I must tell you. Polly thinks Daniel was murdered."

Lydia's shoulders tensed as she waited for Evelyn's stunned response. Instead, Evelyn nodded as though Lydia's news made perfect sense.

"He knew," she whispered. "His last words were 'They did it. They got to me.'"

Lydia shuddered. "Did he say who 'they' were?"

Evelyn shook her head. "I thought he meant his kids aggravating him and bringing on the coronary. He got plenty of fallout after he told them we were getting married."

"When did Daniel tell them?"

"Last week. Denise showed up with Bennett the Saturday before the party to beg for money. She turned ugly when he wouldn't give it to her." Evelyn grimaced. "She obviously told Arnold, because he called here the next day to tell Daniel what he thought of me and our getting married. Then he asked for money for another of his doomed business ventures. Daniel said he was furious when he turned him down.

"Frankly, we didn't expect either of them to show up at the party, but they surprised us. In fact, Arnold drove over to the house before the party while we were getting dressed. Left his family sitting in the van while he tried to convince Daniel to change his mind—about the money, anyway—but Daniel refused to discuss it."

"Lovely children," Lydia murmured.

"Does Polly think her brother or sister killed Daniel?" Evelyn asked.

Shocked, Lydia shook her head. "No, she said nothing of the sort! Daniel told her someone tailed him last week when he drove alone."

Tears welled up in Evelyn's eyes. "Who? Why? And why didn't he tell me, the woman he shared everything with? I'll never forgive him for that. Never!"

Feeling a bit guilty, Lydia said, "Evelyn, Daniel told me he was worried that people he knew years ago might have been involved in a crime. He was very vague, but I suspect it had to do with the body the excavators unearthed in the root cellar. He said he didn't want to upset you because you were busy with the party and the brunch."

"The party and the brunch weren't important! They were only a way of honoring Daniel." Evelyn shook her head. A sob escaped her lips. "I was a fool to make such a fuss about his eighty-fifth birthday. If I hadn't been so occupied, I'd have made him tell me what was troubling him instead of letting him fob me off with platitudes. He'd still be here with me."

"We don't know that," Lydia said gently. "Did Daniel mention anything about the crime he believes was committed?"

Evelyn shook his head. "He told me nothing. He spent hours at his computer. And he called Ron Morganstern."

Lydia's heart took a flying leap. "I just found out from Ron that he and Daniel knew each other when they were kids."

"That's right. Ron, Daniel, and Mick Diminio grew up right around here."

"Evelyn, Daniel grew upset about this old crime right after they found the remains of that boy."

Evelyn nodded slowly. "Of course! Daniel went to talk to you because you were there when the body was discovered, and you helped solve the Weills' murders."

Lydia wasn't crazy about the way Evelyn had phrased things, but at least her pinched expression was fading, a sign she was letting go of her guilt for not having protected Daniel.

"I'm trying to remember Daniel's exact words when he came to ask my advice. Something had happened that convinced him a murder had been committed many years ago. Proof, as far as he was concerned, but no evidence. His dilemma was if he should bring this to the attention of the police or let sleeping dogs lie."

"Of course, we'll tell the police!" Evelyn exclaimed. "It could be the reason Daniel's dead."

"I've already left a message with Lieutenant Molina," Lydia said. "He should be calling me back soon."

"Good." Evelyn stood. "In the meantime, I'd like you to go through Daniel's computer files. Maybe they'll tell us who was after him."

Lydia hesitated. "I don't know." She could well imagine Sol Molina's wrath when he learned she and Evelyn had checked out the files on Daniel's computer.

Evelyn misunderstood her hesitation. "I thought, having owned a business, you'd know the workings of a computer."

"I've worked on computers, of course, but I think we should wait until the police get here."

"Why? It's not as though we're trampling on a crime scene. I can't count how many people have been through this house before and after they rushed Daniel to the hospital." Evelyn's lovely gray eyes, usually so mild, turned cold as steel. "I must know who killed my Daniel. If you won't access the files, I'll find someone who will."

She would, too. Lydia patted Evelyn's shoulder. "In that case, I'll access them, and we can go through each and every one, if you like."

"Thank you, Lydia."

Having won her point, Evelyn babbled as she led Lydia into the den, where she sank into a chair while Lydia booted up the computer. "We got the computer last year. I use it to email my daughter and a few friends. Daniel used it to check his investments and to write his memoirs."

"Write his memoirs?" Lydia was surprised.

"Why not? He was involved in some of the biggest corporate takeovers and mergers."

Lydia mused. "I wonder if the person following him had a grudge against him because of some business venture in the past."

"For Daniel's sake, let's find out."

Going through Daniel's files was easy enough. Most of them were chapters of his autobiography, which he'd entitled "A Man's Life." Evelyn sat quietly beside her as she skimmed through the text. She found it engrossing. Daniel had a pleasant, readable prose style. What's more, the files added up to hundreds of pages. Lydia suspected it was three-quarters complete. Another five files contained copious notes. She wondered if Polly would want to finish the book in memory of her father.

She glanced through the files concerning Daniel's finances and investments and was stunned to discover that his assets totaled close to thirty million dollars.

"I can see why Arnold and Denise weren't happy their father was about to remarry," Lydia said.

"Out of spite. They couldn't care less on a personal level."

Lydia smiled. "I must say, Daniel's new will is the opposite of what we've come to expect in this age of prenup agreements."

Evelyn's nod was knowing. "Believe me, his lawyers worked long and hard to change his mind, but Daniel stood firm. He trusted me more than his two older kids." She laughed. "I don't need his money. Daniel left me this house and our place in Florida, and I intend to make good use of both. As for the money, Arnold and Denise are welcome to it when I'm gone."

With the new will in effect, Lydia thought it preposterous that either Arnold or Denise had murdered Daniel. They simply didn't benefit from their father's death. *Unless one of them was so angry...* Lydia shook her head. She didn't want to contemplate patricide.

"I'm bringing up a file called "suspects."

Evelyn peered at the screen. "It seems to be written in code."

Lydia squinted. She was too caught up in what was before her to get out her reading glasses. "No, simply abbreviated words. There are three paragraphs, each headed by two initials. The first is R. M."

"Ron Morganstern," Evelyn said.

"M. D. That's Mick Diminio, I imagine. And B. E." She looked questioningly at Evelyn. "Do you know who that is?"

"Probably Billy Evans. He was an old friend of Daniel's when they were kids. I think he lived in California until he died several years ago."

"Three childhood friends," Lydia mused. "Was Daniel still friendly with Ron?"

Evelyn shook her head. "I didn't know they knew each other from childhood until a few weeks ago. Ron or Mick Diminio. Daniel called them both. Afterward he told me to invite them to his party, so I did."

"And they came," Lydia murmured. "So Daniel couldn't have accused either of them of murder before the party."

The notes didn't tell her very much. The headings were dates, followed by what appeared to be streets, locations, and times of day. Most of the entries ended with a series of question marks.

Lydia turned to Evelyn, who sat weeping silently into her hands.

"Evelyn, dear," she crooned, putting an arm around her. "We shouldn't be doing this now. You're grieving."

"This is exactly what I should be doing," Evelyn said as staunchly as she could through her tears. "I'm determined to find the rotten bastard who killed my Daniel." She turned imploringly to Lydia. "You'll help me, won't you? You're good at finding murderers."

"I'll do my best," Lydia said, not knowing what else to say.

A framed penciled sketch of a young teenaged boy on yellowed paper caught her attention. It stood on a bookshelf among photos of Daniel and his children, Evelyn and her daughter's family, and Daniel and Evelyn.

"Is that Daniel?" Lydia asked, recognizing the narrow face, the intelligent eyes.

"Yes. Timmy John Desmond drew it," Evelyn replied. "He was a friend of Daniel's when they were young. Daniel said he would have become a famous artist."

"What happened to him?"

Evelyn shrugged. "Nobody knows. He came to live with relatives on Long Island. Then one day he simply disappeared, and no one ever saw him again."

Chapter Seven

Lydia was about to ask Evelyn what she knew about Timmy John Desmond, when her cell phone rang.

"Hello, Lydia. Sol Molina, here. I called you at home, then thought I'd try your cell phone. What's up?"

"Hi, Sol." Flustered because he'd saved her cell phone number, Lydia glanced at Evelyn, who waved and left the room. She appreciated her hostess's tact, considering what she had to tell him.

"A Twin Lakes friend and neighbor died yesterday and was buried today. His name is Daniel Korman. His daughter thinks he was murdered."

"Really? What makes her think that?"

"Polly said Daniel was receiving strange phone calls, and someone was tailing him."

Sol didn't respond. Lydia knew he was thinking. Finally, he asked. "What do you make of it, Lydia? How old was the guy? Do you take her for a hysterical daughter?"

"Daniel had congestive heart failure, but he was in good health. His fiancée threw him a party Saturday night to celebrate his eighty-fifth birthday. And no, his daughter isn't the hysterical type." She paused. "Daniel was worried about something. He came to talk to me last week."

"Lydia, Lydia, how do you get embroiled in these situations?" She heard affection, exasperation, and resignation in his voice.

"It's not something I pursue," she said with some heat. "Daniel needed to air a moral dilemma and used me as a sounding board. He was vague about the details, so I was less than helpful."

Sol sighed. "What are you doing for dinner?"

"I don't know. I haven't given it much thought."

"How's about we go out for a bite, and you can tell me all about it. That is, if you don't mind meeting me. I'll be tied up until close to seven."

"That's fine. Where shall I meet you?"

He gave her the name of a Greek restaurant in the next town and directions to get there. "Let's aim for seven o'clock. I'll call you on your cell if I'm running late."

They said good-bye, and Lydia returned her attention to checking through Daniel's files. There was only one file of interest. It yielded little information other than a log of phone calls made to Ron Morganstern and Mick Diminio.

A glimpse at her watch told her it was after four. She had less than three hours. She asked Evelyn for her Twin Lakes directory and looked up Ron Morganstern's address. "Ron lives on Lake Montaukett," she murmured.

"I don't think it's wise to pay him a visit," Evelyn said. "Let your boyfriend interview him."

"Detective Molina is not my boyfriend. We're friends, nothing more."

"Friends who go out for dinner."

"On occasion," Lydia conceded.

Evelyn gripped her upper arm with surprising strength. "Lydia, don't act rashly! If Ron killed Daniel, why wouldn't he do the same to you?"

"I promise to be careful. I merely intend to ask a few questions about the time when they were kids."

Evelyn grimaced. "If he's guilty, he'll know what you're after. But I can't stop you, can I?" She embraced Lydia in a fierce hug. "Be careful!" she admonished. "And tell me everything he says."

"I will," Lydia promised.

She parked in front of Ron's house and rang the doorbell. Bella Morganstern opened the door. In the small hall, she and Lydia exchanged commiserations, about how sad it was to have attended Daniel's funeral so soon after his birthday party. Bella cocked her head and asked, "Can I help you with something?"

Lydia smiled. "I'd like to speak to Ron if he's here."

"Ron!" Bella called out, and led Lydia into a small den cluttered with photos of children and grandchildren and small figurines of penguins. The birds were made of wood, glass, ceramic, and stone. Bella saw her eying them and smiled. "We collect them, Ron and I."

Bella left and Ron entered the room a few minutes later, rubbing his eyes. He wore khaki pants, a rumpled short-sleeved shirt, and slippers without socks. Lydia must have wakened him from a nap. But he was good-natured enough to offer a small smile as he settled into the brown leather couch that formed an L with the love seat in which she was sitting.

"Hello, Ron," Lydia said. "I wanted to talk to you... about Daniel."

"Sure." Ron leaned back and palmed back what remained of his sparse gray hair. "It's sad how he died so suddenly just before his wedding."

"Yes, it is," Lydia said.

"Makes you wonder..." Ron trailed off.

"Makes you wonder what?" Lydia asked, curious.

Ron laughed. It was a harsh sound that ended in a smoker's cough. "If one of his kids knocked him off."

Lydia shuddered at the track Ron's thoughts were following. At the same time, it gave her the opening she needed. "Polly thinks someone murdered Daniel. Last week he received calls that upset him. And he thought a car was following him each time he left Twin Lakes by himself."

Ron looked at her in alarm. "Really? Maybe she should notify the police."

Lydia nodded, watching his face for any sign of guilt. "She wants the body to be exhumed, but her brother and sister think she's overreacting to their father's death."

Ron got to his feet. "They would—wouldn't they?—if they did poor Daniel in." He called over his shoulder as he walked toward the bar in the far corner, "I think this warrants a drink. Would you like something?"

"No, thanks." Lydia watched him pour scotch almost to the top of a highball glass. She waited until he drank deeply and sat down again before she asked, "What was Daniel like when he was a kid?"

Ron leaned back and smiled. "Danny was the best! An all-around terrific guy. He was a great athlete and absolutely brilliant, in school and out." He grinned. "The kid came up with more ways for us to get into trouble than our whole group put together—never serious trouble, mind you. Sometimes we played hooky and rode our bicycles to the beach. One Halloween we painted the water tower." He chuckled, pleased with himself. "They never caught us for that."

"Was Mick Diminio part of your group?"

"Yep. There were four of us—Danny, Mickey, me, and Billy Evans. Billy moved away to California. He died about ten years ago. I think Mick went to his funeral."

"I suppose you, Mick, and Daniel kept up with one other, seeing that you all ended up living on Long Island."

Ron shrugged. "Mick and I did, off and on, but we kind of lost track of Danny until he moved back to Suffolk County. What a surprise that was, him and me ending up here, a stone's throw from the old neighborhood."

"What about Timmy John Desmond?"

Ron gulped down the rest of his scotch. His hand trembled as he set the glass on the table. "How did you come up with that name?"

Though her heart was racing, Lydia spoke calmly. "I saw a sketch he'd made of Daniel. He was very talented."

"He was a creep!" Ron's eyes narrowed with suspicion. "Why are you asking me about Timmy John?"

"I was wondering if you knew what happened to him."

"How would I know? I'm tired of your questions. I'd like you to go."

Lydia stood, as eager to leave as he was to see the back of her. His vehement reaction meant her assumptions were correct. *Ron and the others were involved with the poor boy's disappearance all those years ago. They must have murdered him!* When his remains were discovered, Daniel put two and two together and must have let his old friends know he was on to them.

And now Daniel was dead. Ron and Mick must have killed him to make sure he remained silent. There was no statute of limitations regarding murder.

Ridiculous! Lydia shook her head as she followed Ron to the door. Eighty-five-year-old men didn't go around killing one another.

Suddenly Ron spun around, making her flinch.

"I'd forget about Timmy John, if I were you."

She forced herself to meet his glare. "The police aren't fools. They'll figure things out and come here looking for answers."

He jutted out his chin so that his face was inches from hers. "If they do, I'll know who sent them."

Eighty-five or not, his angry bulldog expression scared the bejeezus out of her. Lydia dashed out the door and into the street. Maybe a chat with Ron Morganstern had proven to be a dumb idea, after all.

Sol was only fifteen minutes late. He winked as he slid into the booth across from her. "Sorry I couldn't get here any sooner. As it is, I flew."

"And risked a ticket," she said archly.

He studied her face, took in the low V of her silk top, and winked. "It was worth the risk."

"Thank you." Lydia had to restrain herself from getting up and throwing herself into his arms where she'd feel safe and secure after her encounter with Ron Morganstern. Also, because Sol was the sexiest man she knew, and she was half in love with him.

She handed him a menu instead.

They both ordered Greek salads topped with grilled chicken breasts. Lydia was pleasantly surprised. She found the salad crisp and fresh, the chicken tender and moist, and the pita bread warm and nicely grilled. When she'd eaten as much as she could, she found Sol grinning at her over their empty plates.

"Welcome back to earth."

"Sorry," she said. "I didn't realize how hungry I was. Except for the one cookie I grabbed at Polly's, I haven't eaten since this morning."

Sol pitched his voice low so no one but she could hear him. "I figured you must have been near starvation when you didn't ask a single question about the body found in the root cellar."

"Have you finally gotten the report?"

"Finally."

Lydia pushed back her dish and leaned forward. "I'm all ears."

"We have a tentative ID based on sketchy reports from seventy years ago. A fifteen-year-old boy named Timothy Desmond was reported missing and never found. From what we pieced together, he came from Arkansas to live with relatives just a few blocks from the excavation site. After six weeks, he disappeared. At first his aunt and uncle thought he went home, though his aunt didn't think he would because his stepfather was physically abusive—to get the devil out of him. The kid had epilepsy."

Lydia shook her head. "Poor Timmy John."

"What did you say?"

Lydia blinked, disconcerted by Sol's glowering expression. She was getting a bit fed up with men reacting unfavorably whenever she mentioned the boy's name.

"I said 'poor Timmy John,'" she repeated, obviously too loudly because this time Sol put a finger to his lips.

"How did you know his name was Timmy John?"

"Daniel Korman, my neighbor who died, kept a sketch done by Timmy John in his den. I saw it this afternoon when I visited Daniel's fiancée. Evelyn said Daniel had always been troubled by his disappearance and wondered what had happened to him."

Their waiter asked if they wanted coffee and dessert. They ordered decaf and a galaktoboureko to share. When the young man was well on his way to the kitchen, Sol whistled.

"Your neighbor who just died knew the boy whose corpse they dug up at the construction site? That's quite a coincidence."

She nodded and went on to tell Sol about her conversation with Daniel and his dilemma of whether to expose an old crime or let sleeping dogs lie.

"Expose an old crime," Sol echoed. "Interesting."

"Who lived in that house in the 1930s?"

Sol rubbed his forehead as he searched his mind for the name. "A family named Evans."

Billy Evans, she thought, this time careful not to utter the name aloud. Though why shouldn't she tell Sol what she knew? Had Ron Morganstern succeeded in intimidating her? If he and Mick had killed Daniel, it was her responsibility to tell Sol everything she'd learned.

Lydia grimaced. Once she told Sol, he'd be furious that she'd gone to talk to Ron on her own and advise her not to do anything like it again.

"Why does Daniel Korman's daughter believe he was murdered?" Sol asked.

"The week before he died, someone tailed him when he left Twin Lakes. And he'd gotten some weird phone calls."

Sol took out his notepad. "Dan-iel Korman," he sounded out as he wrote. "And his daughter's name, address, and phone number, if you know them."

"It's Polly Ellenberg. She lives in The Knolls, near my daughter, Meredith. I can't remember her address or phone number."

"Did Mrs. Ellenberg call you specifically to tell you her suspicions about her father's death?"

"I paid a shiva call at Polly's house after the funeral and walked in on an argument she was having with her brother and sister, about exhuming Daniel's body. Arnold and Denise thought Polly was overreacting to their father's death and wouldn't agree to it."

"Interesting," Sol observed. "I'll get their names and addresses from Mrs. Ellenberg and speak to them. Please continue."

The note of formality that had crept into Sol's voice made her self-conscious. "I went to see Evelyn Hammond, Daniel's fiancée."

"She wasn't at the shiva?"

"No. Arnold made a nasty remark at the funeral—that Daniel would still be alive if not for Evelyn's birthday party. Evelyn fell to pieces."

"Do you think he did it deliberately? To stir up discord? Gain sympathy?"

Surprised, Lydia shook her head. "Why—I don't know. I never considered it until now."

"Did Mrs. Hammond sense something was amiss with Mr. Korman?"

"Actually, she did. Daniel had been very secretive and upset before his birthday party."

Sol put down his notepad and met Lydia's gaze. "No doubt he tried to find out what really happened seventy years ago. I'm not saying he was murdered, but I intend to do what I can to have his body exhumed ASAP." He reached for her hands. "People die, and not always by natural causes. You see where playing detective can take you?"

"I do." Now was the time to tell Sol about Ron and Mick Diminio. But the police couldn't hold them indefinitely, and then they'd be free to come after her! She'd be better off waiting to see what else developed.

Sol squeezed her fingers. "Go on, Lydia. Tell me the rest."

"That's all there is to tell." Damn it, why did she sound like a teenage boy whose voice was about to change?

Sol let out a belly laugh. "Out with it."

Feeling foolish, she jerked her hands free.

"Evelyn insisted that I open Daniel's computer files. I didn't want to, but she said if I didn't, she'd get someone else to do it. He was keeping records on two people he was friends with at the time Timmy John vanished—Ron Morganstern and Mick Diminio."

"Diminio!" Sol whistled. "Isn't he related to Michael Diminio, our stand-in town supervisor? Of course! The old man's his father. He's an old pol himself."

"So I gather. Ron and Mick Diminio were both at Daniel's party Saturday night. Ron Morganstern lives at Twin Lakes. He had no problem talking about the good old times. But when I mentioned Timmy John's name, he reacted like he'd seen a ghost."

Sol reached over the table and gripped her shoulders. "You did what?"

"Ouch! You're hurting me."

"Sorry. I can't believe you did such a stupid thing. And where did this conversation take place?"

Lydia swallowed. "In his den."

Sol smacked his hand to his forehead. "You're an intelligent woman! You ran your own company, for God's sake! How could you walk into the home of a possible homicide suspect and dangle information in front of him that could make him want to kill you too?"

Lydia found herself babbling. "I wanted to see Ron's reaction when I mentioned Timmy John's name. He nearly jumped out of his skin at Daniel's funeral when someone mentioned the remains were being identified. He told me himself that he, Daniel, Mick Diminio, and Billy Evans were friends when they were kids. When I saw Daniel's notes on Ron and Mick Diminio, I knew they had something to do with Timmy John's death."

"Let me get this straight." Sol took a deep breath. "After you found out all these connections, you let Morganstern know you're on to him, forgetting that, if he already killed two people, he might consider knocking you off too?" He shook his head in disbelief.

"I shouldn't have," she said softly.

Sol's fist pounded the table, making her jump and sending glances their way. "What you should have done was call me! I'm a homicide detective, remember? Or were you planning on solving these murders on your own?"

"I'm sorry, Sol. I won't do anything that stupid again."

"Indeed you won't." His voice remained soft, but it managed to send chills down her spine. "Come on, we're leaving. I'm following you home."

Chapter Eight

Lydia sat on a living room sofa, arms wrapped around her knees, feeling very much like a child who'd been subjected to an unfair tongue lashing. At the same time, she was red hot angry. She wasn't a child, and Sol Molina certainly wasn't her father! While she'd had no business going to Ron Morganstern's home to ring his chimes, blow his cool, or whatever the expression was these days, she'd come away convinced he was involved in Timmy John's death. She'd leave it to Sol Molina to find out exactly what part Ron and his friend, Mick Diminio, had played all those years ago.

Reggie came to snuggle beside her, and she was grateful for his purring companionship. She had hoped for a human kind of closeness to end the evening, but that hadn't happened. Reggie left, and she went into the den and turned on the TV.

She flipped from one program to another, too restless to watch anything for more than a minute. Everything was boring.

Predictable. Turning the TV off, she dialed Barbara's number. Her friend picked up on the third ring.

"Care for some company?" Lydia asked.

"I thought you were having dinner with the handsome detective."

"I did. We had words."

"In that case, come on over. I'll leave the garage door open."

Five minutes later, Lydia was sitting at her friend's kitchen table. Barbara filled a plate with miniature Italian pastries."

"Don't bother with those. I couldn't eat another thing," Lydia insisted. But after downing her second, she laughed as she pushed away her empty plate. "Those were awesome."

Barbara grinned. "I know. They come from the new bakery on Main Street." She got up to fill their mugs with boiling water for tea. "Now tell me what happened."

Lydia shrugged. "I did something dumb."

"Before going off to meet Sol?"

"Actually, yes. We agreed on a time and place for dinner, and I had just enough time to check on something."

"Something you knew would make him angry."

Lydia squirmed under Barbara's penetrating gaze. "Meaning what?'

"Meaning maybe you did what you did for a reason."

"Like?"

"Like you're afraid to get too involved with the guy so you do something you know will set him off."

Lydia opened her mouth to argue then shut it. "You might have a point."

Barbara grinned. "At least you're honest enough to admit it. You may leave my hundred dollar therapy fee on the coffee table as you leave."

"What about Sol? That's the part I wanted to tell you. He got furious."

"Maybe he's afraid you'll get yourself killed one of these days."

"Trust me, Barbara, the man overreacted. I bet he feels threatened because I find out things he knows nothing about. Like the fact that Daniel may have been murdered. And the connection between the dead boy and Daniel's old friends."

"And the fact that you're a strong, effective woman who built up and ran a successful company."

"Whatever." Lydia frowned. "I think Mr. Macho doesn't like my venturing into his jurisdiction, which is pretty childish."

"I'd say all of the above are true, and you both have involvement phobia."

Lydia sipped her tea. She thought a minute, and then said quietly, "It sounds pretty hopeless to me."

Barbara laughed. "The relationship does have a few hurdles to overcome, but I think Sol Molina's worth it."

"So do I," Lydia said softly.

"Then stop provoking him. Talk to Polly and Evelyn as much as you like, but keep away from the bad boys, and pray they keep away from you."

Lydia went home an hour later. Barbara's words of wisdom worked as a sedative, and she slept deeply. The following morning she practiced yoga for forty-five minutes then walked to the clubhouse and swam laps in the indoor pool. The exercise left her invigorated yet calm, and she felt more positive regarding her relationship with Sol. She hummed as she stepped out of the clubhouse and into the May day. A noisy May day, because the gardening service was out in full force, mowing and edging the large expanse of lawn.

"Lydia!"

She turned at the sound of her name. Andrew Varig came trotting toward her, tennis racket in hand.

"Hi, Andrew. Lovely morning for tennis."

"Sure is. Some of the men have gotten up a morning game. Would you be interested in playing later on in the day?"

Lydia laughed as she shook her head. "Sorry, but I gave up tennis ten years ago. Besides, I'm off to work."

"I'm spending a few hours at the construction site this afternoon. They'll be filling in the root cellar and leveling the ground."

She gave him a perky smile. "I'm so glad you're home again, Andrew, so I can leave all that in your capable hands."

Andrew grinned—a shocking sight, since Andrew never smiled. "Fear not. I'll stand guard."

"That's music to my ears," she told him and continued on her way. She'd progressed only a few yards when he called to her. Puzzled, she turned around. "Yes?"

He caught up with her and glanced furtively from side to side before speaking. "When was the last time you were in Manhattan?"

"Let me think. I took the railroad in after my daughter Abbie's wedding in January. Of course! The Women's Club went to the Metropolitan Museum last month."

Andrew seemed to be bristling with nervous energy, which was not like him at all. When he spoke, his words spilled over like a waterfall. "I was wondering, Lydia, would you like to go into the city some time, to take in a play or a show?"

Her eyes widened in disbelief. Was Andrew asking her out on a date?

He added quickly, "Unless you have an understanding with your detective friend."

"No, we've no understanding." She smiled at the quaint use of the term.

He returned her smile, which filled her with trepidation. She hadn't meant to encourage him.

"Then I hope you'll say yes. I didn't realize how much I've missed the city until I visited some of the European capitals with my kids."

He looked wistful, an unusual expression for the confident Dr. Varig. Lydia decided she liked this side of him, liked it enough to say, "I'd love to go to the theatre with you. It's been some time for me as well."

"Wonderful! How about Saturday?"

Lydia was struck dumb. When she found her voice, her impulse was to stall for time. "I—I don't know. I'll have to check my calendar and let you know."

"Meanwhile, I'll see what shows are available, then we can choose something we'll both enjoy."

"All right. Bye." She fled before he could utter another word.

She race-walked home, wondering what she'd gotten herself into. She liked Andrew, but not in a romantic sort of way. She was emotionally involved with Sol, though they argued half the time they spent together. And they weren't lovers, by any stretch of the imagination.

As for Andrew, she hoped he had no designs on her that way because she certainly wasn't interested in him. But how would she know—the perverse thought occurred to her—unless he kissed her?

Lydia shook her head vehemently at the idea. She turned fifty-nine in August and had no desire to return to those awkward dating days of her youth. She'd see a show or a play with Andrew as a friend. A companion. If he wanted more than that, she'd be up front with him, and explain she wasn't interested in anything romantic.

After she rebuffed him, would they end up feeling awkward every time they ran into one another? That would be often, considering they were co-chairs. They lived within the confines of a small community and attended the same meetings and activities.

Take one step at a time, she lectured herself. *You'll go to the city with Andrew and have a good time. If you don't want to go out with him again, you'll say so. He'll get over it. End of discussion.*

Why were relations between men and women so awfully complicated?

At home, Lydia showered and dressed, then drove to work. During the trip she wondered if she should say yes to managing the Carrington Suites. The position would demand a good deal of time and effort, especially at first. Was she willing to give up the luxury of working three days a week at a pleasant job that required limited responsibilities? Then again, she'd enjoy the challenge of starting something brand new. She was good at dealing with people, at resolving crises. Frankly, she found it exhilarating. She'd have to decide soon. Len said they wanted her answer no later than a week from Friday.

Her workday passed quickly, giving her no opportunity to mull about Daniel and Timmy John or her personal life. At five o'clock, Lydia was back in her car heading home. Reggie greeted her by rubbing against her legs. She filled his dish with dried food, which earned her a look of reproach.

"That's all you're getting for now," she scolded. "You're getting fat again."

He must have gotten her message because he began to eat. The doorbell rang.

"Coming," Lydia called out as she walked toward the front door. It was probably Barbara, stopping by to borrow the book they were reading for the next meeting of their newly formed book club.

Mick Diminio stood before her in Bermuda shorts, a short-sleeved shirt, and a Yankees cap. His attire, along with his short, stocky legs and beer belly, was that of an innocuous old man, but his frown of displeasure sent a chill down her back. She resisted the impulse to slam the door in his face.

"May I come in, Lydia? I'd like to talk to you."

"I don't—" Lydia's heart thumped as she searched her brain for a polite way of refusing him. The man had been a powerful politician. For all she knew, he had mob connections. How stupid she'd been, tipping Ron off to her suspicions. She should have realized he'd run straight to Mick Diminio. Who might very well have killed Daniel as well as Timmy John.

Mick read the terror in her face. He raised his palms. "Hey, relax. I'd like us to talk, okay?"

"All right."

Reluctantly, Lydia led the way to the living room, hoping he meant what he'd said. No one knew he was here, except Ron, who must have sent for him to deal with her. She perched on the edge of one of the sofas. Mick Diminio sank heavily into the other. He rubbed his hand along the fabric.

"Nice couches. My wife's been looking for something like these. Maybe you'll give her the name of the place where you bought them."

"Sure."

He glanced around, nodding his approval of her décor. Then he placed his elbows on his knees and leaned forward.

"Ronnie tells me maybe Danny didn't die of a coronary."

"His daughter thinks he was murdered. He told Polly he was getting nuisance calls. And someone followed his car when he was out running errands."

Mick let out a guilty laugh. "That was me tailing him."

Lydia stared at him, dumbfounded by his admission. "Why?"

He shrugged his beefy shoulders. "He pissed me off, coming around asking questions that were none of his business. But I swear on my grandson's head, I didn't kill him."

Of course he'd deny it. "Did Ron Morganstern make the phone calls?"

"How should I know? You'll have to ask Ronnie."

Lydia swallowed. "I'll do that."

"Speaking of which, he said you were checking into business that doesn't concern you."

Lydia pressed her elbows to her sides to control a rising tremor.

Mick continued, his tone now conversational. "I heard you were a big help solving some murders around here. Last autumn was it?"

He stared at her, willing her to speak, but fear kept her tongue-tied. She managed to nod.

"Very commendable, but your snooping days are over, at least where Ronnie and I are concerned." He leaned over the table separating them. Lydia jerked back.

"No little chats with your detective friend about him or me, including what I said before about tailing Danny. Got it?"

She nodded.

Having said what he'd come to say, Mick struggled to his feet. His hoarse breathing made her realize how much it had cost Mick Diminio to come threaten her this way.

He's just an old man used to ordering people around. She was annoyed that she'd allowed his tough-guy manner to intimidate her.

She stood in one graceful move. "The police have ID'd the body found at the demolition site. They know Timmy John Desmond was buried in the root cellar of that house."

"How sad. And what does that have to do with Ronnie or me? Absolutely nothing."

"Then why are you here?" she asked.

"To advise you to keep my name out of it. My son's running for county executive in a few months. We don't want to give the opposition ammunition for their smear campaign."

At last she had the reason behind his visit! Mick Diminio intended to see his son soar to higher pinnacles than he'd ever reached. The knowledge erased her last vestige of apprehension. It was time to burst his bubble.

"The police don't need me to tie you and Ron to Daniel and Timmy John Desmond. They have evidence of their own."

He clamped a gnarled hand around her forearm. "What are you talking about?"

Though his grip was strong, Lydia yanked back his pinky until he let go. "You'll find out soon enough. Now leave my house and don't bother me again, or I'll call Newsday and Channel Twelve to publicize your threats."

"I don't think you want to do that." A sly expression flitted across his face, and Lydia felt her heart fall to her stomach. She'd underestimated the old pol.

"Did our Danny-boy make notes about our little chat?"

She nodded, mesmerized by his intense gaze.

"Sure, we met and talked about old times. A stroll down memory lane." His eyes narrowed. "Anything else is pure conjecture. Let the cops question me. I'll know if you opened your big mouth. Then maybe your family won't be so happy."

Lydia's throat went dry. She had to swallow before she could speak. "What do you mean?"

"Your lovely little granddaughters live—where?—a few miles from here? It would be a pity if something were to happen. Say, if their lovely home burned to the ground."

All breath left her body. Her legs turned to rubber and she crumpled to the sofa, her mind a blaze of white terror. "You wouldn't."

"I certainly wouldn't want to. But I'm sure you'll keep our conversation to yourself, so little Brittany and Greta grow up to be lovely women like their grandmother."

She stared at him as he walked toward the door.

"Good-bye, Lydia. I'll see myself out."

Chapter Nine

Lydia huddled on the sofa, unable to move. Her precious babies! The man was a thug. A monster willing to burn down her daughter's home to shut her up. She shuddered to think he'd made it his business to learn the names and addresses of her family, the people she held dearest in the world.

She finally rose. Her hands trembled as she boiled water for tea. She stirred three teaspoons of sugar into her cup because she'd read somewhere that sugar was good for shock. Reggie, sensing her agitation, settled in her lap and lifted his head for her to stroke him. His purring soothed her, as did the sweet, warm liquid. Her pulse slowed down, and her mind returned to its normal state—alert, curious, and ready to cope with situations and problems.

As Lydia mentally replayed her conversation with Mick Diminio, her fear turned to anger. She discovered she was furious with Ron Morganstern. She'd frightened him, and so he'd set his dog on her. Mick Diminio was frightened, too. Why else would he come on like a goon and threaten her daughter's family, a threat she dearly hoped was nothing more than the words of a desperate man?

She should tell Sol. He had the authority to confront Mick Diminio and put him on notice. But Mick was only a danger if she talked to the police. And Sol would be furious with her for getting into the situation in the first place. No, she wouldn't ask for his help—yet.

Instead, she reached for the phone and called Barbara. Damn! She wasn't in. She left a message for her to call back ASAP, then dialed Ron Morganstern's home.

Bella Morganstern picked up. Lydia greeted her and asked if Ron was there.

"Yes, he is, dear. He's saying good-bye to a friend. Can you hold on a minute?"

"Gladly," Lydia said, hoping her steely tone hadn't upset the older woman.

It didn't seem to. "So much activity lately. Visitors coming and going, and we've tickets with friends for tonight's performance of 'South Pacific' at the Bellport Theatre." Bella giggled. "It serves one good purpose. I'm much too busy to think about my aches and pains."

"I'm glad, Bella."

"Well, here's Ronnie. Bye, Lydia."

"Yes?" Ron sounded wary. "What is it this time, Lydia?"

"Did your goon friend assure you everything's fine? Because it isn't."

"I don't know what you're talking about."

"No? You both must be shaking in your boots to come up with a scheme like burning down my daughter's home."

She heard his intake of air. "That's absurd. I have to go, Lydia."

"We're going to talk, Ron. Now."

"I just told you, I can't—"

Lydia grimaced, an expression her former employees knew was a sign she'd reached the end of her patience. She intended to speak to Ron, and not in her home.

"Meet me in front of the hardware store on Main Street. I'll be waiting. Be there in five minutes and don't call your pal." She trembled with fear and fury. "If you're not there, I'll call Detective Molina and tell him everything your pal Mick said. You'll both be arrested for harassment and menacing, and that's only the beginning of the charges against you. Won't Bella be proud of you?"

"Don't! I'll be there, I swear. As soon as I can."

"You'd better be," she said, and hung up.

The phone rang. That's Ron, canceling, she thought. It was Barbara.

"I need you to turn on your computer and find out everything you can about Mick Diminio, retired politician. Print it all out for me, okay?"

"Are you talking about Michael Diminio's father? The man we met at the funeral?"

"That's exactly who I mean. He was here, threatening to harm Meredith's family if I don't stop investigating what happened to the boy found in the root cellar."

"My God, Lydia! Call Sol. Let him take over."

"Not yet. The threat was meant to keep me from going to the police."

"Sol isn't a fool!" Barbara exclaimed. "He'd never do anything to endanger your family."

"I'm off to meet Ron Morganstern. I'll find out what happened to that poor boy, if it's the last thing I do."

"Be careful, Lydia. I don't want anything to happen to you."

"Me, neither. But if something should, I expect you to make Reggie a good home."

She drove the short distance to Main Street and found a parking spot a few shops down from the hardware store. Ron Morganstern was pacing up and down the sidewalk. He must have jumped into his car and sped the few blocks the second he'd put down the phone.

"Hello, Ron," she greeted him in her crisp CEO tone. "We need to talk." She noticed his shirt was half in, half out of his pants. Sweat rolled down his cheeks.

"Okay, but I want you to know this isn't good for my heart."

Lydia pointed to a bench on a strip of lawn nearby. "Over there. No one will hear us."

He nodded and followed her. Another eighty-five-year-old man, she thought as they sat down. Only this one was soft and pudgy. And guilt-stricken. From Ron's reaction to Andrew's mention of the unearthed body and from their talk yesterday, she knew that whatever had taken place seventy years ago still weighed heavily on his soul.

"Now," she said softly, "tell me what happened to Timmy John."

Ron sank heavily onto the bench. He looked at her with sad cocker spaniel eyes. "I want you to know, it was an accident. We never meant no harm."

"Go on."

He cleared his throat. "Danny, Micky, Billy, and I were friends when we were kids, as far back as I can remember. We were always together—playing ball after school, sleeping over at each other's houses on weekends. Danny, being the smartest, was our leader. Sure, we knew how to goad each other. Insults flew, and sometimes we ended up fighting, but when it came to other kids, we four stuck together like glue. We were a team. Nobody pushed us around. Once, some kid stole Billy's bicycle. Danny planned to get it back and we did. Mickey even beat the kid up, which made Billy forget about his smashed fender."

Lydia nodded, but now Ron needed no encouragement to continue. Mick Diminio wouldn't be happy that his old friend was spilling the beans.

"We were in tenth grade when Timmy John moved in with his aunt and uncle. Right after Thanksgiving. Our group was still close, but we were getting bombarded with changes—our bodies, for one thing. And we started noticing girls. We'd flirt with them on the way home from school. Danny and Mickey were on the school football and baseball teams. Billy was heavily into the thespian group."

"And you?" Lydia couldn't help asking.

Ron shrugged. "I concentrated on doing my schoolwork and getting good grades. I'd decided I was going to college to become a C.P.A., which I did.

"As I said, it was after Thanksgiving when Timmy John came. The weather was turning cold, and the four of us were bored—no sports, no play, no anything. The principal brought him into our social studies class and said he was from Arkansas. The minute he opened his mouth with that funny way he talked, we all cracked up laughing. The next period he had art and so did Danny, and we lost Danny to Timmy John."

Lydia was intrigued. "What do you mean? I thought you said he was a creep. Why would Danny be interested in a kid like that?"

"Because he could draw like nobody's business, this tall, skinny kid with his Adam's apple sticking way out, his teeth as crooked as a smashed-up piano keyboard. He'd squint at a scene or a person, and the next minute get every detail down with his pencil. I'm talking wrinkles, shading, emotion—you name it, it was there."

"I saw his portrait of Daniel. It's an amazing likeness."

"It wasn't just the art. Danny was like bewitched." Ron shook his head. "I'm talking about Danny, who would cut school three days in a row and get the highest grade on a test. Danny was an athlete, for God's sake. In baseball, he could field as well as he could swing a bat, and score runs for our team. But he listened to Timmy John talk about Arkansas, about his bastard of a stepfather who beat him till he was knocked unconscious, about stuff we never thought about. Danny started talking strange, too. Like he was hypnotized. And frankly, we didn't like it."

"You thought Timmy John was taking Daniel from you?"

"We didn't think—we knew. We'd invite Danny over to shoot pool, suggest we ride our bikes to the candy store where the girls hung out, but he was always busy. Studying, he said, but we knew he was with his new friend, talking for hours. Solving the problems of the world, for God's sake."

Ron paused. He covered his face with his hands, and for a moment Lydia feared he wouldn't go on.

"Then Billy had this idea. We'd invite Timmy John over one afternoon after school. Tell him Danny wanted us to get to know him better."

"For what reason? Were you planning to beat him up?"

Ron wouldn't meet her gaze. "Mickey wanted to push him around a bit, let him know we were sore at him for taking our friend away, but Billy and I wouldn't have let him go too far. That's what I mean—we acted like a team. We knew one another as well as we knew our own selves and kept each other in check. Anyway, Billy's parents worked at the factory, his older sisters worked on a neighbor's farm, so we had the house to ourselves."

He took a deep breath and continued. "I caught up with Timmy John as we came home from school and told him Danny said to tell him to meet him at Billy's house. Timmy John was wary. He said that couldn't be since Danny was coming over as soon as he ran an errand for his mother. I told him I'd just talked to Danny, and he'd changed his mind. He wanted Timmy John to meet him at Billy's so we could get to know him better. When he still hesitated, I shrugged and told him to do what he liked, but if he intended to have friends here he'd go along with Danny's plans."

Ron turned pale as he told his tale that ended with Timmy John's death.

"In the end, he came. Billy let him in and took him into the kitchen. Timmy John blinked when he saw the three of us standing side by side, grinning like idiots. 'Where's Danny?' he asked. 'He'll be along soon,' we told him.

"Billy had this dumb braying laugh, and it scared Timmy John even more. He ran for the front door and the three of us went after him. We dragged him into the living room." Ron shook his head. "I swear, I don't know what happened. I mean, we held him down and told him he wasn't going anywhere. His eyes about popped out of his head and Billy brayed again. Timmy John screamed, and Mick slapped him. Slapped his face, I swear, nothing more, but the kid began to buck and moan, and it looked like foam was coming out of his mouth."

"He had an epileptic fit," Lydia murmured.

"At the time, we didn't know what it was, only that we were petrified. We let go of him. Slowly, Timmy John sat up. We thought he was all right. Then he jerked back his head and banged it against the coffee table. Hard. Then he was still.

"We stared at him in shock. Mick felt for his pulse and couldn't find one. I checked his neck, his wrist, but there was nothing. We looked at one another, all of us as frightened as we'd ever been.

"'He's dead,' Billy said.

"'How can that be?' Mick asked. 'We didn't do nothing to him.'

"'He's dead all the same,' I said.

"We heard a noise outside and jumped to our feet. Billy said we'd better pull him outside. Mick said no, someone would see. What about the root cellar? At first Billy didn't go for the idea, but I went down to check it out. The Evans' house was a ranch, and the root cellar went all the way back, though his family never used it. Besides, it was cold down there. I remember how I shivered when I returned to the living room.

"We wrapped Timmy John up in an old quilt and carried him down to the root cellar. Just in time, too, because one of Billy's sisters came home right after. We swore we wouldn't tell anyone, including Danny, about what happened. We were petrified we'd be sent to the electric chair for murder. The cops came and questioned each of us, but we stuck to our story, that we had no idea where Timmy John could be. We met twice to talk about moving the body, but couldn't come up with a good plan, so we ended up leaving it where it was."

Ron gave a hiccup of a laugh. "After that, our group fell apart. Danny asked each of us if we'd seen Timmy John that afternoon, then he pretty much ignored us. I think he suspected we might have roughed him up but couldn't bring himself to think we'd actually harm the kid. Mick started hanging out with a tough crowd. We lost track of one another, but reconnected when my wife and I moved back to Long Island. Billy and his family moved away, after he graduated from high school. I worried a lot when I heard the new owners were doing renovations and putting on a second floor. But I never heard anything about finding a body, so I supposed they left the root cellar alone."

"And Timmy John remained buried there until the house was demolished," Lydia said.

Ron buried his face in his hands. A gut-wrenching sob rose from his throat. "We did a terrible thing, leaving him to rot, his family never knowing he was dead. Every day I wish I could undo it. I think of going to the police, but what good would that do? It wouldn't change a thing, except Mick and I would end up in jail." He looked at her. "And now you'll tell your detective friend everything I just said."

Lydia met his pleading eyes. "I should. He knows I went to talk to you about Timmy John, that Daniel started a file on you and your friend, Mick Diminio."

Ron waved his hand. "Danny didn't know anything, so nothing's in his files. We answered those questions when we were kids. We can answer them again. There's nothing to tie the body that was found in the Evans' house to Mick and me."

"I know that," Lydia said.

Ron gripped her hand. "I swear we didn't kill him! You have to believe me! Mick and I, we don't talk about what happened, but neither of us will ever forget, not one single day. Mick's first grandson was born with a defective heart. The poor kid had one surgery after another and died before his second birthday. Mick made a very generous contribution to the hospital in his grandson's name. For research. I know that was in large part because of Timmy John."

"I'd find that touching if your pal hadn't threatened my grandchildren."

"It's my fault and I'm deeply sorry. I told Mick to come on strong and he went overboard. He likes to talk tough, but he wouldn't hurt anyone. Not since he watched Timmy John die before our eyes."

Lydia nodded, suddenly convinced he was telling the truth. She believed they hadn't killed the boy and, seeing the sweat run down Ron's pasty-white face, knew he suffered for his part in the scheme that had ended so horribly wrong.

"All right. I won't repeat to Lieutenant Molina what you've told me, as long as I have your word you had nothing to do with Daniel's death."

"Thank you, Lydia, thank you!" He squeezed her hand, so tightly she winced in pain.

"What about Daniel?" she persisted.

"What are you talking about? Daniel had a coronary."

"Did you follow him in your car?"

Ron cast down his eyes. All life went from his voice. "Mick did that. And I called his house a few times. Stupid, I know, but we were hoping to scare him off. He was persistent, Danny was. Oh, God! Are you saying that caused his heart attack?"

Lydia moved closer and lowered her voice. "Do you think Mick killed him?"

For a minute Ron didn't answer. Then he shook his head. "Mick's dying. The doctors give him four to six months. Murder's the last thing he wants on his conscience."

Lydia studied Ron's wrinkled face. It was riddled with fear and guilt, his skin the unhealthy color of white paste. She suspected he hadn't much more time, either.

"Thank you for telling me what happened to Timmy John. I'll keep it to myself as long as I can."

Chapter Ten

Lydia drove home slowly, her mind awhirl as she reviewed her conversation with Ron Morganstern. She'd never been privy to a confession of such magnitude and found it impossible to absorb all its ramifications. *Poor Timmy John!* She could visualize him so clearly—a sensitive, gangly boy with a Southern accent, damaged by his stepfather but lucky to have a mother with the good sense to send him north to live with her sister and brother-in-law. Lydia shivered as she realized the poor woman went to her grave never knowing what had happened to her son. The anguish and guilt she must have experienced.

As for Ron, he appeared to be genuinely remorseful for the part he'd played the day of the terrible accident that had led to Timmy John's death. If it was an accident. Lydia felt a pang as she considered that one of the boys—Mick, perhaps?—could have struck the fatal blow, then convinced the others that Timmy John had fallen. Could they have invented the part about his epileptic seizure? Regardless, she had no business—no right—to keep what Ron had told her from the police. Her silence made her an accessory after the fact. If, indeed, Ron, Mick, and Billy Evans had killed Timmy John, which she sincerely doubted.

Seventy years had passed. Billy was dead, Mick was dying, and Ron regretted having lured Timmy John to the Evans' home every day of his life. She'd promised not to tell Sol about his and Mick's involvement, and she'd keep that promise for now.

As she approached the Twin Lakes gatehouse, her thoughts turned to Daniel. The discovery of Timmy John's remains had reawakened his suspicions. He'd gone around asking questions and now he was dead. Ron insisted he hadn't gone after Daniel, and Lydia believed him. He was too jumpy and frail to plan a murder, much less carry one out.

But his friend, Mick, was a different story. As old and ill as he was, Mick Diminio had a brutish quality. He had no qualms about threatening her grandchildren, whether he meant to follow through or not. Daniel could cause more damage than she. He could supply background information about the day Timmy John had died, information no one else was privy to. Not that Daniel had any hard evidence to offer. Despite Ron's assurances, fear for his son's shot at county executive might have given Mick enough reason to kill Daniel as his last paternal deed before going to his final rest.

Lydia pulled into her driveway and waited for the garage door to open. If Mick had killed Daniel, how did he do it? Evelyn certainly would have mentioned if he'd been to see Daniel the morning he'd suffered what appeared to be a fatal heart attack. In which case, Ron was telling the truth.

Lydia sat in her car as the implication of her latest idea struck home. Maybe Polly was wrong. Maybe Daniel had died of a coronary like thousands of other eighty-five-year-old men with heart conditions. Polly assumed someone had killed her father because he'd told her he was being tailed and receiving strange phone calls. Ron and Mick were behind those acts of harassment. Lydia felt a blush warm her cheeks as she remembered how quickly she'd agreed with Polly that Daniel had been murdered. Pure hubris on her part. She had no right to view every death as a homicide and herself as the sleuth, simply because she'd helped solve the murders last fall.

Her ears burned with embarrassment as she recalled how quick she'd been to inform Sol about Daniel's "murder." If only she could call him back to say it was all a mistake. But she wouldn't. He'd reprimand her for interfering with his case. His case? There was no case as far as Lydia was concerned. She'd imagined two murders, and now it seemed there was no murder at all.

Besides, she couldn't call Sol without implicating Ron and Mick. Why had she promised Ron she wouldn't tell Sol how Timmy John had died? Surely Ron and Mick had broken the law by hiding Timmy John's body and not alerting the authorities. They'd lied to the police and were prepared to lie to them again. And now Lydia was part of their conspiracy. What had she gotten herself into? Where would it end? Damn it, the situation was growing more complicated by the minute.

Lydia ate a sandwich for her dinner, then plopped down on the den couch for an hour or two of TV before going to sleep. She felt thoroughly wiped out after her traumatic day.

The phone rang as she was dozing off during a commercial. What now? "Yes?" she asked rather gruffly.

"Hello, Lydia. It's Andrew."

"Andrew?"

"Andrew Varig," he said more forcefully.

"Of course, Andrew." She gave an embarrassed laugh. "What can I do for you?"

"Did you get a chance to look at your calendar?"

Her calendar. "Do we have to set up a committee meeting?"

"I suppose we should—soon, but I'm talking about Saturday night."

"Oh. Right." She remembered. "I'm checking right now. Hold on a second."

The small white squares of her May calendar were infuriatingly empty. No plans, no babysitting dates to watch her granddaughters. Her heart sank as she said, "It looks like I'm free that evening, Andrew."

"Wonderful, Lydia! I went online and discovered there's a new play coming from London. It's supposed to be clever and witty, so I took the chance and ordered us tickets. I hope you don't mind."

"No. It sounds delightful."

He gave a little laugh. "Since I chose the play, it's only fair that you pick the restaurant. What's your pleasure—French? American? Italian?"

"French sounds nice."

"Then French it is. I thought I'd pick you up at four, we'd have a leisurely drive in, and we'd dine at six."

"Sure. But Andrew..."

"Yes, Lydia?"

"We're going as friends, remember? Companions, nothing more."

"Absolutely. Good-bye, my dear! See you on Saturday."

My dear? The words echoed in her ears as she realized she'd never heard Andrew so ebullient before. Maybe his European trip had revived his sense of adventure, and he was looking forward to a night out on the town. She sincerely hoped that was the case, and that his newfound enthusiasm had nothing to do with her.

Ten minutes later, the phone rang again.

"Hello, Lydia, it's Sol."

"Oh. Hello." She pressed the mute button on the remote.

Silence. He let out a sheepish laugh. "You don't sound happy to hear from me."

"I don't appreciate the way you spoke to me last night."

"I apologize, Lydia. I shouldn't have exploded the way I did."

"Then why did you?" she retorted before she could weigh the wisdom of such a question.

"Because I worry about you. Damn it, I care about you, Lydia Krause."

"You have a funny way of showing it."

"I know. I'm sorry about that and I want to make amends. Let's go out for a nice romantic dinner somewhere."

"That sounds promising," she said, then immediately regretted her words. She didn't want to come across as overly eager to accept his apology, so she added, "As long as this dinner won't compromise your case is any way."

He laughed. "Why should it? The case, as you put it, concerns a death that occurred before you were born. Besides, the remains show no sign of foul play, though the lab's testing for poisons."

Lydia sighed with relief. "That's good to hear."

"It still doesn't explain why someone stashed the body in the root cellar. That's a crime, too."

"I know." Lydia's heart pounded in her chest. She could barely get her words out. "Do you think you can find out who put the body there, after all these years?"

"If we can't, it won't be for lack of trying. How about Saturday night?"

"This Saturday night?"

"Yes. Why, are you babysitting?"

She considered saying she was babysitting, but there were too many lies of omission between her and Sol that he knew nothing about. She opted for the truth. "I have a date."

"Have fun."

The line went dead.

"And that's how you left it?" Barbara asked the following afternoon, turning her attention from the road to stare at a despondent Lydia.

"I told you—Sol hung up."

"Without arranging another time for your romantic dinner?"

"There is no dinner!" Lydia blinked back hurt and angry tears. "Lately, Sol has this way of cutting short every conversation we have."

"Why did you tell him you were going out with someone else?"

Distraught, Lydia glanced down at her hands, noticing that her nail polish was chipping. "Because I wanted to be honest with him."

Barbara laughed.

"I know it was stupid, but I feel guilty for not telling Sol what Ron told me about Timmy John. He's the police. I'm withholding evidence. But I promised not to say anything, at least for now. And every conversation Sol and I have turns into a fight. This whole business has left me exhausted."

She felt her friend's eyes studying her. Barbara asked, "Are you sure you're up to a shiva call?"

"I want to spend time with Polly and her family. I barely stayed five minutes after the funeral. That was two days ago. With so much happening in between, if feels like a month."

"Whatever you say. By the way, who is the lucky fellow?" Barbara asked as she turned into Polly's development.

Lydia bit her lip. "I accepted a date with Andrew Varig to take in dinner and a play in the city. I don't want to go."

"Oh, Lydia, Andrew's nice, once you get past his diffident manner."

"Then you go out with him."

"I would, but he asked you."

As she parallel parked, Lydia waited for Barbara to crack a smile. When she didn't, Lydia realized her friend meant what she'd said.

"I'm sorry, Barbara. I had no idea you were interested in Andrew."

"I don't know if I'm 'interested,' but I find Andrew handsome and virile—rare attributes in our community."

"Really? Had I known, I never would have accepted his invitation. I only said yes because I couldn't think of a polite way of refusing."

Lydia's dismay must have been written all over her face, because Barbara squeezed her arm and laughed. "And then you'd have told him to call your friend, Barbara? Sorry, honey, it doesn't work that way."

Feeling foolish, Lydia opened the rear car door. She and Barbara gathered up the bags of prepared food they'd brought and carried them into the house.

About sixteen people sat around the living room, chatting and eating. Nicole, the Good Twin, came over to greet them. Lydia explained they'd brought dinner for the next few nights.

"Thanks so much for thinking of us." Nicole caught her mother's eye, then took two of the packages and carried them into the kitchen. Polly ended her conversation with an elderly man and came to join them. She hugged Lydia and Barbara then led the way to the kitchen where Nicole was already stacking casseroles and salads in the refrigerator.

"This is from the Liebermans, Shari Morgan, and us," Barbara explained.

"Thank you for being so kind." Polly's eyes filled as she hugged them again. "It helps to know my father had good friends at Twin Lakes the few years he and Evelyn lived there."

Her husband, Matt, entered the room to refill a pitcher of milk. "Look who's here!" he exclaimed, opening his arms and giving them each a bear hug.

Lydia and Barbara followed Polly into the living room, where she introduced them to her other guests. Most were elderly relatives and long-time friends of Daniel. Lydia was hoping to see Evelyn here, but there was no sign of her.

"Have some coffee and dessert," Polly suggested. She gestured with her chin to the woman chatting with Denise in the corner. "My cousin Lynn brought the most outrageous pastries from a famous Brooklyn bakery."

"Let's," Barbara said, and headed across the hall to the dining room, with Lydia close behind.

Two elderly men sat at the long table laden with platters of cookies and cakes and a carafe of coffee. They barely looked up from their plates to return Lydia and Barbara's greetings. The women selected slices of cake and pastries. Lydia poured out two cups of decaf coffee.

"Why don't we sit in here?" Barbara suggested, gesturing at the two chairs at the opposite end of the table. "The living room's kind of crowded."

They set down their food and began to eat.

"Mmm, delicious," Lydia said, pointing to her apple strudel.

"Wait till you taste the chocolate blackout cake. It's to die for."

Lydia grimaced. "I wish you wouldn't use that expression."

"Oh—sorry," Barbara said.

Lydia flinched as a wiry arm snaked around her shoulders. "Hello, Lydia. Thanks for coming."

Lydia looked up into Denise's tanned leathery face, then pulled away from the blended fumes of musky perfume and tobacco that threatened to make her gag.

"Hello, Denise. This is my friend, Barbara Taylor."

Barbara turned to Denise. "I'm very sorry for your loss. Your father was one terrific person. He was always so energetic and active."

Denise pulled up a chair and sat down. "His passing knocked us all for a loop. Dad was in good health, then pow." Denise snapped her fingers. "Gone. Eighty-five years old."

"Almost eighty-five, Mater. Tomorrow's his birthday."

Mater? Lydia watched as Denise's son, Bennett, squeezed past his mother to reach the box of Belgian chocolates and pop one into his mouth.

Denise patted his arm. "So sad. I always thought he'd live to be one hundred."

"Life throws us curves when we least expect them," Bennett philosophized as he chewed.

"Lydia, Barbara, this is my son, Bennett. Lydia and Barbara were Grandpa's friends and neighbors at Twin Lakes."

Bennett looked Lydia up and down then winked. "Yes, indeed. We met at Grandpa's party."

Lydia's nostrils flared as they tended to when she was angry, but she restrained the urge to smack his impertinent face.

Bennett switched personas to that of the dutiful son. "Thank you both for coming today and to the funeral. Mom and Aunt Polly appreciate your support."

"I don't see your brother, Arnold," Barbara said to Denise. "Is he here?"

"Oh, Arnold." Denise dismissed him with a wave of her hand. "He and his family are sitting shiva in New Jersey. He said coming to Long Island was too much of an inconvenience for his friends and neighbors."

Bennett was working on a brownie. In between bites, he said, "Mom, I have to go to work now."

"Then eat something nourishing, Benny. Aunt Polly has plenty of food in the kitchen."

"Mom." His tone sounded a warning. Denise let loose a carefree laugh as false as a three-dollar bill. "I know, you're a grown man and I have to stop nagging."

"Would you like me to drive you home so you can get your car?"

"That won't be necessary."

"You're sure? Tonight's my late night. I can't come back here for you until after ten. Aunt Polly might want to go to sleep before then."

Startled by the steely undercurrent in his voice, Lydia and Barbara exchanged glances.

Denise chucked Bennett under the chin. "Darling boy, don't worry about me. I'll get a ride when I'm ready to leave."

"With who? Stefano?"

Another false laugh. "Yes, as a matter of fact. He's coming by later to pay his respects."

Bennett's handsome face burnished red. "He's the Twin Lakes handyman, for God's sake! He has no business coming here!"

"Of course he does, Benny. Stefano's my friend. Besides, your grandfather liked him."

Bennett threw his mother a look of disdain. "He wouldn't if he knew the guy was getting into your pants."

"What a terrible thing to say!" Denise blinked furiously but couldn't stop two fat tears from rolling down her cheeks. She dabbed at her heavily mascaraed eye as Bennett stormed out of the room.

"Don't pay any attention to my silly son," she said to Lydia and Barbara, as if Bennett were twelve and had just stuck out his tongue in defiance. "He hates every man who comes into my life. Except for his father, of course, now that he's dead. Benny conveniently forgets Chet used to gamble away whatever money he earned and left us to fend for ourselves."

What a dysfunctional pair! She's as outrageous as her son is rude. Lydia picked up her coffee cup, determined to escape, when Denise's moment of mortification changed to one of watchful cunning. She moved her chair closer to Lydia.

"I'm glad you came today, Lydia. We need to talk."

"Oh?" Lydia caught Barbara's wink as her friend crossed the hall to the living room.

Denise glanced over at the two old men recounting stories of their youth before she began to speak in a low voice.

"Arnold and I are upset because Polly's convinced someone killed Daddy. She said you agreed to go with her when she reports her foolish notion to your friend on the police force."

Lydia felt a pang of guilt for having already told this much to Sol. "I'm beginning to think Polly's overreacting to your father's sudden death."

"Dad was eighty-five, for God's sake. He died of a coronary! Talk to Polly, Lydia. Explain that there's no need to exhume the body. The man was just laid to rest."

"I'll talk to her," Lydia said, "but I don't know what good it will do."

Denise's smile held a tinge of mockery when she said, "Polly thinks you're an expert on crime because you helped solve the murders last fall. Trust me, this was no crime."

"I certainly hope not," Lydia murmured.

"Polly regarded our father as some kind of immortal god. She revered him in a most unhealthy way. And he encouraged it. Boy, did he encourage it."

The venom in Denise's tone would have shocked Lydia if not for all she'd learned from Daniel's friends the night of the party.

"I suppose they were very close."

"You might say that!" Denise snapped. Then she remembered she needed a favor, and her tone softened. "So you'll talk to Polly?"

"Talk to Polly about what?" Polly asked, resting her hand on Lydia's shoulder.

Lydia squirmed. She wished she could fly out the door and disappear.

"About your far-fetched idea that someone killed Dad," Denise said. "Lydia agrees it's ridiculous."

"You do?"

Lydia flinched under Polly's scrutiny, the shock of betrayal in her eyes.

"I don't believe it! You knew Daddy was upset about something serious."

"That's true, but I've been thinking it over...." Lydia found she was unable to finish the sentence. She couldn't very well explain that while Daniel's old friends had admitted to harassing him, she believed them when they swore they hadn't harmed him. "The fact that your father was upset doesn't prove that someone killed him. In fact, the emotional turmoil might have brought on the coronary."

Tears of frustration glistened in Polly's eyes. "The other day you were on my side! Now you're treating me like a kid who's made up a wild story because she can't cope with her father's death!"

Denise, suddenly composed, patted her sister's arm. "You have to calm down, Pol. You don't want to work yourself into another stint in the hospital."

Matt appeared and wrapped his arms around his sobbing wife. "Polly, honey," he crooned.

"I'm so sorry," Lydia said. "I didn't mean to make matters worse." She moved to comfort Polly, but Polly stuck out her hand to ward her off.

Mortified, Lydia fled to the bedroom where the sweaters and jackets were strewn across the bed. She grabbed hers and Barbara's.

"What's the matter?" Barbara asked as Lydia thrust her jacket at her.

"I'll explain in the car," Lydia said, making a beeline for the front door. She breathed a deep sigh as she stepped onto the porch, then stopped short to avoid crashing into Nicole and Gillian, who faced one another with the antagonism of spitting cats.

"Sorry," Lydia apologized.

In silence, the twins moved apart to let them pass. Despite her own agitation, Lydia knew something was terribly wrong. Before stepping into Barbara's car, she turned to observe them. The girls practically touched foreheads as they argued in whispers. Finally, Gillian threw up her hands and stormed inside the house. Nicole ran past the two women, to a car parked halfway up the block. The driver stuck out his head. Lydia recognized Nicole's scruffy boyfriend from Daniel's party. A minute later, the two were entwined in a passionate embrace.

Once they were in the car, Lydia turned to Barbara. "I wonder why Nicole's boyfriend didn't go into the house… and why were the girls fighting like that?"

"I've no idea," Barbara said, turning the ignition and backing out of the parking space. "Before you strong-armed me away, I heard Nicole's cell phone ring and saw her run outside. Gillian chased after her a minute later, looking mighty determined."

"Clearly, Polly doesn't approve of Ringo, or whatever his real name is."

Barbara stared at the two lovebirds, still lip-locked, as they drove by. "But why is Gillian so angry? Unless her sister stole her boyfriend. This Ringo looks more her type than Nicole's."

Lydia shook her head and sighed. "Today's so full of calamities, I can't even begin to imagine what's troubling the girls."

As they passed Meredith's house, Lydia felt a wave of gratitude that she and Merry had ironed out their difficulties. There were enough people angry with her as it was.

"What on earth did Denise want from you?" Barbara asked. She shuddered. "That woman gives me the willies."

Lydia sighed. "She asked me to help convince Polly there's no need to exhume Daniel's body. Though I don't much care for Denise, her son, or her brother, I tend to believe they're right—that Daniel died a natural death—so I agreed to talk to Polly. At which point, she joined us and was hurt and angry because I'd changed sides. I gather from a comment Denise made that Polly once had a nervous breakdown. At any rate,

Polly now sees me as a traitor and wants no part of me." She rubbed her temples. "I think I'm getting a headache."

"Poor Lydia," Barbara said, patting her knee. "Today isn't your day."

Chapter Eleven

L ydia refused Barbara's dinner invitation, preferring to stew in private. She punched in her garage door code with a vengeance. Her headache felt as though several elves were pounding on her skull with tiny hammers. She wanted to close the drapes in her bedroom, crawl under her quilt, and fall into a dreamless sleep.

What was happening to her? Had she lost all her managerial know-how in the one short year since she'd retired as CEO of Krause's Gifts and Furnishings? Had her people skills withered away, now that she was no longer a player in the business world? Lydia shuddered as she reviewed the way she'd leapfrogged from one calamitous situation to another in the last few days, leaving unhappy or furious victims in her wake.

She splashed water into a glass and downed two aspirins. Reggie came in, tail high, meowing loudly for both a show of affection and his dinner. Lydia scooped him into her arms and pressed her face against his furry haunch.

"Thank God I have you, Reginald Redcoat."

He butted his face against hers, then struggled to be free.

"Your meow is my command. Dinner's coming up," Lydia said, following him to the kitchen.

The essence of her problem occurred to her as she watched Reggie gobble down his chicken in gravy in a most un-feline way. She wasn't anyone's boss any longer. Why had it taken her almost a year to realize this fact?

Lydia stumbled into the living room and dropped onto a sofa. Running her company all those years, she'd grown accustomed to making unilateral decisions. She'd issued orders, which her employees had carried out. Not that she'd ever related to her family or her friends in this manner.

Now this side of her—this CEO persona—reared its head when she played detective, seeking information regarding what were murder cases—what she thought were murder cases—with dire consequences. She felt the heat of a blush as she recalled how she'd encouraged Polly to view her father's death as a homicide. How she'd badgered Ron Morganstern until he told her about Timmy John. She was relieved to learn that he and Mick hadn't murdered him, but uncovering such information was the police's job, not hers. No wonder Sol was furious at her. She'd give him a few days to calm down, then call to beg his pardon for interfering in his business. And hope he hadn't decided to kiss their relationship good-bye.

His meal finished, Reggie set about cleaning himself. Lydia checked her messages. Nothing. The phone rang. Her heart thumped away as she lifted it, hoping it was Sol. Her spirits plummeted when the caller identified herself as Evelyn's daughter, Gayle.

"Lydia, I hope I'm not imposing on you, but my husband and I are leaving for Atlanta. We'd hoped to stay longer, but our daughter, Lynn, has been taken to the hospital." Gayle made a sound between a laugh and a sob. "Why does everything happen at once?"

"I'm so sorry!" Lydia exclaimed. "What can I do to help?"

"Lynn will be all right. She has a chronic medical condition that requires frequent hospitalization. Her husband's in the Far East, and we want to be there for the little ones. I've asked Mom to come back to Atlanta with us, but she refuses.

"What I want to ask you," Gayle went on, "is would you please spend some time with my mother? She's been turning away friends and neighbors, but she feels comfortable with you. I know she'd welcome your company."

"I'd be happy to," Lydia reassured Gayle, pleased that at least someone wasn't angry with her. "I'll stop over later."

"Thank you, Lydia. You're an angel."

I'm no angel, she thought as she put down the phone. Still, it was nice to be called one after being driven from the home of a mourner.

Evelyn put up little resistance when Lydia called and offered to bring over dinner for both of them.

"That would be lovely, Lydia. I've plenty of cake, so don't bother with dessert."

Lydia agreed to come at seven so Evelyn could fit in a nap. She'd been sleeping badly at night and was thoroughly exhausted.

At first, Lydia contemplated ordering a variety of dishes from the take-out Chinese restaurant in town. Then she decided that cooking a meal would be just the thing to take her mind off Daniel and Timmy John's deaths and the people she'd recently upset. She sautéed chicken breasts, which she then placed in a deep dish, alternating the chicken with tomato slices, grilled eggplant slices, mushrooms, peppers, and cheese. While the casserole baked, she made a rice pilaf and a salad. When everything was done, she placed the three dishes in the refrigerator, along with a nice bottle of chardonnay, and went into the den to watch the news. When she got to Evelyn's, she'd pop the casserole and the pilaf into the microwave oven.

Dusk was darkening the sky by the time Lydia carefully placed the two shopping bags filled with dinner into her car. She felt ridiculous driving the short distance, but she couldn't manage to carry everything on foot. She pulled into Evelyn's driveway, surprised to find the house in darkness. Evelyn was one for lights, and plenty of them. But maybe she'd taken a pill to help her sleep and was still off in dreamland.

Lydia grabbed her pocketbook and knocked on the front door. "Evelyn!" she called, loud enough to be heard inside. Silence. She went around to the back and tried the kitchen door. The knob turned easily. Lydia switched on the light and stepped cautiously into the house. Something was wrong. Evelyn never left the door unlocked.

"Evelyn!" she shouted. "Can you hear me? Are you awake?"

She turned on the hall light and started down the narrow hallway toward the bedrooms. The door to the master bedroom was ajar. Lydia approached the queen-sized bed and gasped. Evelyn lay on her side as still as a stone. A dark stain spread on the pillow beneath her head. Though the light was dim, Lydia knew it was blood that had seeped from a wound on the back of her head.

"Evelyn!" Lydia trembled as she knelt beside the motionless woman. Her moan was barely audible, but Lydia exhaled with relief. Her friend was alive.

"Stay calm, dear, while I call for help. You'll be all right, I promise."

Lydia squeezed Evelyn's hand and was heartened by the slight return of pressure. She turned on a lamp and peered down at the wound. It appeared to have stopped bleeding, but there was no telling if there was internal damage.

The sound of footsteps, of the front door opening, chilled her to the quick. Lydia remained frozen, her heart pounding against her ribs as she realized how close she'd come to being swatted as well. She'd walked in while Evelyn's attacker was still in the house!

She waited for what seemed like minutes before venturing into the hall to close the door. Still trembling, she called 911 from her cell phone. She relayed Evelyn's age and the extent of her injuries, gave her own name and Evelyn's address, and told them to send an ambulance as soon as possible. Next, she punched in Sol's cell number, grateful that she'd entered it into her cell phone's memory. She held her breath while the phone rang three times.

"Molina."

"Sol, it's me, Lydia."

"Lydia." She cringed at the impatience in his voice. "I can't talk now."

She felt her ears burn but forced herself to continue. "Someone's attacked Evelyn Hammond, Daniel Korman's fiancée. She was expecting me at seven with dinner. When she didn't answer the bell, I figured she was napping. I went around to the back and found the door unlocked." Lydia faltered. "Evelyn's in her bed, barely conscious after being struck on the head. I called for an ambulance, then I called you."

"Damn it, that place is a war zone! Sorry," he apologized before she could protest. He paused, then asked, his voice deadly calm, "Is anyone else in the house?"

She fought to control the tremor rippling through her body. "Not any longer. The intruder made a run for it while I was with Evelyn."

"You've got to stop playing detective! One of these days something terrible will happen, and I won't be around to help you."

She bit back the retort on the tip of her tongue. She'd been trying to be a good neighbor, not play Sherlock Holmes! But now wasn't the time to argue.

"Stay with Mrs. Hammond. I'm on my way. What's the address?"

She told him. "It's a few houses past mine, on the other side of the street. My car's in the driveway."

"See you."

Lydia checked to make sure Evelyn was breathing, then sank into the armchair in the corner of the bedroom beside an antique armoire. Such a lovely room, she thought, as tears welled up in her eyes. Would Evelyn be well enough to live here? Would she want to live here after all that had happened?

The shrill whine of a siren growing louder startled her from her reverie and she went to open the front door.

Three young emergency medical technicians, two men and a woman, entered the house. The woman—a buxom, cheerful type—checked Evelyn's vital signs, examined her wound, then nodded. The two men lifted Evelyn onto a stretcher.

The EMT in charge, a bearded bear of a man, asked Lydia several quick questions, which she answered as best she could. Then she said, "I'd like to go with her in the ambulance."

"Are you a relative?" the woman asked.

"I'm her friend and neighbor. Evelyn's almost eighty and she lost her fiancé a few days ago."

"Sorry," the bearded man said. "Our rules won't allow you to ride in the ambulance."

Lydia opened her mouth to argue, when she felt a tug on her arm. She turned and was astonished to see Sol Molina. When had he arrived?

"I'll drive you to the hospital after the crime scene team arrives. Meanwhile, I'd like you to fill me in on everything you know."

Half an hour later they were traveling swiftly along Sunrise Highway on their way to Brookhaven Hospital. Lydia glanced over at Sol, but his face was as unrevealing as a mask. She found it both surreal yet oddly appropriate that she should be riding beside him in his unmarked car on their way to see Evelyn. He'd questioned her in detail regarding what she'd seen and heard before entering the house—if she'd heard cars pass while still at home or if she'd noticed any parked on the street. As she had nothing to offer, the interrogation lasted five minutes. When Sol asked her to accompany him to the hospital, she was puzzled but saw no point in asking him why. Of course she agreed to go.

Sol pulled up to the curb of the emergency room entrance. "Lydia, why don't you go and find where they've put Mrs. Hammond. I'll park and catch up with you."

She nodded and stepped out of the car. She stopped at the security desk for her visitor's pass and learned that Evelyn was being attended to in the ER. She could go right through.

She found Evelyn being cared for in one of the cubicles set off by vinyl curtains.

"How is she?" she asked the young woman taking Evelyn's blood pressure.

"In and out of consciousness. Breathing on her own."

The nurse moved aside and indicated Lydia could take her place. Lydia reached for Evelyn's hand. "Hi, Evelyn. It's me, Lydia."

Though Evelyn's eyes remained closed, Lydia was gratified to see a ghost of a smile.

"You'll be fine," Lydia said emphatically to cheer them both up.

A volunteer—a sweet-faced woman in her late sixties—asked Lydia if she had the patient's information. When Lydia said she did, the woman directed her to a secretary seated behind the round office in the center of the ER. Lydia pulled out Evelyn's Medicare and secondary insurance cards from her wallet—which Sol had reminded her to bring along—and handed them to the secretary. She answered what questions she could and gave the secretary her phone number and that of Evelyn's daughter, whom she intended to call as soon as she found a spare moment.

Sol strode into the ER and returned the greeting of an attractive young nurse with a wink and a smile, causing Lydia's heart to thump with jealousy. His smile faded as he caught sight of Lydia.

"How's Mrs. Hammond doing?"

"Coming along. They'll take a CT scan and keep her overnight for observation."

"Good. Be right back." Sol disappeared inside Evelyn's cubicle. It was minutes before he rejoined Lydia. "I hope you don't have anywhere important to be for the next two hours."

"Not really," Lydia said. "What's happening?"

"The doctor's in there with her. He expects her to be fully conscious in an hour. When she is, they'll put her in a semi-private room. I'll post an officer outside her room throughout the night."

Lydia's heart quickened. "Do you think whoever did this will come to the hospital to finish what he began?"

Sol grimaced. "I've no idea, but I intend to keep her safe while we find out."

Lydia shuddered. "Maybe Polly was right. Maybe someone did kill Daniel and now he's after Evelyn."

"First things first. When the doctor gives his okay, I want to ask Mrs. Hammond a few questions. And I'd like you to be there."

"So that's why you had me come along." Despite her willingness to help Evelyn any way she could, Lydia felt deflated. She should have known his request had nothing to do with her!

"Of course. Your friend will feel more comfortable with you beside me." He offered her a half smile. "I'm sorry for snapping at you before. I tend to do that when I'm worried."

Lydia nodded. "Apology accepted."

"Why don't you go ahead to the cafeteria? I'll catch up with you there after I make a few phone calls."

"Sure." Lydia forced a smile, but Sol was gone, off to hold his conversations in private.

She checked on Evelyn. Reassured firsthand that her friend was indeed recovering, she called Evelyn's daughter. In the calmest tone she could conjure up, Lydia left a message for Gayle to please call her on her cell phone as soon as she arrived home, and gave her the number. Then she headed for the hospital cafeteria.

Something rankled her, and she was determined to figure out exactly what it was before Sol joined her because she knew damned well it concerned him. But what troubled her exactly? He hadn't coerced her into coming to the hospital. She would have come, regardless.

And she had no objection to being on hand while Sol questioned Evelyn. But all this waiting around in a hospital cafeteria was maddening. That was it, she realized! Sol was calling the shots—giving her orders and expecting her to follow them.

Trying to be fair-minded, she regarded the situation from his point of view. Why shouldn't he be the one issuing orders? She'd called on him in his professional capacity, and he'd rushed over ASAP. It was his job to find Evelyn's assailant and to ascertain if he was the same person who had murdered Daniel. If Daniel had been murdered. Sol was making it clear he was in charge because Lydia had interfered so often in the past.

Interfering, hah! Lydia let out a huff of exasperation, causing a passing resident to stare at her. It wasn't her fault people around her were dying or being attacked! She couldn't help but act. She was a take-charge kind of person. As CEO of her company she'd acted on the principle that every problem had a solution. Just as every murderer had an identity. Which would reveal itself, she was firmly convinced, after enough poking and prodding.

It dawned on her that Sol knew exactly how her mind worked. He was aware of the force within her and felt challenged by it.

Or was he threatened?

Lydia hoped that wasn't the case. Especially since his coolness toward her had another, more personal component. He'd finally asked her out and she'd told him she had a date, of all things!

In the almost deserted cafeteria, she bought two coffees and a tuna salad sandwich, which she carried over to a table in the corner of the room. A thought struck her, and she burst out laughing. She and Sol had gone out a total of two and a half dates—the half being the other night—and the dynamics of their relationship were as complicated as those of a four-year marriage. Which was totally ridiculous! It was unfortunate she hadn't been free when he'd asked her out, but she'd make up for it by inviting him to dinner. There! She bit into the sandwich, pleased to have solved her problems so quickly, and hoped Sol would make it to the cafeteria before his coffee cooled off.

Chapter Twelve

S ol showed up twenty minutes later. "Sorry I took so long. A call came in regarding another case and required my attention." He took a gulp of his coffee and frowned. "Ice cold. I'll get me another."

When he returned, he downed the hot coffee and cake he'd bought in record time. His cell phone rang. He listened a minute. "Okay, thanks." He got to his feet. "Let's go, Lydia! Mrs. Hammond's awake and alert."

She nodded and followed him out of the cafeteria. She practically had to run to match his stride. "So this is a typical day of a homicide detective?" she asked, glad that at least she wasn't panting.

"Typical? There ain't no such animal." He flashed her a smile, the first of the evening. "But today's a good day because you saved your friend's life. Tomorrow we go after the bastard who bashed in her head."

Evelyn was sitting up in bed as a towering, lanky Black doctor examined her eyes with a flashlight. Lydia felt Sol's pent up energy pulsing, his eagerness to question Evelyn.

The doctor advised his patient not to move her head. When he was done, he said in a musical West Indies cadence, "You may now see your visitors." He turned toward them. "Lieutenant Molina, you have five minutes with Mrs. Hammond. We don't want to tire her out."

He left them. Sol stepped back so Lydia could stand beside Evelyn.

"I'm so glad you're awake," Lydia said.

"I am too," Evelyn said, her voice faint. "My head aches something awful."

"It's no wonder, Mrs. Hammond. I'm Lieutenant Molina."

Evelyn smiled. "Yes, I know. I remember when you came and spoke to us last fall."

"Did you see who struck you?"

Evelyn shook her head, then winced. "No. I was fast asleep. Lydia offered to bring dinner. At seven, we said. I figured I'd be awake by then, and if I wasn't," she smiled, "well then, Lydia would awaken me."

"You mean you left the door unlocked?" Sol asked.

Evelyn stared at him. "Certainly not! Lydia has a key to our house."

"I didn't think to bring it with me," Lydia admitted. "The house was dark when I got there. I rang the doorbell. When you didn't answer, I went around to the kitchen door."

"And found it was unlocked," Sol said.

"I locked it before I went to lie down."

"Who else has a key to your house?" Sol asked.

"Let's see—our neighbors, the Bronsteins. They're away. Stefano—he checks on our house when we're in Florida—my daughter, Daniel's daughters, and our cleaning woman, Flora."

Sol had whipped out his notepad and was writing furiously. "Anyone else?"

"No one I can think of—oh, yes, Gillian, the Devil Twin. Oh, sorry. I shouldn't have said that."

Lydia gaped. "You actually call her that?"

"It's something the twins cooked up, a takeoff on the good twin-bad twin thing, which, frankly, I'd never heard of before. Nicole and Gillian call themselves Angel and Devil. They love to dress for their roles."

"Come to think of it, they do look like day and night," Lydia said.

Evelyn gave a weak smile. "Gillian asked if she could study at our place when we were in Florida this past winter. Study, my eye. She wanted a place to be alone with her boyfriend, and who am I to stop young love?"

"I didn't realize Gillian has a boyfriend," Lydia commented. She caught Sol's frown and was sorry she'd spoken.

Sol must have thought better of stopping the flow of conversation because he waved his hand. At any rate, Evelyn hadn't noticed either the frown or the wave because she went right into her story.

"Had a boyfriend. Kyle Mendoza's his name. He looks like Satan, with his jet-black hair and brooding eyes. Loves to wear black leather like Gillian." Evelyn laughed, then winced in pain. "They made quite a pair. Polly thought he was a bad influence on Gillian, while I think they were mostly playacting. They both thrived on coming off as scamps."

Scamps! When was the last time Lydia had heard that word? "Did Kyle use the nickname Ringo?" she asked.

Evelyn thought a moment. "Ringo? Isn't that the boy Nicole brought to Daniel's party?"

"Yes. And I saw her talking to him outside when I paid a shiva call."

"That's because Polly won't let him in the house. Gillian tells me he's really bad news. He takes drugs."

Lydia was about to ask another question, but Evelyn was having trouble holding back tears.

"Have you any idea who broke in and struck me while I slept?" she asked.

"Not yet," Sol said. "We found your jewelry box open, and items scattered over the bureau. We've no idea what he took, if anything. Lydia's arrival must have caught him in the act."

Evelyn gave a feeble wave. "The only thing I value is my engagement ring, and I was wearing that, thank God."

"Do you have any enemies, anyone who might want to hurt you, Mrs. Hammond?"

"Of course not." Evelyn blinked, puzzled by the direction the detective's questions were taking. "But there's the matter of the will."

"Your will?" Sol said.

"No, Daniel's. His two older children get the bulk of their inheritance after I'm gone."

"Meaning they stand to gain if something were to happen to you."

"Exactly, and they're both desperate for the money." Evelyn's grimace turned fearful. "Dear God, I hope they don't come after me here!"

Sol patted her shoulder. "Don't worry, Mrs. Hammond. There may be no connection between your assault and Mr. Korman's demise, but I'm posting an officer outside your room for the length of your stay."

"And then I'm going to Atlanta to be with my daughter." Evelyn yawned. The last of her energy seemed to give out and she closed her eyes. A moment later she was gently snoring.

Lydia and Sol left the cubicle. Evelyn's doctor approached to say a room had just become available and Evelyn would be moved there within the half hour. Lydia said she'd call the hospital in the morning to find out when she could drive Evelyn home, while Sol arranged for Evelyn's guard. Minutes later they were back in Sol's car.

"Care for a bite of dinner?" he asked.

She laughed. "I've dinner for two waiting at home. Want to try my latest chicken dish?"

"Wouldn't mind if I did."

Lydia never could decide if it was the wine, the time spent with Evelyn in the ER, or her decision to put a lid on her old CEO persona, but suddenly she and Sol were in sync. After agreeing to put a moratorium on all discussion of deaths and attacks, both deliberate and accidental, their conversation lost any semblance of rhyme or reason. At home, she warmed up the chicken dish and rice pilaf in the microwave. Fifteen minutes later they were eating and imbibing their way through dinner and dessert.

One kiss led to another and, without much ado, Lydia took Sol by the hand and made straight for her bed. Their lovemaking started out slowly, then turned fast and urgent. When it was over, Sol stroked her face, a lazy smile lighting up his face.

"I've been wanting to do that from the first day we met."

"Me, too," Lydia said, grinning.

He kissed her fingers. "I've been lusting after you, not to mention the pining part. But you see how my days play out. They often run into night. You might get sick and tired of broken appointments."

"I'll take that chance," she answered lightly.

"Well, that's good, because I was thinking—"

As though to prove his point, Sol's cell phone rang. "Molina," he answered crisply, then turned away to carry on a short conversation. "I'll be down at the station and question him myself." He glanced at his watch still on his bare arm. "I'll be there in twenty minutes. Keep his lawyer there, whatever he says." He was about to click off, when he growled, "I'll tell her."

But when he turned back to her, he was grinning. "Your old friend, Officer McKlusky, sends his regards." He gathered up his clothes and made a beeline for the bathroom.

Lydia giggled. "It's a good thing this wasn't a video call."

"You could say that again," came through the closed door over running water. Lydia stretched her arms overhead, knowing the smile on her face was gelling into a permanent feature. It had been so long since she'd been joyous with a man. The last year of Izzy's life had been given over to his care and comfort.

Sol emerged from the bathroom, dressed and looking gorgeous. Lydia stretched out her arms and he kissed her. He ran his hands down her breasts, and she wanted him all over again.

"I hate to make love and run, but two of my men brought in a possible suspect in a case we've been working for months, and I can't give up the chance to talk to this guy."

He kissed her nose. "Thanks for dinner and for everything else. Are you free Friday night? Or is your other admirer taking you out then too?"

Lydia burst out laughing. "Friday's fine. As for my admirer, I believe I'm Andrew Varig's excuse to have a night out on the town. My plan is to shift his attention to Barbara. She wouldn't mind giving him a try."

Sol shook his head in mock dismay. "And we guys think we make the moves. Talk to you later."

Lydia was too exhilarated to sleep much that night. She kept reliving the evening again and again in her mind, each time telling herself not to get carried away. She and Sol lived such different lives. His work consumed him day and night. What's more, he bristled whenever she crossed the line to enter what he considered his domain. Still, she was happy, happier than she'd been in months, and she had no intention of squelching her high spirits.

She managed to fall into a deep sleep around four, and slept until a quarter to nine, when Reggie awoke her by licking her face as he meowed his complaint that she was late with his breakfast. She felt a moment of panic, then sighed with relief. Today was Thursday. She didn't work today.

She slipped into her robe and padded down to the kitchen to feed her hungry cat. She called the hospital to check on Evelyn's condition. She was put through to Evelyn's section and told to wait for Evelyn's nurse, who finally came to the phone to say the doctor had just examined Evelyn and declared her well enough to be taken home. Lydia said she would come for her within the hour.

Next, she called Carrington House and punched in Len's extension. She waited through his message, knowing he never answered his phone, then said, "Len, it's Lydia. Please pick up if you're there."

He did. "Hi, Lyddie. What's up?"

"Len, a neighbor's had a bad accident and I have to take care of her. I won't be coming in tomorrow."

There was a stunned silence, and then Len exploded. "You gotta be kidding! We're up to our ears in affairs, and days behind on the paperwork. Jessica can't possibly manage the front desk and send out contracts by herself."

"Then hire more help," Lydia said calmly. "I'm sorry I won't be able to come in—really, I am—but that has no bearing on the fact that you never replaced the women who left months ago. Jessica's doing the job of three."

An expert at changing tacks, Len asked, "Have you come to a decision regarding the position you've been offered? Tom called this morning, asking if you have."

Sure he did. "I'll call him as soon as I've decided."

"Gotta go," Len barked, a sure sign he'd ceded the battle. "See you on Monday?"

"I hope so," Lydia answered, and hung up before he could squawk about that.

She showered and dressed quickly, her happy mood dampened by the realization that someone had tried to kill Evelyn. Her attacker was patently evil and without a conscience, for who else would strike a sleeping woman and leave her for dead? Could it have been a robbery? Somehow she doubted it. Instead, she wondered if Arnold or Denise were capable of attacking Evelyn and if either of them had murdered Daniel.

Lydia set aside her speculations and called Evelyn's daughter to give her an update on her mother's condition. Gayle had returned her call her late the night before, the moment she and Roger arrived home from the airport. The news had thoroughly upset her, and both Lydia and Roger had to work hard to convince her not to return to Long Island on the next plane out of Atlanta.

Gayle was relieved to hear Evelyn was well enough to leave the hospital.

"I don't like the idea of your mother staying in the house by herself," Lydia said. "I'm going to invite her to be my houseguest until she leaves for Atlanta."

"Lydia, you're an angel! Thanks so much for looking after Mom. Daniel's death was a terrible blow, and now this. Do the police have any leads?"

"None that I know of," Lydia said.

"And you'll be the first to hear. Thanks again, Lydia. I'm so glad Mom has you as her friend."

Did everyone know she and Sol were seeing each other? Lydia wondered as she put down the phone. Her cheeks grew warm as she wondered further if everyone assumed they were sleeping together. She shrugged. She couldn't monitor people's imaginations.

At the hospital, Lydia was appalled at how pale and diminutive Evelyn appeared, her lovely hair hidden by the white dressing wrapped around her head. A nurse reviewed the printed instructions for Evelyn's care and said someone would be calling that evening to check on her condition. Finally, the nurse instructed Lydia to drive her car up to the hospital entrance and wait for the patient, who would be escorted outside in a wheelchair.

Lydia and a volunteer not much younger than Evelyn settled her in the passenger seat. Lydia, mindful of her fragile passenger, started slowly for home.

"How are you feeling?" she asked.

Evelyn, who hadn't spoken two words since Lydia had arrived, said, "My head hurts."

Lydia forced herself to sound cheerful. "That's to be expected. You're doing fine. The doctor found you well enough to come home."

Tears welled up in Evelyn's eyes. "I won't go back to that place! It's not my home, not without Daniel."

Lydia reached over to pat her shoulder. "You'll stay with me until you feel better. Then you can visit Gayle in Atlanta."

Evelyn gripped Lydia's hand hard, nearly causing her to swerve into the right-hand lane. "They killed Daniel and now they're trying to kill me!"

"We don't know that," Lydia said with more enthusiasm than she felt. "Whoever broke in helped himself to some of your jewelry. It could have been a random robbery."

"Robbery, my eye!" Evelyn said bitterly. "It was Arnold or Denise—or the two of them together. They'd do anything for money they think belongs to them."

Eager to redirect the conversation to a less volatile subject, Lydia said, "We need to stop to fill your prescription. Which pharmacy do you use?"

"The Drug Market in town. No, don't go there! Bennett works there and I don't want to see any of Daniel's miserable relatives. Take me to the other drug store on Main Street, please."

"Of course." It suddenly dawned on Lydia that the reason Bennett had looked familiar was because she must have seen him in the large drug supermarket in town.

"Is Bennett a pharmacist?" she asked.

"Are you kidding? He's a manager or holds some such cockamamie title, though Denise acts like he's president of the company."

"She dotes on him."

"And spoiled him rotten in the process. But at least he's now gainfully employed instead of—"

Lydia never was to hear the rest of the sentence because Evelyn had fallen asleep.

She stirred awake as Lydia drove up to the pharmacist's window. Embarrassed, Evelyn said, "Sorry, I must have dozed off."

"Who wouldn't, after all you've been through?" Lydia handed Evelyn's prescription to the woman and was told it would be ready in an hour.

"That's taken care of." Lydia put the car into gear and headed for Twin Lakes. "Why don't we stop by your house and pack some clothes and things you'd like to have while you visit?"

Evelyn's eyes filled with anxiety. "Only if you come inside with me."

"Of course, I will. Afterward, I'll make you a cup of soup for lunch, then you can take a nice nap in my guest room."

"Sounds good to me." Evelyn yawned.

Lydia approached Evelyn's house, her heart thumping at the sight of an oversized SUV smack in the middle of the two-car driveway. Her fear turned to annoyance when she realized she couldn't let Evelyn out close to the front door as she'd planned. Instead, she pulled in behind the mammoth vehicle and killed the motor.

"That's Arnold's SUV," Evelyn croaked. "Why is he here?"

"I'll go inside and find out. Evelyn, dear, hand me your door key. It's in your pocketbook."

Lydia unlocked the front door and followed the trail of lights, through the living room and dining room to the den. Arnold had his back to her as he tried his best to yank open a jammed desk drawer.

"And what do you think you're doing?"

Arnold spun around, his hand over his heart. "My God, Lydia! You nearly scared me to death."

"I repeat, what do you think you're doing?"

"Looking for some papers." He pointed to the desk drawer. "I know Dad kept them there, but the drawer seems to be stuck."

"Or locked. You're trespassing, Arnold. You'd better leave."

Arnold's face turned red. "Now see here, this is my father's home. I have a key. How do you think I got in? I knocked and knocked, and when I realized Evelyn wasn't home, I unlocked the door. Nothing sneaky about that."

"It's Evelyn's home now. She's in my car and was disturbed to find you here."

"Then ask her for the key to the desk so I can get what's mine. I'm talking about stocks my father bought and put in both our names. Regardless of anything, that money comes to me."

"If I find anything that's yours, I'll put it in the mail. Now get out of my house!"

Lydia and Arnold turned to Evelyn, leaning against the wall for support. Lydia gasped and ran to her.

"Evelyn, you should have waited for me! You might have fallen."

"I want him to leave."

Arnold's mouth fell open as he took in Evelyn's bandaged head. "My God, what happened to you?"

Lydia helped Evelyn to the living room and sat her down on a chair. "Rest here while I move my car so Arnold can back out and disappear."

"Thanks, dear, for getting rid of him."

Lydia patted her hand. "My pleasure," she said softly and was rewarded with a faint smile.

"What happened to her?" Arnold asked Lydia once they were outside.

"Someone struck her head while she was sleeping and left her to die. I'm sure the police will come to question you about it."

His eyes bulged out behind his glasses. "You can't imagine I had anything to do with it! I haven't seen Evelyn since Dad's funeral."

"Tell that to the police." She held out her cupped palm.

"What?"

"Your key to this house, please. You've no right to it any longer."

Arnold opened his mouth as though to remonstrate, then thought better of it. He fished in his pocket for the key and placed it in Lydia's outstretched palm.

"Here! Please see to it that Evelyn sends along those stocks. They're mine, now that Dad's gone."

"Evelyn will do what's right, which is more than I can say about your behavior."

Lydia got into her car and slammed the door on Arnold's indignant protests. It felt good to help Evelyn throw him out, after the way he'd treated her at Daniel's funeral. She backed out of the driveway and waited until Arnold drove away before pulling up as close to the front door as possible. She'd ask Barbara to pick up the medicine, she decided as she walked back inside the house. That way she wouldn't have to leave Evelyn alone.

Chapter Thirteen

Lydia settled Evelyn into her guest bedroom, where she fell asleep immediately. Barbara was more than happy to get Evelyn's medicine, along with the few items Lydia needed.

"Thanks. I can't let her wake up in an empty house," Lydia explained. "She's terrified."

"Of course she is," Barbara agreed. "This on top of Daniel's death."

"Which I'm back to considering a homicide."

As Evelyn slept, Lydia occupied herself with domestic chores, her mind chugging ahead like a locomotive, trying to figure out who wanted both Daniel and Evelyn dead.

If Daniel's old friends hadn't killed him, as Lydia now believed was the case, the murderer had to be someone in his family. Arnold and Denise had serious issues with their father. *But would they actually kill for an inheritance? What inheritance?*

Lydia suddenly wondered, since Daniel had changed his will before his death. But perhaps the murderer hadn't known this. At any rate, how had he or she managed to poison Daniel and make it look like a heart attack?

Lydia grimaced as it occurred to her that Evelyn had the best opportunity to kill Daniel. *Ridiculous!* Evelyn adored Daniel. She had nothing to gain from his death but millions of dollars, which she didn't need.

She had been devastated at the funeral! And she certainly hadn't caused her own injuries. On the other hand, Arnold and Denise needed money, which they'd have if Evelyn died.

Lydia sighed with frustration. She was going around in circles and getting nowhere. Determined to put the matter to rest, she concentrated on preparing a cheese omelet for her dinner, which she ate as she watched the six o'clock news.

Her thoughts strayed to work, and she wondered how Jessica had managed without her, and hoped that Len was considering getting more help. He was a workplace bully toward Jessica and everyone beneath him, and needed to be taken down a peg or two. But, to be fair, he was being taxed beyond his capabilities. Because of the expensive Carrington Suites about to be built, the board was trying to keep expenses as low as possible—despite the fact that Carrington House was hosting more parties than ever. Not replacing the office workers might have been a directive from above.

Did she want to become a frazzled manager, too—come home exhausted, often frustrated, after solving problems all day? She didn't need to prove she could do it. She'd achieved her working success when she took on Izzy's family's business and turned it into a thriving enterprise. Besides, she enjoyed her present part-time job of showing prospective customers around the mansion, explaining the various packages available and writing up contracts as well as doing the bookkeeping. She had nothing to prove—but she thrived on challenge, and managing the hotel would keep her on her toes.

Evelyn finally awoke shortly after seven o'clock. Though she insisted she was fine, Lydia noted she wasn't steady on her feet and escorted her to the bathroom. Then Lydia sat her down at the kitchen table to eat chicken soup and toast and gave her her medicine. Five minutes later, Evelyn was back in bed, fast asleep.

The following morning, Lydia tiptoed into the guest bedroom. She was surprised to find Evelyn dressed in slacks and a blouse.

"Evelyn, why are you up? You should stay in bed and rest."

The grin she flashed was almost up to par. "I feel much stronger. I'm going home to take care of things."

"But—"

"I need to see what's been stolen, call a locksmith to change the locks and the security company to upgrade my security system. I'll be damned if I'm driven from my home!"

Lydia swallowed the argument she was about to make. Instead, she offered a few suggestions she hoped Evelyn would follow.

"At least stay for breakfast. Then, if you like, I'll go home with you."

Evelyn gave her a bittersweet smile. "Lydia, dear, I can't impose on you a moment longer. I certainly don't want you to miss any more work on my account."

"I told them I wasn't coming in today. We have your doctor's appointment this afternoon."

Evelyn patted Lydia's arm. "What would I do without you?"

After breakfast they walked to Evelyn's house, and she made some calls. A locksmith would be there no later than noon. The alarm company was sending over a technician to add to her security system first thing Saturday morning.

"Now for the hard part," Evelyn said as she headed for her bedroom.

Lydia remained in the den, flipping through the newspaper without noticing the headlines. She hoped Evelyn's ordeal wouldn't prove too stressful. After all the poor woman had to endure, the loss of her cherished possessions might send her over the edge.

Some minutes later Evelyn sank onto the couch beside her. "Not too bad. Three hideous antique pins an aunt gave me are gone. They're worth quite a bit, but Gayle didn't want them, and I don't wear them." She grimaced. "Still, I should have sold them instead of letting that animal—"

She covered her face with her hands. Lydia put an arm around her. Evelyn fought to regain her composure and continued.

"He also took a ring, a bracelet, and two brass figurines my parents gave my husband and me for our third anniversary. I'll notify the police and my insurance company."

Lydia knew she was being dismissed. "I'll pick you up at three for your appointment. Call if you need anything before then."

"I have to regain control of my life." Evelyn took Lydia's hand as though she was comforting her. "I'm sure you understand."

"Of course I do, but I hope you'll continue to spend the nights at my house until you leave for Atlanta."

"I'll feel safer if I do," Evelyn admitted.

The phone was ringing as Lydia arrived home. It was Sol looking for Evelyn.

"She's gone back to her place," Lydia explained. "As we speak, she's writing up a list of what her assailant stole."

Sol laughed. "That's one feisty woman. I'll call her there, see if she's up to answering some questions. Also, I noticed the computer in the den. I'd like to have our tech expert check it out."

Lydia's pulse quickened at the mention of Daniel's computer. "Do you think there's a connection between the attack on Evelyn and Daniel's death?"

"You mean do I think he was murdered? I don't know. I'll speak to his three children, find out how they feel about the body being exhumed."

"Speaking of which, when I brought Evelyn home yesterday, we found Daniel's son in her house. He was rummaging through drawers searching for stocks he claims his father had in trust for him and kept in the desk. We threw him out."

"Good girl. How did he gain entrance?"

"He had a key, which I took from him. That's one of the reasons Evelyn's changing the locks."

"Quite a few people had access to that house. I intend to talk to every one of them." Sol paused. When he spoke again, his voice took on a deeper, more intimate timbre. "And how are you feeling these days, Ms. Krause?"

"I feel wonderful, lieutenant, though I'm concerned about Evelyn. I've convinced her to stay over the next few nights."

"Have you?" He pretended to groan. "That puts a crimp in our activities."

"She's flying to Atlanta just as soon as the doctor gives his okay."

"In that case, I look forward to next week."

"I'm looking forward to tonight," Lydia said.

Sol laughed. "Me, too. Shall I pick you up around seven?"

"Seven's fine," Lydia said, and hung up, as giddy as a teenager looking forward to her first date.

Evelyn's doctor had her take a CT scan, and then gave her the good news. Her head wound was healing, there was no sign of swelling, and she could fly to Atlanta on Sunday.

Evelyn joined Lydia in the waiting room, a perplexed expression on her face.

"He says I can fly to Gayle and Roger's on Sunday."

Lydia laughed. "Aren't you glad?"

Evelyn waited until they got into the car to explain. "I'm delighted I'm on the mend." She took a deep breath, then continued. "The fact is, now I don't want to leave. When I came to after being half dead, I was terrified and couldn't wait to get away. But I have to get used to living alone."

"And you will, but it will do you a world of good to get away for a week or two. And, hopefully, by the time you're back, your assailant will be behind bars."

Evelyn's eyes glittered with anger. "My assailant and Daniel's. Your friend, Sol, is taking Polly's claim that he was murdered very seriously."

"Polly wants Daniel's body to be exhumed for a postmortem, but Arnold and Denise are against it."

Evelyn made a sound of disparagement. "They would be, if they killed him. Frankly, I wouldn't put it past Arnold or Denise. Each inherits over seven million dollars when I'm gone."

"That's a lot of money," Lydia agreed, turning the ignition.

"They're both desperate for it, always have been. Which is why Daniel set up his will this way." Evelyn sighed. "I told him not to do it, that I was fine with what my husband left me, but he insisted. And now he's gone."

She wept quietly. Lydia wrapped her arms around her. She felt fragile, her bones as brittle as a bird's.

"Sol and his men will find out what happened. Meanwhile, build up your strength at Gayle's. You'll return to Twin Lakes in a better frame of mind."

Evelyn nodded. "You're right, of course. I'm too worn out to do otherwise." She smiled sweetly. "And it will be heaven, spending time with my grandchildren. I miss the little ones so."

Lydia dropped Evelyn off at her own house and got ready for her date with Sol. "Friday night's a fun night," Sol called to say, "so dress casually. I'm wearing jeans."

He looked sexier than ever in his worn jeans, boots, and Ralph Lauren polo. She must have looked fine in her jeans, too, because his eyes lit up when she opened the front door.

"Good evening to you, Ms. Krause." He swept her up in his arms and kissed her deeply.

"Ah," Lydia sighed when she could speak. "And hello to you, too. But don't do that again or we'll never leave."

"Oh, we're leaving, all right. We've places to go."

They drove to a restaurant facing a marina. Though it was too cold to eat outdoors, Lydia gazed out at the water, imagining how it would be in the summer.

"We'll come back on a hot summer's eve and watch the sun go down," he said, as though reading her thoughts.

She sipped an apple martini then ate most of her salad, coconut shrimp, and sweet potato fries. Though she felt filled to the gills, she gave in to Sol's coaxing and agreed to share a chocolate lover's dessert. Two bites was all she could manage. She set down her fork and watched him devour the rest of the cake.

"Hey, this is real whipped cream," he crowed, offering up a dollop. "You have to taste it."

She shook her head no, but he insisted.

"Delicious. Now you finish the rest."

"Oh, I will," he promised, and polished off the rest of the rich dessert in no time. They drove slowly back to Lydia's home, hands entwined in comfortable silence.

At a red light, he turned to say, "Do you realize you haven't asked me one question about the case all evening?"

"I thought I'd give you a break."

"Much appreciated and worthy of a reward. I've contacted Daniel Korman's three children. They've all agreed that, in view of his sudden death and the attack on Mrs. Hammond, an autopsy is in order. It's scheduled for Wednesday."

Lydia nodded. "I'm glad."

"Do I take it you're back to thinking Mr. Korman was murdered?" A probing undercurrent had crept into his voice.

Now was the time to tell him about Ron and Mick Diminio, only she couldn't. She felt a pang of guilt for having to dissemble. "After what happened to Evelyn, I certainly do. Before, I thought I was letting Polly's fears along with my sense of the dramatic convince me someone had murdered Daniel."

"Though you also knew something was troubling him."

Lydia gave a little laugh that sounded false to her ears. "He was troubled, yes, but that doesn't mean someone wanted to kill him."

The light changed and Sol accelerated. His hand slid from Lydia's and went to the steering wheel. *Damn! He sensed she was hiding something and was annoyed that she wouldn't say what it was.*

Still, when they reached her driveway, he took her in his arms and kissed her deeply. He drew back to study her face. "That will have to do for now."

She nodded. "The house is ablaze with light, which means Evelyn's here."

They entered the kitchen through the garage. Evelyn called out to them. "Lydia, is that you?"

"Yes, I'm home. Lieutenant Molina is with me."

"I wanted to make sure it was you. I'll be in my room. Just pretend I'm not here."

Lydia burst out laughing. All this tiptoeing around her relationship with Sol made her feel she was back in high school. "Don't be silly. Come out and say hello."

"Well, if you insist."

Evelyn emerged from her room, dressed in black trousers and a silk V-necked turquoise sweater. She bussed Lydia's cheek and smiled at Sol. "Lieutenant Molina. Enjoy your dinner?"

"Mmm, it was terrific."

Lydia led them into the living room and remained standing, while Sol and Evelyn sat on the sofas facing one another. "Would anyone like something to drink?" She had the bizarre sensation she was following a script in a play.

They both declined. Lydia dropped down beside Sol. She longed to reach for his hand but didn't.

"I went out for dinner, too, as it turns out," Evelyn explained. "Rosalie and Allen Holtstein heard about the break-in and left a message at the house. You remember them, Lydia—they sat at your table at Daniel's party. Anyway, I phoned them back, and when they realized I was up and about, they insisted on taking me out."

"Sure, I remember them." Lydia pictured the couple: the old friend who had made a toast to Daniel's good health, his pleasant wife.

"Allen Holtstein," Sol mused. "Is he a Twin Lakes resident?"

"No," Evelyn said. "They've recently sold their home in Syosset and will be renting an apartment not far from here. Why, do you know him?"

Sol shook his head. He got to his feet and reached into the pocket of his jacket for his cell phone. "If you ladies will excuse me, I'll call in and find out what's been happening in my absence."

When he returned, the three of them chatted for a few minutes, then Evelyn excused herself.

"I like that woman," Sol murmured in Lydia's ear. "She knows when to leave a happy couple alone."

"Are we a couple?" she asked teasingly, though her heart was pounding.

"You bet." He nuzzled her ear, then whispered. "I'm going now. Walk me to the door."

In the small entrance hall, he drew her close and kissed her. "That's something to remember me by till next we meet."

Lydia grinned. "Oh, I'll remember you, all right. By the way, why did Allen's name sound familiar?"

For a moment Sol remained silent, and Lydia thought he wasn't going to answer. "Mr. Korman mentions the Holtsteins in his memoirs."

The memoirs. Lydia hadn't read them and had no idea what they contained.

"I talked to them at Daniel's birthday party. Allen and Daniel worked in the same shoe store in the city. Years later they ran into each other when both couples were living on Long Island and resumed their friendship."

"I suppose neither of the Holtsteins mentioned that Allen was suspected of murdering his former boss and released for lack of evidence. No one was ever brought to trial for the homicide."

"Oh, no! The man who owned the shoe store?"

"The very same."

She gulped. "If only I'd known! They took Evelyn out for dinner tonight."

"And they'll be living just down the road." Sol's tone turned mocking, but she knew it wasn't directed at her. "Remember, Lydia, he was never charged with the crime. In the eyes of the law, he's an innocent man."

"Why did they suspect he killed his boss?"

"The victim owned a few shoe stores and was living the good life. He and his wife gave lavish parties and occasionally invited their sales staff. At one such party, Allen Holtstein was upstairs looking for a bathroom and came upon his boss mauling his wife, Rosalie. There were words and the Holtsteins departed. A few days later the boss was found dead in his Manhattan office. A few people remembered the fracas between the two men and Holtstein was brought in for questioning. He was a serious suspect because his brother was an exterminator and used the kind of poison found in the dead man's body. But nothing could be proven, so Holtstein wasn't charged with the crime."

"Oh." Lydia blinked, trying to digest Sol's story.

"Before you start imagining you're surrounded by murderers, I'll add that the victim, Peter Rittenberg, had his finger in every dirty scheme. He had heavy debts. The shoe stores were a cover but, ironically, they proved to be his only success."

Sol sighed as he pulled away. "I must leave you to your beauty sleep for your date tomorrow night."

"Ah, yes, my date," Lydia said. "I'd almost forgotten."

"I haven't," Sol said, reminding her that her date with Andrew Varig was the least of the issues separating them. She hated to think how angry Sol would be if he found out she'd been withholding information about Timmy John's death.

"Talk to you soon," Sol said and went out into the balmy May evening.

Chapter Fourteen

Saturday morning, Lydia prepared a light breakfast for Evelyn and herself. Afterward, she sponged the table as Evelyn stacked the dishwasher.

"One more day, and you'll be rid of me," Evelyn teased.

"I'll miss you," Lydia said. She'd enjoyed having a guest who provided interesting conversation yet didn't feel compelled to fill every silence. "How long will you stay with Gayle?"

"Two weeks, at least. Gayle's youngest granddaughter turns two and there's a party in the works."

"The weather will be nice and warm when you come home. And your time away will give you the necessary break between all that's happened."

Evelyn sighed. "I feel I should be here, at least until we find out the results of the autopsy."

"Now, Evelyn, Sol promised to call the moment the results come in. I'll take in your mail and water the plants twice a week."

Evelyn went home to pack for her trip. Lydia headed for the clubhouse for a much-needed session in the indoor pool. With all that had been happening lately, she'd been neglecting her daily routine of swimming laps. She ran into George, Benny, and Andrew in the lobby. They halted their animated conversation to greet her.

"We're about to go over to the construction site," George informed her, "to keep an eye on things." He winked. "Not that we're expecting any more dead bodies to turn up."

"I should hope not," she said.

Andrew patted her shoulder. "On behalf of our committee, I promise to keep an eye on the crew. You needn't set foot on the site until the clubhouse is up and ready for your decorating talents."

"Much appreciated," Lydia said, moving around him to open the glass door and go downstairs to the pool. "Bye, fellas."

"I'll pick you up at four-thirty," Andrew called after her. "That will give us plenty of time for a relaxed dinner before the play."

She turned around to nod in agreement, wishing Andrew had shown some discretion, and was disconcerted by the opened-mouth astonishment on both Benny and George's face.

Let them be shocked, she told herself. It was no one's business whom she saw. It was her life to run as she chose! *She was a grandmother—almost fifty-nine years old, for God's sake! Andrew was seventy.* Suddenly, the whole thing struck her as hilarious, and she giggled all the way to the pool.

To her surprise, Lydia found herself chatting easily with Andrew as he drove swiftly and competently westbound on the LIE to Manhattan. He must have experienced an epiphany during his trip abroad because his usual uptight demeanor was gone, replaced by a warm and friendly manner. As they stopped at a light before turning onto the street leading to the Fifty-Ninth Street Bridge, she felt comfortable enough to ask, "What happened on your European trip that changed you?"

He turned to her and winked. "You've noticed."

"Who wouldn't?"

Andrew remained silent as they moved along with the traffic. When they were halfway across the East River, he said, "I fell in love."

"Oh." Lydia was stunned. *Andrew? In love? Then again, why not?*

He laughed at her fluster. "That's right. I fell in love with a beautiful Italian woman thirty years my junior. We had four unforgettable days."

"I'm happy for you, Andrew."

Lydia waited to hear that the bella donna was coming for a visit, or that Andrew was planning a trip back to Italy. Instead, he grinned.

"It was great while it lasted. My kids had the good sense to keep out of our way and resisted making comments about my robbing the cradle. When we said good-bye, Francesca and I agreed we'd shared a magical interlude in our very different lives, one we'll always cherish.

"I miss her, of course, but not in a morbid way. The experience opened my eyes to the fact that I have a damn good life right here at Twin Lakes, among people my own age."

Lydia cleared her throat. "Andrew, I'm very fond of you, but—"

"But you're involved with Lieutenant Molina. I know."

She turned to stare at him. "You knew! Then why did you ask me to go with you into the city?"

"Because you're a delight to be with. And you agreed to go, so I figured things weren't that set between you and your paramour."

"They are now. I mean," she quickly amended, "there's nothing official. We're just... involved," she finished lamely.

"I hear you," Andrew said. "Frankly, I asked you out first because I figured you're so cool, you'd know about this senior dating."

"I don't have a clue," Lydia admitted.

They laughed. Andrew continued. "I figured I'd work out the dating kinks, then gather up my nerve to ask out a specific someone and avoid all serious bloopers."

Lydia was both amused and, surprisingly, hurt. "Oh! So, I'm the guinea pig!"

"Sort of." He reached over to squeeze her hand. "Only in the kindest of ways."

"Thanks a lot!"

Andrew stared straight ahead, apparently concentrating on maneuvering uptown on the East Side Drive. He was oblivious to the fact that he'd wounded her pride. Or if he knew it, had no intention of uttering another word on the subject. In truth, her pain was merely a twinge, and Lydia decided she'd be better off ignoring it herself.

"Andrew?"

"Hmm?"

"Is there someone you want to ask out, someone you like?"

He hesitated. "Please don't say anything, but I was thinking of getting to know your friend, Barbara, better."

Lydia grinned. *Men!* "And you figured you'd get to know her better by asking out her best friend."

*   *   *

"We sure had a hell of a time," Andrew said six hours later as he pulled up his emergency break in Lydia's driveway.

"We sure did, Andrew. Everything was great, including the company." Lydia leaned over to kiss his cheek. "Thanks so much for inviting me. I enjoyed myself thoroughly."

He grinned. "Maybe next time we'll make a double date of it."

"That would be nice," Lydia agreed, though she doubted that would ever come to pass. Sol Molina's days off were always subject to change.

Reggie came to greet her as she entered the darkened house. He accepted her stroking, then turned around. Tail in the air, he led the way to her bedroom.

"You bet we're off to dreamland, Reggie Boy, because tomorrow we rise early."

She washed up and changed into her nightgown, then put an ear to Evelyn's door. She smiled when she detected the sound of her steady breathing. Evelyn was fast asleep. Soon she'd be asleep, too. Lydia returned to her bedroom and set her alarm clock for five-thirty. She switched out the light and, nudging Reggie to make room for her, turned on her side.

"A beautiful day for flying," Lydia commented as she placed Evelyn's two suitcases in the back seat of her Lexus.

"You have my new key?" Evelyn asked, her face puckered into a frown.

"I do. I'll bring in the mail, check your phone messages, and water the plants twice a week." Lydia patted her hand. "You're not going to the North Pole. We'll talk on the phone."

Evelyn smiled. "Silly, aren't I? And I should mention, Gillian has a key to the house, so don't be surprised if you see her stopping by. She's back with her boyfriend. I gave Stefano a key, too. He finally has time to put in the shelves in our—I mean—my small TV room."

Lydia froze. "You did?"

"Of course. Stefano's been our handyman and caretaker since we moved to Twin Lakes. Daniel had him keep an eye on the house when we went to Florida. Why? Don't you trust him?"

"I've no reason not to," Lydia said, the image of Stefano and Denise embracing vivid in her mind. What was it about that twosome that set her teeth on edge? "I supposed, after what happened, you wouldn't give your house key to anyone but me."

Evelyn gave a little laugh as she brushed aside Lydia's concern. "Gillian's family, and Stefano's honest as the day is long. Besides, Daniel was very fond of him."

How fond of him would Daniel have been if he knew Stefano was involved with his daughter? "Whatever you think is best," Lydia said as she opened the car door on the passenger side and helped Evelyn into her seat.

"What I think is that I can't go around being suspicious of every person because of what happened," Evelyn said as she fastened her seatbelt.

Lydia fastened her own seatbelt and backed slowly out of the garage. She felt uncharacteristically jittery this morning. She told herself it was probably because Evelyn was leaving, and the sensation would pass once she saw her safely into the airport.

It was a bright, clear morning. "A perfect morning for flying," she mused aloud. "Not a cloud in the sky."

She drove through the community and turned onto Bellewood Road. There was no traffic in sight except for the red pickup truck approaching from the opposite direction. The vehicle gained speed as it drew closer. Lydia's heart leaped into her mouth as the truck veered onto her side of the road and came barreling toward them.

"Lord-a-mercy! A drunkard!" Evelyn exclaimed.

Lydia spun the wheel hard to the right. The Lexus crossed the shallow shoulder and bumped along a patch of low bushes until it came to a stop. Lydia jerked around in time to watch the truck disappear over the rise behind them.

"He's gone," she told Evelyn, who sat huddled against the car door. "Are you all right?"

"Yes. Please take me to the airport."

"Of course." Lydia reached for her cell phone. "After I call Sol."

Chapter Fifteen

Lydia sat down in the visitor's chair and watched Sol take his place behind his desk. It had felt strange when he'd called early that morning, asking her to come down to the police station, even stranger to be facing him across his desk strewn with papers and empty coffee cups. She'd never been inside his office, and the experience was filling her with dread. His impassive expression told her nothing. He cast his eyes on the papers before him, preventing her from seeing the shade of green they were right now. He was making this interview official and impersonal, and she had no idea why.

"Mr. Korman was poisoned. We received the results this morning."

Lydia nodded, too stunned to speak. Thinking Daniel might have been murdered and hearing verification that he was were two very different kettles of fish. Suddenly, she was downing deep gulps of air.

"I'll get you some water."

When she could manage a few words, she said, "No need. I'm okay."

Sol was already at the door, shouting out his order.

"Please don't argue with me, Lydia. We've some ground to cover so I'd appreciate your cooperation."

Ground to cover? She nodded, though she had no idea what he was talking about. When he handed her a glass, she sipped dutifully.

"Does Evelyn know?"

"I've spoken to her."

"How did she take the news? Poor thing, she's still shaken from our experience Sunday morning, and now this." Lydia was babbling, but she couldn't seem to stop. "I talked to her last night. She's dizzy and very frightened. Gayle took Evelyn to see her doctor. He's ordered bed rest for at least seventy-two hours."

"Lydia, the poison was administered in candy. In Bertran's Best crèmes."

She stared at him. "Oh, no! You don't mean in the box of chocolates that Barbara and I gave Daniel!"

"That's not what I said."

"How can you know the poison was in the candy we gave him? Other guests dropped off gifts and left them on the table in the cloakroom. I saw two other boxes of Bertran's Best chocolates. Not the same shape, which means they weren't crèmes, but I recognized the iridescent blue wrapping paper."

It suddenly hit her. "Oh, God! Ours was the only box of crèmes!" She turned to Sol. "I swear, Barbara and I didn't poison Daniel!"

"Lydia—"

"Are you positive Daniel ate one of the crèmes?"

"There's no doubt. It's what his stomach contents revealed."

Stunned, Lydia fell silent, her thoughts scattering too fast to catch. "I don't understand how that could be."

Sol came to stand beside her. He put his hand on her shoulder. "I know you didn't put the poison in the chocolates, but Evelyn's certain Daniel opened the box of Bertram's Best crèmes because the chocolate crèmes were his favorite."

"I know they were. Someone else knew it, and—oh, my God!" She stopped, too distraught to continue.

Sol grimaced. "Lydia, it's not your fault Daniel's dead. Take another sip, then tell me everything you can about the box of candy—from the time of purchase until you brought it to the party."

Drinking water helped calm her. She drew a deep breath, then related the mundane facts of how she and Barbara had bought the candy one afternoon in the Bertran's Best chocolate store while shopping at the mall.

"We told the salesgirl the kind of candies we wanted, and she pointed to a stack of boxes. It was already wrapped in their special shiny blue paper. I took it home with me and left it on the dining room table until the evening of the party."

"Could anyone have touched it in the interim?"

Lydia shook her head. "No one broke into my home, as far as I can tell. Besides, the wrapping was undisturbed."

"Did you or Barbara hand the box of chocolates to Daniel?"

"No. Like everyone else, we left it on the table in the cloakroom. Though Evelyn had put 'no gifts, please' on the invitations, there were already some gifts on the table when we arrived."

"And that's the last time you saw the chocolates?"

"I suppose." Lydia thought back. "I passed the cloakroom later in the evening, on my way to the ladies' room, but I didn't get a good look at the gift table. Daniel's kids were in the room, holding what appeared to be a meeting. Actually, they were arguing."

"What about?"

"Money."

"Interesting. Who was present?"

"Arnold and his wife, Polly—I can't remember if her husband was there or not—Denise. Oh, and Bennett."

"Any other grandchildren?"

"Sorry, I don't remember."

"Were the gifts still on the table?"

"I'd imagine so. The hosts usually collect them when they're ready to leave." When he said nothing, Lydia said, "You're thinking someone in the room arrived early and injected the poison somehow?"

"Or substituted a box of doctored chocolates for Daniel's favorites, which happened to be what you and Barbara brought."

Lydia shivered. "How diabolical! The killer exchanged boxes, attached our birthday card, and that was that."

She thought a minute, then asked, "But how would he know when Daniel would eat the candy? Though Daniel finished off a Bertran's Best box pretty quickly, and the crèmes were one candy he wasn't willing to share."

Sol's eyes were a dull green. "A good thing in a way, because I imagine the killer must have doctored every candy in the box to ensure Daniel died."

"Who would do such a thing? A family member?"

"Maybe, though any guest could have made the candy switch some time during the party."

Lydia nodded. "The murderer intended Daniel to die, and soon. Which means, if it was a family member, he was operating under the premise that Daniel was going to change his will when he married Evelyn." She stared up at Sol. "Unless they knew he'd already changed it."

Sol shook his head. "I asked Evelyn about this very issue. Daniel only told his children that he and Evelyn were getting married. The murderer assumed he or she had to act before the wedding, not knowing the will had already been changed."

Lydia continued. "Then, when the murderer found out the terms of the new will, he or she went after Evelyn."

"Went after her twice."

"Thank God she's safe in Atlanta," Lydia said.

Sol frowned. "She wanted to come home. I had to all but threaten her with protective custody to get her to stay put, at least for a few weeks."

"I'm glad she's out of harm's way." She stood.

"I want you to be careful as well."

"Nobody's after me." She shuddered. "Or was that red pick-up truck after two birds with one stone?"

"I'd say that was the murderer's final attempt to get at Evelyn before she left Long Island. But there's no saying whoever it is won't go after you, should you start to snoop around."

Lydia grimaced. "I have no intention of—as you put it—snooping around."

"Good. No investigating, no following up hunches. Promise?" He raised her chin with one finger.

She thought he was about to kiss her, and was disappointed when he didn't. "I promise," she said, feeling like a child.

"Talk to you soon," Sol said, opening the door.

"You never told me—what kind of poison was in the chocolates?"

"It wasn't poison exactly, but a powerful dosage of digitalis. The same medicine Mr. Korman took to keep his congestive heart failure under control."

"Something a close friend or relative would know."

"Exactly."

This same person would happen to know Evelyn was catching an early Sunday morning to Atlanta, Lydia thought, but didn't say aloud.

Lydia drove slowly to Carrington House, her mind awhirl with everything Sol had told her. Daniel was dead because someone had injected a strong dose of digitalis into his chocolate. Her birthday gift, which she and Barbara had chosen with Daniel's preferences in mind. She was overcome by a sense of rage, so powerful she almost sailed past a red light. *How vile, to kill a man while pretending to celebrate his life! Who, among Daniel's family and friends, was that intent on wiping him off the face of the earth? Was the murderer after Daniel's money, or was there a personal vendetta involved?*

As soon as she stepped inside the business office, she knew that Len had gotten word of Daniel's postmortem. He cut short his conversation with Jessica and Betty, the head of the wait staff, to glare at her.

"A Lieutenant Molina called to say your friend, Mr. Korman, was poisoned, possibly right here at the mansion. He's coming by later to question as many of the staff as I can round up who were on duty the night of his party." Len's small eyes bore into her. "That's your Mr. Korman, Lydia."

Lydia resisted the urge to smack him. "Yes, Len, Mr. Korman was my friend and neighbor. I'm just coming from the police station, where Lieutenant Molina gave me the sad news."

"Jeez!" Len rubbed the bald spot on his head, messing up his comb-over. "I hope you told him we run a respectable facility. Nobody who works here had any reason to kill the old geezer. Nobody even knew him—except for you."

Lydia's nostrils flared. "Daniel Korman was a wonderful person and not a 'geezer,' as you put it."

Len waved his hand. "It's an expression, that's all. No need to be so thin-skinned. The point is, we don't want adverse publicity. The board hears about it, and there goes the money I practically had to beg them for to do our much-needed renovations."

You're afraid they'll blame you if the suites aren't a moneymaker, and you're chewing me out to let off steam. Well, buster, you picked the wrong patsy.

"Tell you what, Len. I'll make today my last day at the mansion and turn down the offer to manage The Carrington Suites.

That way you and the board won't be tainted by any connection to me because someone I recommended was poisoned."

"No, Lydia, you can't leave!" Jessica wailed.

Lydia felt a pang of remorse. She was fond of Jessica, who was young enough to be her daughter. Though she held the title of office manager, Jessica was overworked and understaffed. Lydia held her ground.

"I'm sorry to leave you in the lurch, Jessica, but I can't work here knowing Len blames me for bringing trouble to the mansion."

"I never said—"

"Then I quit, too," Jessica broke in staunchly. "I can't manage without Lydia."

Len's eyes rolled like a wild man. "Don't say that, Jessica. I'll raise your salary fifty bucks a week."

"Oh, sure," Jessica said. Tears streamed down her face. "Just like you said you'd hire two more people. Well, now you'll have to hire four more." She fled from the room.

Len chased after her. "You can't go, Jessica! What will I do without you?"

Jessica swirled around, making him stop in his tracks to avoid crashing into her. "You'll get what you deserve!"

"Please stay, Jessica."

"I won't—unless Lydia stays, too. She helps me with things you should be teaching me, things you have no time for with your precious renovations."

Len paused. Lydia nearly laughed at the agony he was going through, stewing in a situation he'd created. He swallowed once. Twice. He cleared his throat.

"Would you reconsider staying, Lydia? I didn't mean to speak harshly about you or your friend. I've been burdened with business concerns—"

"You haven't been taking care of your home office," she broke in smoothly. "That should always be your first concern. I'll come back if you make the hiring of two office workers a priority. Jessica can't go on as she's been doing." Lydia grinned. "She's a terrific asset. You'd be a fool to let her slip through your fingers."

Driving home hours later, Lydia reexamined her exchange with Len and all that had ensued. She wasn't proud of having allowed herself to be sufficiently provoked to offer to quit, though the results were mostly positive: a raise for Jessica, and ads for more personnel were placed online and in the papers. The downside was Len now saw her as a threat to his authority and was bound to seek retribution somehow. She shook her head. No matter. If he made things unpleasant, she'd quit and find a job in a more congenial workplace.

She stopped at a gourmet market and bought fruits, vegetables, and flounder for dinner. She ate her dinner, stacked the dishwasher, and was planning to call Barbara when the doorbell rang.

"Coming!" she called out, hoping to see Sol when she opened the front door.

Her smile disappeared when she saw Ron Morganstern and Mick Diminio standing there instead. They looked grim. Her heart jumped to her throat, but she refused to show her apprehension.

"Good evening, gentlemen. I've nothing to say to either of you."

Mick met her gaze. "But we have something to say to you—if you'll let us."

He lowered his head, awaiting her decision. Ron nodded reassuringly.

Puzzled but no longer frightened, she shrugged. "In that case, come on in."

She led them into the living room, and they sat side by side on the sofa opposite the one she favored.

Ron cleared his throat. "First off, Mick and I want to thank you for not running to the cops about Timmy John."

"Something I hope I don't live to regret," she said wryly.

Mick reached across the table, as though intending to pat her hand, and thought better of it. "I'm deeply sorry for making asinine threats against your family. That was stupid and unconscionable, and I certainly didn't mean it."

Lydia glared at him. "It was the most awful thing anyone ever said to me."

He gave her a thin smile. "I regretted it the moment the words left my mouth. Will you forgive me?"

Lydia thought a minute. On a visceral level, she'd never forgive him, but there was no point in refusing his olive branch. She nodded. "Apology accepted. It's rare to hear an old pol say he's sorry."

Mick sighed. "Thank you. Ronnie and I have a lot to be sorry for, but I swear to you, we didn't kill Timmy John. I've regretted that afternoon these seventy years."

"We're sorry we can't undo what we did that day," Ron said, "but we want to help set things right—by finding Daniel's murderer."

"Yeah, we want to make sure the rotten skunk gets what he deserves!"

Lydia gave a start. "How did you find out he was murdered?"

Mick winked, giving Lydia a glimpse of what a charmer the man must have been in his prime. "You underestimate an old pol's connections. My son called me as soon as he heard the news, and I called Ronnie."

"Can you believe it—Danny done in by one of his own flesh and blood?" Ron shook his head in disapproval. "I thought that all along, ever since he died."

"So you did," Lydia mused, remembering his comments about Daniel's mercenary children the day of the funeral.

"Now, Ronnie, don't go jumping to conclusions," Mick admonished his friend. "There are a few other possibilities. That fellow, Allen Holtstein, has a real murky past."

"Excuse me." Lydia held up her palms. "I think it's admirable that you want to help find Daniel's murderer, but the police are on top of it. I'm sure they'd appreciate hearing whatever you know about any guests who attended Daniel's party."

"Are you kidding?" Mick got to his feet and paced a bit before turning back to her. "The last thing Ronnie and I want is to draw attention to ourselves. If we went to the cops, they'd go digging into our personal histories."

"They'll find out you were both at the party. I'm sure they'll question you along with every other guest. They're bound to ask how you knew Daniel."

"No doubt they will," Ronnie said. "And we'll tell them we knew him when we were kids, which is true enough. But that's them coming to us, not us going to them. Makes a big difference to the cops."

Mick came to stand beside her. "The thing is, Lydia—may I call you Lydia?"

She nodded.

He smiled. "Ronnie here tells me you're pretty friendly with Lieutenant Molina in homicide. Is that right?"

"I am," she said, feeling the blood rise to her ears, "but—"

"And you're no slouch yourself when it comes to finding crooks and murderers."

She nodded, wondering where this was going.

"The thing is, I have the ways and means of learning everything there is to know about people—the real dirt, not the face they show to the world. I can tell you what I dig up, and you can pass it on to your friend."

Lydia bit her lips so she wouldn't laugh aloud at the absurdity of his suggestion. "I don't think it's a good idea. Sol will want to know the source of my information."

Mick put up a hand to halt her objections. "Let me give you a "for instance." You know Danny's grandson, Bennett?"

Lydia nodded.

He let out a humorless laugh. "The kid's thirty-five and has been involved in more crooked deals than you could shake a stick at."

She nodded again, though she couldn't see what shaking a stick had to do with anything.

"In high school he hooked up with a gang of thieves and started selling some of their booty to his classmates. Until a kid ratted them out." Mick's eyes narrowed. "Bennett arranged for one of the gang's goons to teach the kid 'a lesson.' The kid almost bled to death. He required thirty-nine stitches. Bennett ended up in juvie hall."

Lydia knew enough about the law to be impressed by this piece of information. Juvenile records were closed. "Nice guy," she commented. "It's difficult to believe he's Daniel's grandson."

Mick frowned. "The kid's father was a drunken sot who tried his hand at forging checks instead of working. The first time he got caught, Daniel hired a top lawyer who got him off with a slap on the wrist. The second time, Daniel told Denise to divorce the guy, and she listened. She cleaned up her act for a while then met husband number two, a druggie who got her hooked on pills."

"Maybe you should have been a detective," Lydia said.

Mick laughed, this time with genuine pleasure. "In my line of work I had to know everything about everyone I dealt with. Right now I'm making it my business to check out the people in Daniel's circle." He turned serious. "The way I see it, someone at the party poisoned Daniel. I intend to find out who."

Mick's intent—with her as a conduit to the police—took on a new gravity that appealed to her sense of morality. With or without her assistance, the old pol would find a way to get his information to the police. But Lydia suddenly saw this as her chance—her obligation—to assist Mick and Ron for Daniel and Evelyn's sake.

"Okay, I'll do it," she said as she stood.

To her astonishment, Mick enveloped her in a bear hug that swept her off her feet. "Good girl! We'll get the mother—er—person who poisoned Danny."

They left shortly after. Lydia dropped down onto the sofa and considered the logistics. She'd promised Sol she wouldn't get involved in playing detective. Well, she wasn't—merely acting as a messenger girl. The trick was to offer up whatever information Mick gave her as something she'd learned in the course of conversation with Twin Lakes' residents.

"He wants me to tell him what the neighbors are saying," she said aloud. It wasn't quite true, but it helped assuage her guilty conscience for defying Sol's instructions, which, if he found out, would create a rift between them.

Chapter Sixteen

E velyn called her that evening, spilling over with apologies.

"I'm so sorry, my dear, for repaying your hospitality by implicating the box of chocolates you and Barbara gave Daniel."

"Please Evelyn, that's the least of it. Sol figures the murderer must have switched boxes and replaced our gift with doctored chocolates. Be sure to tell Sol everything you can remember about the night of Daniel's party and the morning after."

Evelyn gave a rueful little laugh. "Which isn't very much, I'm afraid. I think I threw out the box of candy laced with digitalis." She paused. "At least I must have. I don't remember seeing it after I came home from the hospital."

Lydia's pulse quickened. "Maybe the murderer took it with him after he struck you."

"I couldn't say."

"Try to remember when you last saw the box of candy, and tell Sol when he calls again."

"I will, dear."

"I'll keep an eye on everything." Lydia drew in a breath, then ventured to say what was at the forefront of her mind. "Stay in Atlanta and enjoy your family. There's no reason to hurry home."

Evelyn sounded forlorn when she said, "So Gayle keeps telling me. Goodbye, Lydia. Thanks for everything."

Lydia placed the phone down, and ignored the newspaper she'd been reading. Instead, she called Polly to make amends for what Polly considered her cruel betrayal. Polly's fear that some-one had murdered her father had proven correct. While Lydia could never explain why she'd changed her mind about Daniel's death, she felt obliged to offer her sympathy and support.

Polly dismissed her apologies almost perfunctorily and laid all her resentment at Denise's feet.

"She's a snake, always conniving and wheedling men for drug money."

"I thought she'd stopped using."

"Denise? Never. Oh, she pretends to stop. My sister's great at dissembling and lying. I know for a fact she tried to hit Dad up for money a few days before the party. And you know what? I'm beginning to think she killed him."

"Polly!" Despite all she knew about Daniel's family, Lydia was shocked.

"Who else could it be? Denise knows all about hypodermic needles. And getting hold of Dad's meds would be easy enough. She used to raid the medicine chest when we were little."

"Still. This was a deliberate act of homicide."

"Patricide, you mean." Polly's voice grew shrill. "Denise hated my father, and she wanted his money. I know she did it!"

"Polly, dear, please calm down so we can discuss this. I agree Denise is a possible suspect, but you've no proof that she's guilty."

"Maybe not for a court of law, but I've seen enough to know what I'm saying. The night of Dad's party, Arnold wanted us to hold a meeting at ten o'clock. I didn't want to, but he insisted. I figured it would be easier to go along, stay for fifteen minutes at the most, then leave. Just before ten, I went into the ladies' room off the entrance hall. You know where it is."

"Of course," Lydia said, remembering her own visit there minutes later, in time to overhear Polly's siblings arguing about Daniel.

"Denise was standing at the sink when I came in, her purse was wide open. She jumped when she saw me. I figured I'd startled her as she was touching up her makeup, but now that I know the poison in the candy must have been administered with a hypodermic needle, I suddenly realize that's what I saw in Denise's purse."

"Are you certain, Polly?"

Polly paused. "I saw something long and thin, thinner than a cigarette. It had to be a hypodermic needle!"

Lydia remembered Polly's psychiatric history and sighed. "Really? You never mentioned this before."

"I know. I mean, it didn't occur to me at the time."

"But Polly, you said Denise is probably using again. She wouldn't want you to see the hypodermic needle and know she was shooting up."

"You're not listening to me! Denise used that hypodermic needle to kill my father!"

Lydia drew in breath then spoke slowly, not wanting Polly to think she was betraying her a second time. "Sometimes we make an assumption without having all the facts."

Polly's voice grew shrill. "Then I'll find out! I'll talk to Denise, make her tell me if she did it!"

Lydia gripped the phone to stop her hand from trembling. "You'll do no such thing! Even if Denise had a hypodermic needle, it doesn't mean she killed your father. And if she did, she'd have no compunction about killing you! Tell Lieutenant Molina what you suspect. Let him take it from there."

Silence. Lydia held her breath. "Polly?"

"Well..."

"Promise me you won't confront Denise! You'll leave everything to the police."

Silence.

"Polly! I know you're distraught, but I don't want to see you get hurt. Think of your family. The girls."

"The girls." Polly let out a braying laugh that ended in a whimper.

"Polly, is something the matter? Is Gillian giving you a hard time?"

"No more than usual. It's Nicole I'm worried about. She's threatening to move in with that Ringo. And if she does," Polly sniffed, and Lydia realized she was crying, "I don't know what will become of her!"

Before Lydia could think of a soothing response, Polly went on quickly, "I have to go. Thanks for calling, Lydia."

"But I didn't do—"

I'll be talking to your Lieutenant Molina," Polly interrupted. "Just remember—Denise is a pathological liar. If she calls you, don't believe one word she says."

***

Two days later, Lydia rose with a brilliant June sun. She swam laps in the pool, then hurried home to dress for work. There was something to be said for working, even when one didn't need the money. In her particular case, it kept her from dwelling too much on Daniel's murder.

She waved to Jessica in passing, glad to see her in the midst of an interview. In her own office, she glanced at the slew of phone messages she had to return, and started making calls in order of their importance. From the looks of things, she'd have an hour or two to work on the books in the afternoon. And hopefully, one of five applicants Jessica was interviewing today would work out.

At eleven-thirty, Lydia was on the phone with an excited mother-of-the-bride, taking down the final number of guests for her daughter's Saturday night wedding, when Denise strode into her office reeking of cigarette smoke. She paced up and down as furiously as a penned-in tiger until Lydia held up a finger to indicate one minute more and waved her outside. The mother was telling her for the third time about the bride and groom's honeymoon trip to the Far East, when Lydia interrupted to say a call she absolutely had to take had just come through. The woman said she understood, then embarked on another story. Having reached her limit, Lydia broke in to offer congratulations once again and disconnected before the woman could reply.

Whew! How prenuptial nerves affected some people! And what had brought Denise to Carrington House? Lydia repressed a shudder as she recalled Polly's insistence that Denise had killed their father. Though Lydia held little stock in what Polly considered "proof" of her sister's guilt, she assumed Denise's unexpected appearance was related to Daniel's death.

She found her visitor on the broad top step of the front entrance, puffing furiously on a cigarette. At the sound of her name, Denise tossed the butt aside and followed Lydia into her office, where she perched precariously on the edge of a visitor's chair. Only when Lydia sat facing her across her desk did she notice the tears streaming down Denise's gaunt cheeks.

"You have to help me, Lydia! There's no one else I can turn to."

Was Denise about to confess to the murder, or had she landed in a completely different mess of trouble? Regardless, she had overstepped boundaries by coming to Lydia's workplace. Lydia bit her lip to stop herself from expressing her displeasure. Denise was Daniel's daughter. She owed her the courtesy of hearing her out.

"What's the matter, Denise?"

"It's Stefano. The police arrested him this morning." Denise reached across the desk and clutched Lydia's arm. "Please, Lydia. Talk to your friend, the police detective. Tell him Stefano didn't do it!"

Lydia disengaged her claw-like grip and Denise sank back into the chair. "What are you talking about? They suspect Stefano killed your father?"

"No, of course not!" Denise shook her head vehemently, whipping her dark hair back and forth. "They're accusing him of running you and Evelyn off the road the morning you drove her to the airport."

"Accusing him?" Lydia echoed.

"All right, questioning him. It's the same thing, isn't it?"

Lydia thought a minute. "Does Stefano have a red pickup truck?"

"Yes, but I swear he never came after you and Evelyn. Why would he?"

"I've no idea why anyone would want to hurt us, but someone was behind that wheel."

"It wasn't Stefano," Denise insisted. "You would have recognized his mustache."

"I couldn't make out the driver's face, so I can't help you there."

"But if you didn't see his mustache, then it can't be Stefano," Denise insisted. "Besides, he was with me that entire weekend. We got to bed late Saturday night and slept till noon Sunday morning. I've no idea why someone reported his license plate—unless they had it in for him."

Lydia's antenna went up. "Someone reported his license plate number? That's odd. There weren't other cars on the road when the truck tried to sideswipe me."

"Odd? It's as phony as a three-dollar bill!" Denise shrieked.

Lydia closed her door, and hoped Len was out of earshot and not speculating what she might be saying to antagonize a potential client.

Denise went on. "The cops who took Stefano down to the station said an anonymous witness called in, claiming he'd seen the incident, then rattled off the license number."

"Days after it happened?" Lydia mused. "The police sure took their time tracing the number."

"Because they screwed up. Whoever took the message at the station left it on Detective Molina's desk, but it got misplaced until this morning."

Lydia thought a minute. "I've seen Stefano leaving work in a black Honda, never a red pickup."

"That's right. He never takes the truck to work."

Then what does he need it for? Aloud, she asked, "Could anyone else have taken it Sunday morning without his knowledge?"

"I don't see how. He parked it outside my house and left his keys on the bureau. Though when he came back from buying groceries for our lunch he mentioned the truck felt different somehow. Like someone had adjusted the seat. Frankly, I was worried about a car bomb."

"A car bomb?"

Denise nodded. Reluctantly, she explained. "Stefano fought for his country during the Balkan war. He came to the United States to escape his enemies." Her eyes widened. "They swore they'd come after him, no matter where he went, and kill him." Denise paused, then went on. "He's pretty sure he saw one of them the other night outside his apartment."

"Won't he tell this to Detective Molina?"

"No." Denise grimaced. "Stefano doesn't trust the police. He'll be furious if I tell them. But it's a different story, coming from you."

Lydia failed to see the logic in this, but said, "I'll speak to Lieutenant Molina and explain it as best I can."

Denise came around to Lydia's seat, her arms open to embrace her. "Thank you, Lydia!"

Lydia suffered her smothering, cigarette-reeking hug. "I'll call you tonight."

"With good news, I hope."

"I can't promise anything."

Denise frowned, clearly disappointed that Lydia hadn't offered to vouch for her lover's innocence after hearing his tale of woe. Then she remembered her manners and flashed an artificial smile. "Thank you, Lydia. I knew I could count on you."

Lydia noted Denise's unsteady gait as she left. *Was she drinking again? Downing pills? Shooting up? The woman was repugnant. Interesting how she insisted it hadn't been Stefano who'd tried to run Lydia's car off the road on Sunday morning.* Lydia shook her head. She'd never given much thought to Stefano's background. She had no idea if he was Croatian, Bosnian, or Serb. If he'd indeed been a soldier in the midst of those troubled times, he must have witnessed unspeakable horrors. And might have taken part in them himself.

Maybe Stefano had grown so immune to killing that he had no compunction about poisoning Daniel and finishing off his fiancée so his lover could receive her inheritance. Lydia wondered if Denise was so devious and amoral that, after their plan had failed, she was nervy enough to seek help from the very person Stefano had nearly killed.

Lydia decided that pondering these matters would serve no purpose. She called Sol, got his tape, and left a message to call her. She then sat down to tackle the work she'd intended to complete before lunch.

Lydia and Jessica ate their sandwiches at a corner table beside one of the tall windows in the library. Jessica was bubbly because Len wanted to meet with her about the women they'd interviewed.

"Will you be leaving here to manage the Suites?" Jessica asked.

Lydia shrugged. "I haven't given it much thought. I've been too busy with the fallout from Daniel Korman's murder."

She returned to her office, vowing to make a list of pros and cons regarding the position to help her decide. Daniel's murder was foremost in her mind. She wanted to call Sol again but didn't. He'd speak to her when he could. He called her at a quarter to five as she was about to leave for home. Lydia told him of Denise's visit.

"A witness places his red pickup at the scene on Sunday morning. Ligoris swears up and down it wasn't him. We're not convinced he's telling the truth, but we don't have enough to hold him."

"Denise will be thrilled Stefano won't be spending the night in jail. She told me about the misplaced information."

Sol muttered something under his breath. "We spoke to the witness, and he confirmed what he'd reported on Sunday. He was at the other far end of Bellewood Road traveling toward the incident. He saw the red pickup nearly swipe your car. He caught the license number as it sped past him, but he didn't get a good view of the driver, either. He thought it was a DWI. Called it in because his sister was nearly killed by a drunk driver some months ago."

"Could someone have stolen Stefano's truck that morning?" Lydia asked.

"He didn't notice it was gone, though he claims something about the truck felt different when he drove it later that day. Trouble is, he has an elaborate alarm system. Unless the guy who swiped it knew how to disarm the system, it would have made a racket."

"Denise told me Stefano has enemies from his native country who want to kill him. She said he saw one of them the other night."

"I've asked immigration to check him out. If his papers prove to be phony, as I think they will, he'll end up being deported. In the meantime, given his involvement in the Korman homicide, I want him around. Meaning, he can go back to being the Twin Lakes groundskeeper."

"Maintenance engineer," Lydia said automatically. "Did Polly Ellenberg call you? She's convinced Denise killed Daniel."

"Yup, she ran it by me but, as you see, I haven't charged her sister with the crime. Though I intend to ask her a few questions about her mustachioed lover."

Lydia laughed and said good-bye, feeling virtuous for having shared all she knew with Sol. Not that it made up for her unholy alliance with Mick and Ron, but it was something. She locked her office and headed for the main entrance of the mansion. When she passed Len's office, she stuck her head in the open doorway and called out, "Good night. See you tomorrow."

Len and Jessica paused in their discussion, which sounded animated but friendly.

"See you tomorrow," Len echoed, and turned back to Jessica.

"'Night, Lydia," Jessica sang out, her fingers forming an "o" behind her back. Lydia grinned. *Good for you, girl!* Len was finally hiring more help.

The Mercedes idling at the start of the circular driveway caught her attention as she stepped outside. Lydia squinted to see if she could see the driver through the windshield, but the tinted glass and glaring sun made that an impossibility. Wary because of the events of the last few weeks, she gave it one last glance before starting down the footpath leading to the parking area. She told herself she had nothing to fear. Carrington House was a well-known place of business. People often drove through the grounds to scout out the mansion, even if they weren't planning a social affair.

The Mercedes followed her to the parking lot. It honked as it inched closer. Terrified, Lydia walked quickly toward her car then realized she was committing a tactical error. She had to return to the mansion where she'd be safe! She spun around and double-backed. Once she passed the trees, she'd run like hell to the rear of the building, to the kitchen. The staff preparing for the evening's affairs always left the door propped open.

Chapter Seventeen

"Lydia! Wait."

Her heart jumped into her throat as she turned and saw Ron Morganstern waving to her from the open car window.

She downed deep gulps as the car pulled up beside her. "My God, you gave me a scare!"

"Sorry about that," Mick said from the driver's seat. "We got to talking and almost missed you when you came outside."

"Why were you waiting for me?" she asked as Ron struggled out of the passenger seat and held the door open for her.

"Have a seat," he said.

Lydia paused. While she was no longer concerned about her safely, she didn't like being shanghaied in this manner.

"We've things to tell you," Mick explained, "and figured we'd do it over an early dinner—or a drink, if you prefer."

"All right. Dinner's fine. I am hungry." She stepped into the car. Ron closed her door then climbed into the back seat.

Amused now, she asked, "How did you know what time I was leaving today?"

"Your friend, Barbara," Mick explained, a grin splitting his face.

Accepting that she'd been outnumbered and outmaneuvered, Lydia sank back against the leather seat and smiled. "I'm all yours, for the next hour or so."

"You won't be sorry," Mick said as he maneuvered the car through traffic, changing lanes with the quick reflexes of a man thirty years his junior. He turned into a strip mall and parked in front of a pizza parlor. Lydia knew better than to say a word. Sure enough, a young woman greeted Mick with an affectionate peck on the cheek, and led the three of them to a dining room in the rear. Lydia blinked in the dim light, as they sat down at a corner table dressed in crisp white napery. The food, she knew, would be delicious.

A man with a white apron wrapped around his considerable paunch clapped Mick on the back. He introduced himself as Luigi, and listed the specialties of the day. They all ordered an antipasto salad, homemade crab, lobster ravioli, and iced tea.

When Luigi left, Mick winked at her. "You're about to taste the best food in town." He nodded to Ron. "Let's bring Lydia up to date."

Ron reached for the clipboard he'd carried into the restaurant and referred to his notes.

"Here's what we've got so far: Stefano Ligoris. Real name Stefano Tadic, Serbian nationalist. Ligoris is his dead brother-in-law's name. Accused of atrocities but escaped to the U.S.

before being brought to trial. We're assuming he'll be sent back once the police do a thorough investigation of his ID."

Lydia gasped. "Once Denise told me his background, I suspected he might have committed atrocities. But knowing that he did is a shocker. I don't mean to sound naïve, but it's difficult to absorb. Stefano's always been so pleasant." She shuddered. "And flirtatious. Half the Twin Lakes women swoon when he flashes his smile."

"Assassins can be charming," Mick pointed out. "With his background, the last thing he'd want is to draw attention to himself."

"Bennett hates him," she murmured. "Could he have taken Stefano's truck to menace us, knowing Stefano's past would come out and he'd be deported? It would be one way of disposing of his mother's lover."

Mick shrugged. "With Bennett, I'd say anything's possible. Let's move on."

"Matthew Ellenberg, attorney and investor. Went in over his head, suffered losses, and owes a bundle. The Ellenbergs recently took out a second mortgage on the house."

"Poor Polly."

Ron threw her a speculative glance. "Think he did away with Daniel for the money?"

"I certainly hope not," Lydia replied.

"Two years ago Allen Holstein borrowed money from Daniel," Ron said.

"I found no indication that he ever paid it back," Mick said, "and he paid Daniel a visit the day of his party."

"How do you know?" Lydia asked, casting him a look of pure admiration.

"Easy," Ron said. "I checked the security gate's record for that day.

"Ah ha," Lydia said. So Ron was no fool, either. "Smart move."

Ron nodded his appreciation.

"That's just for starters," Mick said. "I left Bennett and his mother for last. Nothing's checked out yet regarding Bennett, but a kid with his past doesn't take to the straight and narrow that quickly."

"Denise has a job," Ron said. "I don't know if she's using. Either way, she's one explosive woman."

"She sure is," Lydia agreed. "She came to see me earlier today. She was so hyper, she might have been high."

"Denise came to see you at Carrington House?" Mick asked, shaking his head in disbelief. "What did she want?"

"She was frantic about Stefano's being arrested, and asked me to put in a good word for him with Lieutenant Molina. I can only imagine how she'll react if he's deported."

Their antipasto arrived and the three set to eating with gusto. When their plates were cleared, Luigi brought large steaming plates of homemade ravioli with vodka sauce. Lydia tasted it. "Delicious."

Mick gave her a dazzling smile. "I only invite special people here."

A warm, cared-for feeling spread through her body. "I'm honored."

She ate two of the five ravioli and pushed her plate away.

"Is that all you can manage?" Mick asked.

Lydia nodded. His gaze rose past her and Luigi appeared immediately at her elbow.

"Shall I wrap this for you, *Signora*?"

"That would be lovely," Lydia said.

"Ours, too, Luigi," Mick said.

Lydia glanced at their plates. Both were untouched.

"The salad was enough for me," Ron admitted. "Bella and I will share this for dinner tomorrow."

"The same for Caitlin and me," Mick said. The two men exchanged glances and laughed heartedly over a shared secret.

Lifelong friends who have been through hell and back together.

Five minutes later they were in the car speeding toward Carrington House.

Behind her, Ron asked, "Lydia, any thoughts regarding who might have killed Danny?"

The question, coming so unexpectedly after their congenial lunch, stunned her into silence. Mick patted her arm. "Don't worry. We won't hold you to it."

"I've no idea," she finally said. "Logic says it's one of his children. Not Polly, of course," she quickly added, "but maybe Arnold. Or Denise. Though frankly, I can't see either of them plotting to poison their father."

"Arnold's strapped for cash," Ron pointed out. "And he resented Danny."

"I don't dispute that," Lydia said. "But injecting medicine into his favorite candy? My gift, I might add."

"I'm sure the killer meant nothing personal," Mick said kindly.

"I don't know about that," Lydia said, remembering when a killer had used her car as a murder weapon with the intention of making her look guilty a few months back.

"I think it's safe to say the person who killed Daniel also tried to kill Evelyn," Ron added.

"I suppose," Lydia agreed.

"Another indication the assailant was after money he or she could only acquire when both Danny and Evelyn were dead."

"That makes sense," Lydia said. "Unless it was meant to look that way."

"Go on," Mick said. "We're all ears."

"Well, for example, I hate to accuse anyone of killing Daniel without proof, but let's say his friend Allen owed him money, a lot of money, which he couldn't or didn't want to pay back."

"But would he go after Evelyn, too?" Ron asked.

"I don't know," Lydia mused. "If she were no longer in the picture, I'm not sure if the estate lawyers would check that carefully to see what money Daniel might have loaned someone."

"Maybe Evelyn knew about the loan," Mick offered. "And if Allen killed his boss, then killing again might not be that difficult."

Lydia nodded. "That's the crux of the matter, as I see it. Whoever murdered Daniel considers murder a viable means of getting what he wants."

"Let's not forget Matt, Polly's husband," Mick said. "Polly collects millions more when Evelyn dies. He probably needs at least two million to set his finances back on course."

"Matt's a family man," Lydia demurred, the memory of Matt comforting a sobbing Polly at Daniel's funeral vivid in her mind.

"You can't let your emotions cloud the facts," Ron said.

She nodded. "You're right, but it's depressing how you guys turn every friend and relative into a suspect."

Five minutes later they dropped her off at her car in the parking lot. Lydia picked up her doggie bag and bussed Mick and Ron. "Thanks for dinner, fellows."

"It was our pleasure," Mick said. "We'll keep on working and digging. Something has to turn up. Meanwhile, get Lieutenant Molina to check Allen out, if he hasn't already."

"I'll do my best," Lydia agreed.

She drove home, aware that the Mercedes kept two cars' distance discretely behind her. Her elderly squires, she thought with affection. Mick and Ron had spent several hours gathering information about the possible suspects. She was dismayed by how many suspects there were! In every case, the motive was financial gain. Every suspect except Stefano had attended Daniel's birthday party, and had the means and opportunity to switch the boxes of chocolates. During her next conversation with Sol, she'd introduce—as a question or a possibility—what Ron and Mick had told her, though she was certain he must have checked out everyone's past and financial history already.

Who was desperate enough to resort to murder? Lydia wondered as she turned onto Bellewood Road. She ran down the list of suspects, trying to decide whom she could question without appearing too obvious. She had an excuse to call Denise—and she would later that evening—and try to find out if she was using drugs again. Right now, Denise was probably smoothing Stefano's feathers, helping him come up with ways to stop immigration from tossing him out of the country.

There was Bennett, though, who worked nearby. Lydia drove to the Drug Market, a well-lit, well-stocked enterprise that sold everything from stationery to household cleaners, and included a pharmacy and a photo center. Several customers were shopping while others stood in line waiting to pay for their purchases at the cash registers. Lydia meandered up and down each aisle, hoping to spot Bennett. She found him in the hair color section, chatting with a beautiful girl with long blonde hair who held up a box of hair coloring in each hand. From afar, Lydia watched what was clearly a flirtatious conversation that included a good deal of laughter and rippling blonde hair as the girl continuously shook her head. Finally, Bennett pointed to one box. The girl set the other back on the shelf and headed for the registers at the front of the store.

"Bennett!" Lydia called out, noting his furtive expression as he glanced about trying to determine who wanted him. When he caught sight of her, he broke out in a grin.

"Ah, Mrs. Krause. Can I help you find something?"

"I need some shampoo," Lydia said.

Bennett gestured with his chin. "The next aisle over. We've a wide selection." He stepped away.

"Your mother must be relieved," Lydia threw out to catch his attention.

It worked. "What do you mean?"

"She came to see me today. She was very concerned because Stefano had been arrested. Someone identified his pickup truck as the one that nearly drove Evelyn and me off the road on Sunday. But it seems the police have released him."

Bennett frowned. "That's too bad. Mom would be better off without that guy." He stepped closer and Lydia smelled a strong aftershave mingled with something else, something musky and dark. "Did you know he tortured people back home?"

Lydia shook her head as though she doubted his word. "Really? Stefano's always been so nice and helpful to the Twin Lakes residents. Your grandfather was very fond of him."

Bennett's look of condescension made her want to kick him hard in the butt. "It's all a performance." He laughed derisively. "If you saw him with his Serbian pals, you'd know what Stefano's all about. Besides," he fixed his gaze on her, "what are you defending him for, after what he did to you?"

Lydia shook her head. "I'm not defending him. If it was Stefano. I couldn't see the driver through the tinted glass."

"What do you want—a neon sign?" Bennett's face was contorted in fury. "A witness ID'd his truck at the scene. I'd put two and two together, if I were you."

Lydia froze. As sure as she knew her children's birthdays, she was certain Bennett had taken Stefano's pickup truck to frighten Evelyn and her. Refusing to be intimidated, she stared into his eyes until his false outrage melted into a sardonic grin. Bennett was better at this than she was. Still, she had inner resources, and taking the offense was one of them.

"I hear Stefano will probably be deported. You must be glad," she said as calmly as she could manage, "since you don't approve of him as your mother's boyfriend."

Bennett averted his gaze, but not before she noted a strange expression she couldn't quite read. Was he apprehensive? Dissembling? A moment later he chose to laugh off her comment.

"I sure as hell don't. My mother deserves better. She's never known how to pick her men, starting with my father."

There was nothing to be gained here. "I'm glad Denise has such a devoted son. Goodbye, Bennett." Eager to get away, Lydia started down the aisle for the exit.

"Mrs. Krause, you forgot your shampoo."

She shook her head—at her stupidity and Bennett's derisive tone—and made a quick U-turn. "So I did, Bennett. So I did."

She spent the five-minute ride home berating herself for coming off as a snoop without gaining anything in return. That wasn't quite accurate, Lydia surmised as she waited for Twin Lakes' security gate to rise. Bennett's comments and reactions told her he was disreputable through and through. But he wasn't as good at concealing his secrets as he thought. He had something against Stefano a bit more personal than the man's relationship with Denise, though Lydia was sure that entered into it as well.

At home she fed Reggie, then made herself a cup of coffee. It was a balmy night—warm with a delightful breeze. Lydia wondered if Sol would call or, even better, stop by, though she had no intention of waiting at home for that possibility to occur. That's why cell phones had been invented. Lydia grabbed hers, checked to make sure it was on, then draped a sweater around her shoulders and locked her door behind her.

She decided to stroll around Lake Nissaquoge and work off her dinner. She waved to neighbors, walking or chatting with other residents, all enjoying the spring weather. One woman stopped Lydia to ask if she'd spoken to Evelyn, and if the police were making any headway finding Daniel's assailant.

Their conversation reminded Lydia to stop by Evelyn's house to water her plants. When she got there, she was surprised to see a black Honda parked in the driveway. For a moment, she thought it might be Arnold breaking in again. But then she remembered—Stefano had a black Honda. He was probably fixing whatever Evelyn had asked him to do. She decided to leave him in peace. She'd water the plants in the morning.

She stretched out on the den couch to watch a movie about to begin in five minutes. A sudden urge for ice cream sent her into the kitchen. She scooped a portion of chocolate ripple onto a plate. She turned out the kitchen light and, on impulse, peered through the blinds. Across the street, a young girl was getting out of a car. Lydia smiled as she remembered that Polly's daughter, Gillian—the "bad twin"—sometimes used Evelyn's house as a lovers' nest. Lydia shrugged. The girl was over twenty-one. If Evelyn didn't care, who was she to mind?

But was that Gillian? Lydia looked to check as the girl, now walking arm-in-arm with a young man, passed under the streetlight before turning up the driveway. A long blonde ponytail spilled behind the baseball hat. Nicole! The Good Twin, whose behavior was upsetting Polly. And the young man was her boyfriend, Ringo. Presumably, Gillian had handed Evelyn's key over to her sister.

The young couple turned to glance at Stefano's car in the driveway, but never paused as they approached the front door. Lydia watched as Gillian turned the doorknob, and she and her boyfriend disappeared inside.

They were expected! Stefano expected them.

She stifled her impulse to fly across the street and demand of the three intruders what the hell they were up to. For she had no illusions. They were up to no good. She reached for the telephone and dialed Sol's number. He picked up on the second ring.

"Sol, it's me. Stefano Ligoris, or whatever his real name is, is in Evelyn's house. And Polly's daughter, Nicole, just went inside the house with her boyfriend, Ringo Something-or-other."

"Ringo Sheridan?"

"I don't know his last name. Do you know him?"

Instead of answering, Sol cursed under his breath. "Lydia, stay put. I'm going over there." He cut the connection before she could ask any of the several questions on the tip of her tongue.

"What's happening?" she muttered to herself as she shut off every light. Then, checking that no one was stirring in Evelyn's house, she crossed the street to find out what the hell was going on.

Chapter Eighteen

There was little need for stealth or silence, Lydia observed a minute later through a crack between two vertical blinds. Nicole and her boyfriend were sprawled out on Evelyn's living room sofa, wearing expressions of spaced-out ecstasy. Stefano lounged against a wall looking pleased with himself.

Pieces of one puzzle, at least, fell into place. Ringo took drugs and had hooked Nicole into using them. Lydia's memory flashed back to her shiva call, when the twins were bitterly fighting. Gillian, despite her outrageous vampire look, had more common sense than her twin. She must have been warning Nicole that her boyfriend was bad news, but Nicole wouldn't listen. And Stefano? Lydia shivered. He was the dealer. He had probably gotten Denise using again. He took up with her, knowing she'd inherit a large sum of money when her father died. And even more when Evelyn was dead.

Lydia stormed back into her own house, furious to think that only hours ago she'd defended Stefano to Bennett! That she'd listened sympathetically to Denise's sob story about her poor, misunderstood lover.

She watched from her kitchen window as Sol's unmarked car stopped across the driveway, blocking Stefano's exit. Two black and white police cars screeched to a halt behind him. Sol, another man, and six officers in uniform poured out of the cars and rapped on Evelyn's front door. *Good! Now Stefano and Ringo would be arrested and get what they deserved!* Stefano must have been one of the dealers who'd used the old house before it had been torn down. Now he'd be deported for sure. She hoped Ringo would be thrown into jail for a long, long time—long enough for Nicole to get back on the straight and narrow. What was that girl looking for? Thrills and excitement?

A few neighbors gathered in the street in time to see the police take Nicole, Stefano, and Ringo into custody. Poor Nicole seemed dazed by the whole incident. Lydia decided to call Polly and Matt to let them know Nicole was on her way to the police station.

Gillian answered the phone and told Lydia that her parents weren't home.

When Lydia hesitated, Gillian asked, "What's wrong? Is it Nicole?"

"As a matter of fact, it is. How did you know?"

"That idiot! She took the key to Grandpa's place—the new one Evelyn gave me. I figured she was going there to get high with her dumb boyfriend."

"It's worse than that. The police came and took them, along with Stefano Ligoris, down to the station."

"God! I'd better call Dad on his cell. Let him play lawyer and bring Nicole home. Oh, God! I hope Mom doesn't have a breakdown over this! Now she'll really buy into her dumb obsession that she's the worst mother in the world."

"Why does she think that?" Lydia asked.

"Because I was always a rebel, but at least she had Nicole, the perfect child who led the perfect life. Then Nicole decided I was having all the fun, so she'd do what I did, actually what she *thought* I was doing. Only Kyle and I don't do drugs or half the things her warped Ringo gets her to do."

"I'm sorry, Gillian. I hope Nicole's learned her lesson," Lydia said, feeling twinges of guilt for having called the cops on Polly's daughter.

"Dad will make sure nothing happens to her," Gillian said cynically. "Gotta go."

Hours later, Lydia had given up hope of hearing from Sol and was about to go to bed, when she heard a knock at the door. A disgusted Sol strode into the house.

"We couldn't hold them. Ligoris and the girl had keys to the house, so there went breaking and entering. And though the kids were as high as kites, we didn't find any drugs on them. We tested them, though, and called the Ellenbergs. Matt came for Nicole. One of my men dropped off the other two. End of story."

"I'm sorry, Sol. Would you like some coffee?"

"No, thanks, but this will help." He took her in his arms and held her close. "It's damn frustrating knowing Ligoris and Sheridan are up to their necks in drugs, but we've yet to catch them with evidence."

Lydia sat down beside him on a living room sofa. "Are you saying this Ringo kid has a record?"

"He does. His juvie record's closed, but he's well known to dealers when he has the money. He's not gainfully employed."

"So, either he steals or gets the money from Nicole," Lydia mused.

Sol cast her a look of admiration. "I'd say you're two for two."

"I'd say Polly's upset about her daughter for good reason."

"If she's smart, she'll make sure that guy's never within ten feet of Nicole. And she'll see to it her daughter enters a drug rehab ASAP."

Lydia shivered. "I'm glad that's one worry my daughters never put me through."

Sol yawned and quickly covered his mouth. "Sorry," he apologized. "It's been a long day. Thank God it's over."

Lydia grinned up at him. "Ready for bed?"

He returned her grin and pulled her to her feet. "I thought you'd never ask."

***

After they made love, Sol fell into a deep sleep. Lydia watched his chest rise and fall, listened to his breathing. She washed, got into her nightgown, and curled up next to him. When she awoke at four in the morning, he was still asleep, snoring gently on his back. She was filled with the wondrous knowledge that the man she adored was lying beside her, sharing the passing of night into day.

What else are you prepared to share? The question popped into her mind, startling her because she had no answer. What did she hope to have with Sol? A romantic relationship, to start with.

Lydia grinned, remembering last night's sexual antics. Sol was a wonderful lover who made her feel young, beautiful, and desired. She'd forgotten the ecstatic joy of early love.

But was this love she was feeling? More important, was Sol someone with whom she could share her life? Attend plays and movies? Share holiday meals? Their time together was extemporaneous. Sporadic. Always dependent on Sol's work.

"Lyddie."

His hand reached out for her, and she wrapped herself around him, feeling him harden as they began another cycle of lovemaking.

At six-thirty she awoke with a sense of panic. Sol was gone! She was alone in her bed. She was relieved to find him behind the closed bathroom door, singing slightly off-key, in the shower. When he caught sight of her, he slid open the glass door. "I didn't mean to wake you."

"I woke up and missed you." Oh, God, had she actually said that? Was it too clingy? Too possessive? "Let me get you a fresh towel."

She hurried down the hall and pulled a bath sheet from the linen closet. Thank goodness she hadn't gone into overly feminine colors like pink or lavender. She raced back to deliver it.

Her heart started to pound as she wondered what came next. Breakfast, of course. She set the table and had coffee brewing by the time Sol came into the kitchen. He kissed her lightly on the lips.

"Good morning, Ms. Krause. Did you sleep well?"

"Very well. What would you like to eat—toast? Cereal? I've all types. And very nice jams that my daughter—"

"Lydia."

She stopped her prattle to stare at him. Sol sat her down in a kitchen chair, and then pulled up a chair alongside to sit beside her.

"I realize my spending the night was unexpected, but it's nothing to be nervous about."

"It isn't?" she asked, and then laughed at how silly that sounded.

He took her hand. "Come on, Lydia, you look more frightened now than when you faced a murderer."

"This is different. I'm not sure how I'm supposed to act."

Sol tossed back his head and roared with laughter. Lydia grimaced and flexed her fingers. She sorely wanted to smack him.

"I'm sorry, but it's like finding out Wonder Woman's petrified of frogs."

"Frogs! You equate your staying overnight to frogs?"

"You know what I mean. We care about each other. I stayed over. It's the natural order of things. Try to take it in stride."

Lydia nodded. "I will. It's just that this is all new to me. You're the first man who's been in my life since Izzy. I don't know the rules of the game."

"The rules are whatever we set up, okay?"

She nodded again.

"We'll talk about them some time soon, I promise. But meanwhile, could you please pour me a cup of coffee? I have to get down to the station."

Lydia smiled and filled two cups with coffee. A minute later, his cell phone rang. From Sol's few comments, she knew he'd be leaving momentarily.

"Talk to you later," he said as she walked him to the door.

"By the way, did any of Evelyn's stolen jewelry ever turn up?"

"No, though I have men checking the usual pawn shops and other places."

"Strange, don't you think?"

Sol kissed her briefly. "Not really. The thief could have a fence in the city or any place in the world, for that matter. We've seen stolen goods show up on eBay."

"eBay," she repeated as she closed the door behind him.

Five minutes later, Lydia was in her bathing suit and heading for the indoor pool. She swam her laps with more energy than usual and noticed that more of her fellow residents were using the pool. Probably, she thought, in anticipation of the outdoor pool opening in two weeks. She stopped to greet Benny, George, and Andrew before exiting the clubhouse.

"I heard the police were at Daniel and Evelyn's house last night," George said.

"What was that all about?" Benny asked.

Lydia's natural reticence to share information gave her pause, but only for a moment. The board had every right to know what Stefano's true character was like.

"The police took Stefano down to the station, along with Daniel's granddaughter and her boyfriend. It appears he sold them drugs, but by the time the police got there, there were no drugs in evidence, so they let everyone go."

George's face was grim. "Evidence or not, we don't want a drug dealer here at Twin Lakes. I'm calling a board meeting now.

Stefano will be out just as soon as we vote and make it official. We would have fired him after he came after you and Evelyn, if not for the fact that you insisted you hadn't seen him inside the truck."

"Of course," Lydia said, knowing Denise was bound to come whining to her, begging that she help get Stefano reinstated.

"By the way, the new construction's going gangbusters," Benny said. "Come and see for yourself."

"I will," she promised. "I've been very busy at work. And if I don't hurry, I'll be late this morning."

She went home and was about to step into the shower when the phone rang.

"My God, if I don't catch you in the morning or late at night, I never get to speak to you," Barbara said.

"Lot's has been happening." Lydia proceeded to tell her friend about Stefano's arrest, her encounter with Denise, dinner with Mick and Ron, and the police coming to take Stefano, Nicole, and Ringo down to the station.

"My, you've been busy!" Barbara crowed.

"That's not all. Sol stayed over, and I'm kind of bowled over by it."

"Why? You care about the guy. Have fun."

"Sure. Right. Only it changes everything. I don't know how I feel. I mean, I'm crazy about Sol. It's just that..."

"You don't know if you want to be in a committed relationship."

Lydia nodded. A piece she just realized had been floating around in her head suddenly slid into its rightful place. "That's exactly it! I care about Sol, I really do. But we're so different. I've a job with regular hours. He works all hours, day and night. On one hand, I feel I should want a typical life with him—dinner at seven, Saturday night out with friends. But frankly, Barbara, I've gotten used to having time to myself. I like having time to myself."

"Ah, yes, the independent widow. I know exactly how you feel."

"Do you?"

Barbara laughed, obviously pleased with herself. "Certainly. I've told Andrew I need my personal space."

"Andrew? Are you talking about Andrew Varig?"

"I am. What other Andrew do we know?"

Lydia paused. She felt happy for Barbara, and at the same time hurt that her friend was just now sharing what was obviously an established relationship. "But why didn't you tell me when he first asked you out? I just saw him at the clubhouse," she added as a non sequitur.

"Lydia, dear, between your job, Sol, and looking after Evelyn, you're hardly around anymore."

"Sorry," Lydia said. "But I'm delighted that you and Andrew have found each other."

"We've only gone out a few times—to dinner and the movies. We've been keeping a low profile, in case things didn't gel. But we've decided to go to the Fifties Pool Party next month. Do you think Sol might like to go?"

"I honestly don't know," Lydia admitted, not bothering to add that she wasn't sure if she wanted to invite him to the event. It was so... public. "His hours are totally erratic."

They chatted a few minutes more and made plans to go out to lunch on Saturday.

Lydia drove to work on automatic, her thoughts jumping from Stefano to Nicole to Barbara. Why did people keep changing? Stefano had turned out to be a war criminal, a drug pusher, and maybe a murderer. Nicole was fast on her way to becoming the Bad Twin. And Barbara had begun a romantic relationship without telling her best friend, and was managing it a hell of a lot better than Lydia was handling whatever she had with Sol.

It was a relief to put her efforts into helping Jessica train the new secretary. Her name was Rosalinda Gómez. She was twenty-five years old, spoke English with a lilt of a Spanish accent, and mastered each new task easily and competently. At noon, Jessica left her to man the phones and ran into the library to do the happy dance with Lydia.

The day moved smoothly ahead. For Lydia that meant no phone calls or sudden appearances of anyone connected to her personal life. Working was essential to her well-being, she realized. Maybe she would take the Carrington Suites managerial position, after all.

She drove home thinking about Sol, hoping he'd call her that evening. She had the odd sensation someone was following her. She checked her rearview mirror as she changed lanes, and was relieved that no car behind her stayed on her tail. *I must be imagining things.* She decided to stop at the organic food mart to pick up some groceries. Maybe she'd invite Sol for dinner tomorrow night.

Lydia parked and went inside, where she filled her wagon with an assortment of fruits and vegetables, then wandered over to the chicken and meat department where some of her favorite cuts were on sale. At the cash register, she nearly gasped. The total was a staggering amount of money. Deciding she wanted every last item she'd bought, Lydia handed over her charge card then signed the transaction. She wheeled her wagon past the automatic doors and paused to remember where she'd parked.

Lydia gasped when she caught sight of her car. The right side of the Lexus was keyed from fender to fender. She touched the deep gash in the metal, and tears welled up in her eyes. Someone had been following her. Stefano. Or perhaps Ringo.

Her hand shook as she called Sol and told him what had happened. His voice sounded flat when he asked if she'd seen anyone she recognized in the vicinity. She said she hadn't. He told her to drive home slowly, that he'd be sending a patrol car to meet her there. When she hung up she realized the lack of affect in Sol's voice was because he was frightened for her. For the first time she completely understood why he wanted her to butt out of his homicide cases. He wanted to keep her out of harm's way. She'd become a liability.

She drew a deep breath and turned on the ignition, then drove home slowly, keeping an eye out for trouble. A police car was parked in front of her house. Lydia waved to Officer McKlusky, and pulled into her driveway. He came over and whistled after seeing the side of her car.

"Hey there, Mrs. K. I see the perps keep on damaging your cars."

"Don't they," she said grimly.

He insisted on entering and checking out the house before waving her inside. The answering machine was blinking. Lydia pressed the button and listened. It was Denise, frantically demanding to know why Lydia had arranged for Stefano to be fired, and swearing repeatedly that "her Stefano" never touched any drug whatsoever.

Disgusted, she was about to erase the message when Officer McKlusky grabbed her hand. "Don't touch that. We'll need to make a copy of it."

Lydia nodded and swooped a meowing Reggie into her arms. He squirmed to be let down. "All right," she said, and proceeded to open a can of cat food.

Officer McKlusky questioned her about the keying incident, but, as she hadn't seen a car actually following her, left soon after. Lydia mixed a margarita, which she carried to the small patio outside her living room. The car would cost at least five hundred dollars to repair and paint. She told herself it was a minor inconvenience, a venting of hostility. But it had been vented against her!

She wondered if Stefano was responsible. Or was it Ringo? It was the kind of petty revenge a young person with little regard for the law would take. People like Ringo resented being called to account for their behavior and acted out against anyone who blew the whistle. The keying was the cost of her involvement. She gripped her arms to stop a sudden bout of shivering that had nothing to do with the breeze cooling the early evening. She gulped down the rest of her drink and thanked God that nothing worse had occurred.

Sol called to say he'd stop by around eight to take her out for dinner, if she could hold out that long. Lydia said she'd take a rain check, and offered to make him a meal from some of the food she'd bought instead. She was glad he'd agreed to her suggestion, because five minutes later she realized she was starving. She prepared her dinner and filled a glass with chardonnay. After she'd eaten and finished her second glass of wine, she felt decidedly calmer. She decided to call Evelyn and tell her about last night's events before an excited neighbor phoned to offer her an overblown version of the incident.

Evelyn's breathing sounded labored when she answered the telephone.

"Lydia, dear, I've just spoken to Polly. She and Matt are frantic. Nicole's gone!"

Adrenalin shot through Lydia. "Are they certain?"

"Oh, yes. Nicole went to take her last final of the term. Graduation's in ten days. When she didn't come home for dinner, Polly went up to her room and saw half her clothes are gone. She called the bank. Nicole withdrew every penny in her account."

Foolish girl. "I suppose she went off with her boyfriend. He's certainly a bad influence. The police found them in your house, high on drugs. Stefano was with them. It turns out he's a dealer. The board's fired him."

"Yes, dear, so I've heard. A few of my friends called with the news." Evelyn released a deep sigh. "To think Daniel and I trusted him. Now I wonder if he was the one who hit me and left me for dead."

Lydia decided not to tell Evelyn about the keying incident. "Life is full of surprises."

"And poor Nicole, letting herself be hoodwinked by that boyfriend of hers. I'm afraid I'm partly to blame there. Polly was all for taking away Nicole's car and cell phone when she started seeing that Ringo, but I pointed out that Nicole was over twenty-one and would probably move out if she did." She sniffed. "I even suggested that she let Nicole bring him to Daniel's birthday party."

Daniel's birthday party! Could Ringo have doctored the chocolates, knowing that, with Daniel dead, Nicole's mother would soon inherit much more money—money she might be willing to share with her daughters?

"Evelyn," Lydia said aloud, "you gave Polly sound advice, so please don't think you have anything to do with Nicole's breaking out of her perfect image. Gillian thinks it's a reaction to years of being regarded as the good twin."

"The Angel Twin," Evelyn mused. "We never knew she hated it so."

Chapter Nineteen

"**S**tefano's dead."

Lydia stared up at Sol standing in the doorway.

"Oh!" She felt light-headed, as though she was about to faint. Sol grasped her in a tight embrace. She closed her eyes and imagined he was a tree she could burrow deep inside of, protecting her from the next assault or murder.

He helped her to the sofa, where she sprawled against the back cushion as weak as an invalid. "I can't believe it," she whispered.

She began to weep. Tears rolled down her cheeks. Annoyed by the intensity of her response, Lydia swiped them away with the backs of her hands.

"Why am I'm crying?" she demanded. "Stefano turned out to be an awful person. He tortured people in Yugoslavia. Here he sold drugs." She pointed to the paintings hanging around the living room. "And he put up every damn one of them."

Sol went to the liquor cabinet and poured out a healthy dose of scotch. "Here, drink this."

She nodded, swallowed, and asked, "Do you want some?"

"Not tonight. I have to get back to the precinct. We saw the body and looked around his apartment. The body's been removed for autopsy, and the crime scene team's checking out his place. My men are lining up interviews. I'll be at it till all hours of the morning." He sat down beside her and gave her a bittersweet smile. "I had to stop by and tell you."

Lydia blinked, trying to take it all in. "But why? Who?"

"Someone shot him in his apartment around six o'clock. A neighbor heard the weapon discharge and called 911. No one saw anyone."

"But it was still light out," Lydia said.

Sol frowned. "Many illegals live in his neighborhood. I doubt anyone will come forward to testify, even if he saw the killer."

"Denise said Stefano had enemies from his country who wanted to kill him."

Sol raked a hand through his wavy hair. "We'll talk to her, but I suspect that's a story he made up to explain away some of his drug activities."

"Do you think this has anything to do with Daniel's murder?"

Sol shrugged. "It's too soon to say. Most likely it was a drug deal gone bad."

She noticed his five o'clock shadow, and it struck her that he probably had to shave twice a day to keep it at bay.

With an effort, he got to his feet. "I'll go grab something at the diner then go back to the station."

"Don't be silly. Your meal's all prepared." She saw him hesitate. "You have to eat, Sol. Please. I'd like you to stay."

He nodded and followed her into the kitchen. They didn't speak as she heated up what she'd prepared in the microwave. Lydia watched him eat, taking neat, precise bites. When he was finished, he used the bathroom then headed for the front door.

"I'll call you tomorrow," he said, and kissed her quickly on the mouth. She stood in the hall and heard him drive off, feeling as though she was seeing him off to battle. What had driven him to choose this dangerous line of work that dealt with the dark side of society? She felt a wave of empathy for the wives and children of policemen everywhere.

The phone rang at ten o'clock, startling her from her nap. It was Mick.

"Hi there, Lydia. I hope it's not to late to call."

"No, no," she demurred automatically.

"What did Molina have to say about Allen Holtstein?"

"Allen?"

"Right. You were going to bring up his name, find out if the cops have checked him out as a suspect."

"Mick, I didn't get a chance. Stefano Ligoris is dead. Someone shot him."

"You don't say! When did this happen?"

"About four, five hours ago. I don't know anything else."

"I'll make a few phone calls, find out what I can, and get back to you."

"Thanks, Mick."

But he'd already hung up. She wished he hadn't sounded like a little boy setting off to an amusement park.

True to his word, Mick called back almost an hour later. "The cops have no leads, but they think the shooting was drug-related."

"Thanks, Mick. I'm going to sleep now."

"Hold your horses. I haven't told you the news. They found digitalis and a hypodermic needle in Ligoris's apartment, along with pieces of antique jewelry. From the description the police have, it's what Evelyn said was taken when she was hit over the head."

"It sounds too good to be true," Lydia said dryly.

"Come on, Lydia, you give criminals too much credit. Actually, they're a lot stupider than they make them out in books."

"Why would he keep evidence of a murder he committed weeks ago? And not fence the jewelry?"

"Who knows why? Maybe he was saving it till he could show the antique pieces to someone in the city. What's important is that it looks like this guy attacked Evelyn and killed Daniel."

To Lydia's astonishment and dismay, the official reaction to Stefano's murder was the same as Mick's.

"I can't believe Stefano killed Daniel, attacked Evelyn, and came after us that Sunday morning," she told Sol Saturday evening as they sipped wine and awaited their appetizers in the new French restaurant on the bay.

Sol leaned along the banquette to kiss her neck.

"My dear, the evidence points the way. There it sat in Ligoris's apartment, waiting for us to bag it and close the case."

Between the wine and Sol's attentions, Lydia felt her resolve melt away. "That's wonderful, only it seems too pat, somehow. All that proof just waiting to be found."

"Try not to think, Lydia—at least about homicide cases. We're here to enjoy ourselves, remember?"

She nodded, determined not to bring up the subject again. Sol deserved an evening free of distractions. And, miracle of miracles, since he'd picked her up almost two hours ago, his cell phone hadn't rung once.

Their escargot appetizers arrived, and they ate them with relish as the chatted about other topics. Non-homicide topics. Lydia talked about Barbara and Andrew's budding romance, of her upcoming trip to visit Abbie, her newly married daughter in London. Sol spoke of his daughter Heather's visit during the month of July.

Their main courses arrived. When they'd finished tasting each other's dishes, Sol said, "I've plenty of activities planned when Heather comes." He paused. "And I'd like her to meet you."

Lydia was touched. "I'd love to meet your daughter."

They went home in a mellow mood and made passionate love until two in the morning. Afterward, Lydia fell into a deep sleep, from which she emerged when Sol shook her shoulder.

She opened her eyes and saw him smiling down at her. He was dressed.

"I have to go."

She felt panicky, as though she'd overslept for something important. "What time is it?"

"Eight-thirty. Go back to sleep."

"No, I'll get up. Make you some breakfast."

"No need. I'll stop for something on the way into work."

"Work?" Lydia pulled her curls behind her ears, thinking she must look a fright. "It's Sunday morning."

"I know, but I've tons of paperwork to catch up on." He bent down to kiss her cheek. "And I want to have another chat with Denise. I'll call you later."

Reggie entered the room and jumped on the bed. Lydia stroked him as the front door closed. She felt saddened. Abandoned. Was this how it was going to be with her and Sol—a night together and then off he'd go, working all hours of the week to solve yet another murder?

She used the bathroom, then went into the kitchen to prepare breakfast. As she filled the coffee pot with water—enough for one person—Lydia berated herself.

What did you expect—a proposal of marriage? An offer to spend Sunday together? No to the first, yes to the second.

She still knew very little of Sol's life when he wasn't chasing after clues and interviewing suspects. She had no idea what his apartment looked like.

But he wanted her to meet his daughter, which was more than she'd offered. Get a grip! she told herself. Sol cares for you. He wants to spend time with you. Stop acting like one of those wimpy women, and find something to do by yourself. Like you've been doing since Izzy died.

She got dressed and found herself mulling over Daniel's murder and the events that had followed. If Stefano had killed

Daniel, then the only thing that made sense was that Denise was equally guilty—which was why Sol wanted to question her.

But what if Denise wasn't guilty? It was a ridiculous question, given that she'd suspected Denise of murdering her father only days ago. Denise had been on drugs for most of her life, was probably using currently. From what Polly had once implied, she'd prostituted herself when she and Bennett had nothing to eat. But would she agree to be part of a plot to kill Daniel and Evelyn? Lydia didn't know. She only knew that it made no sense that Stefano was the murderer.

And if Stefano wasn't the murderer, then someone else was.

Lydia speed dialed Barbara's number. Her friend sounded groggy when she picked up on the third ring.

"Good morning, my dear," Lydia greeted her.

"Hi, Lyddie. What time is it?"

"Time to get out of bed. Are you busy today?"

"Andrew's going to his grandson's baseball game. I'm joining them for dinner."

"Are you up for some sleuthing in the interim?"

"Of course! What did you have in mind?"

An hour later they were breezing along Rte. 97 on their way to Whispering Pines.

"How do you know the Holtsteins are home?" Barbara asked.

Lydia smiled. "I tried calling them twice and the line was busy. If Rochelle was doing the talking, as I suspect, she's indulging in long conversations. Meaning, she's not in any rush to leave the house. And if they have plans for the afternoon, she'll need at least an hour to get dressed, put on her makeup—stuff like that."

Barbara grinned. "Great deduction, Sherlock. And our story's that I've a sister looking for a nice apartment, not too far from me."

"We'll check out the models first, to be on the safe side."

"Fine with me," Barbara said. "I always love to look at models."

Lydia drove past the Whispering Pines Luxury Apartments sign and parked in one of the sand-covered spaces allotted to visitors viewing the models.

"They're actually apartments," Barbara mused, gazing at the three-story building. "I hope my sister likes apartment living."

A slender young woman, her long blonde hair rippling down the back of her pink cashmere sweater, welcomed them and introduced herself as Mindy. Lydia and Barbara smiled and headed for the tiny models on display, but Mindy blocked their way, a pile of forms in her hand.

"We ask each visitor to please fill these out first," she said sweetly but firmly.

"It's for my sister," Barbara explained, hoping to avoid the paperwork.

"Please fill out whatever you can," Mindy instructed, waving a two-caret engagement ring adorning her French-style manicured hand. "The owners like to have everything on record."

Barbara frowned, but did as instructed. Only then did Mindy direct them toward the four model apartments.

"We've only twenty units left," she said, "and five of those have holds on them. So if you think your sister might be interested, have her call me ASAP."

"Will do," Barbara tossed over her shoulder.

They burst into giggles as soon as they were alone, then got down to the serious business of checking out each apartment.

"Some lovely decorating touches," Barbara commented as she moved closer to inspect a wall unit.

"Right," Lydia agreed, "but the furniture doesn't come with the apartment." She bent down to feel the carpet. "Cheap. And the walls are paper-thin. I bet you can hear your neighbors' conversations."

"Or worse," Barbara agreed. "And the rooms are small."

Lydia opened the folder and checked the prospectus. "Still, the rent for a two-bedroom apartment isn't astronomical. Not a bad deal for a couple over 55 who have sold their home and don't want to put all their money into buying another house or condo."

"Like the Holtsteins," Barbara said.

Ten minutes later they were back in the office, and had to wait until Mindy finished talking to other potential renters.

"Very nice, especially the large two-bedroom," Barbara said. "I'll have my sister call you."

Mindy graced her with a huge grin. "My favorite. Have her call me ASAP. They're going like hotcakes."

"We're friends of Allen and Rochelle Holtstein," Lydia said. "They told us it's wonderful living here."

Mindy's grin dissolved into a frown. "Really? You'd never know it from the hard time they're giving us." Her diamond-adorned hand covered her mouth. "Sorry! I shouldn't have said that. It's just that they've decided to move and they're using every trick in the book to break their lease."

Lydia feigned surprise. "I didn't know they were moving. We were planning to stop by and say hello."

"They're going to Arizona, where living is cheaper."

"Really?" Lydia exclaimed, no longer pretending to be shocked.

Mindy placed her hand on Lydia's arm. "They are, and please, please don't repeat what I've just said!"

Lydia gave her a motherly pat. "Don't worry, dear. We won't breathe a word."

Mindy sighed with relief. "Thank you! I need this job until my wedding, and that's practically an entire year from today."

Outside, the two women looked at one other and shook their heads.

Barbara said, "And what does she intend to do once they're married—sit at home and eat chocolates? Live on their wedding gifts?"

"Perhaps have a baby," Lydia said as they got into her Lexus. "In which case, she'll have to cut those talons. But Mindy was most informative. Evelyn said Rochelle and Allen were buying a condo on the island."

"Maybe they want to economize. They say living in Arizona is less expensive than living up here."

"So they say," Lydia said. She took out her cell phone and dialed the Holtsteins' number, which she'd jotted down before leaving the house. The phone rang twice, and then Rochelle picked up. Lydia identified herself, explained that she and Barbara were at Whispering Pines checking out an apartment for Barbara's sister, and were wondering if they could stop by and ask Rochelle a few questions about the place. Rochelle said to come right over.

Chapter Twenty

"The place is a dive," Allen said. "The plumbing stinks, the walls are paper-thin, and since there aren't enough bins, garbage often overflows into the street. Then you have low-class neighbors shouting at all hours, day and night. I wouldn't recommend this place to a homeless person."

He lifted the coffee urn. "Anyone for more?"

"I'm fine," Lydia said.

Cup in hand, Barbara reached across the tiny round table where the four of them were sitting. "Thanks, I'll have a bit more. This coffee is delicious."

Rochelle beamed. "I'm so glad you like it. I buy the beans in Fairway."

"As for the apartments here, I'm glad you told me about the noise factor," Barbara said. "My sister's very sensitive to sounds."

"And they're giving me a tough time breaking the lease." Allen pointed to a stain on the ceiling. "See that? It leaks every time it rains. Management doesn't give a damn once you've signed on the dotted line."

Rochelle reached over to pat her husband's shoulder. "Allen dear, don't aggravate yourself. It's not good for your heart. I've told you, I'll take care of it—like before."

Allen leaped to his feet with amazing agility for a man approaching eighty. "Time for your nap, dear."

He tried to raise his wife from her seat, but Rochelle held fast. A beatific smile graced her lips. "A small fire in their office would convince them to see things differently. Or maybe—"

"Rochelle, don't talk foolishness!" Allen's false sounding laugh sent chills down Lydia's back. "The girls might get the wrong impression."

Rochelle waved her hand and laughed. "Oh, poo, Ally. You're always so concerned when there's nothing to worry about. No one ever found out."

"You're tired and need to take a nap."

Allen made another effort to lift her from her chair, and this time Rochelle cooperated. She yawned.

"Yes, I am sleepy." She turned from one startled woman to the other. "Thank you for coming. Please stop by again."

She walked meekly beside her husband as he escorted her to their bedroom. Lydia and Barbara rose, eager to flee this madhouse.

"Please wait," Allen said over his shoulder. "I'll be with you momentarily."

They sighed and sat down again.

When he returned ten minutes later, he looked exhausted. "I gave her a pill and she's fast asleep. Poor Rochelle. She's in the first stage of Alzheimer's. She'll be fine one minute—clear-headed and witty as always—then start talking gibberish."

"I am sorry, Allen," Lydia said. "It must be very hard on you."

"I hope you don't believe a word of that nonsense she was spouting." There was that awful laugh again. "When she's not in her right mind, the most outlandish statements pour from her mouth. I don't know where she dreams them up."

Barbara offered a smile of commiseration. "I understand. I've an aunt who had Alzheimer's. My heart goes out to you both."

"Thank you," Allen murmured.

They stood to leave. This time he didn't stop them.

Lydia paused to say, "I'm sure if you mention Rochelle's condition, they'll be more amenable to letting you out of your lease. Where were you planning to go?"

"Arizona," he answered. "It's been our dream these last few years, and now we've the money to make the move. I want to do it as soon as possible—while Rochelle's still lucid a good part of the time."

Lydia nodded as she considered the most tactful way to ask her question. She tried for humor. "That's wonderful, Allen. Did a rich uncle leave you a bundle of money?"

Allen laughed. "At our age? Come on, Lydia. Get real!"

"Sorry," Lydia apologized, and looked so remorseful he felt obliged to explain.

"The long and short of it is we've had—expenses. Now we're no longer in debt."

That was as vague an answer as any. Lydia decided not to push it. Instead, she glanced at her watch.

"My goodness, I didn't realize it was this late. Barbara has an appointment. Don't you, Barbara?"

"Er—yes," Barbara agreed. Though this was the first truthful thing either of them had said during their visit, it came out as a blatant lie.

"I'll give Evelyn your regards when I speak to her," Lydia said.

"Please do that," Allen said. "She's been very kind to Rochelle and me."

"She appreciated your taking her out to dinner after that awful incident," Lydia said.

"When is she coming home?" Allen asked.

Lydia controlled the tremor that ran down her spine. "Soon, I imagine, now that the police have decided the man who attacked her and killed Daniel is dead."

Allen stepped closer to Lydia. She flinched. He wasn't a tall man, but at seventy-eight, he was in good physical condition. For all she knew, he'd had a hand in killing two people and attacking another. She was grateful he hadn't picked up on her anxiety. Instead, he sounded outraged when he said, "That Ligoris guy got what he deserved. He killed one of the greatest people I ever knew!"

Lydia and Barbara said quick good-byes and hurried out of the apartment.

"Whew!" Barbara exclaimed in the elevator. "Sounds like Rochelle killed Allen's boss all those years ago! What kind of people do you take me to visit, Lydia Krause?"

Lydia smiled at her attempt at humor. "We don't know for sure. It could be the Alzheimer's speaking."

"Maybe, but Allen sure was wigged out by what Rochelle was saying. I bet the cops never considered her a suspect."

"I'll have to tell Sol what she said, though he'll be furious that we set foot in the Holtsteins' living room."

As they stepped into Lydia's car, Barbara asked, "Do you think either of them killed Daniel?"

Lydia shook her head. "I doubt it. They weren't in line for an inheritance."

"But maybe they figured that if Daniel were to die, Allen wouldn't have to repay his debt."

Lydia drove, her eyes fixed on the road. A few minutes later, she said, "Barbara, you bring up an important point: it's what's going on in the murderer's mind that provokes the crime, how he or she perceives a situation. Not necessarily what's real. Do you see what I'm getting at?"

"Of course. Only we have to work the other way round."

"Right." Lydia sighed. "We deduce from facts, clues, and evidence. Stefano's dead, and we've spoken to the Holtsteins. I feel like we're back to square one."

She dropped Barbara off at her house and wished her a fun evening with Andrew.

"Let's make it a foursome one night," Barbara called back.

"Good idea," Lydia agreed, but somehow she doubted it would ever happen. Barbara and Andrew were retired, their time was their own. Sol's work was his top priority. Besides, while she considered him the man in her life, she had difficulty picturing Sol at her daughter Meredith's for dinner, or going to the movies with Barbara and Andrew.

She drove home, wondering if Sol would stop by tonight. She clicked the garage door opener. As the door began to rise, a figure approached from the shadows. Lydia's rush of panic subsided when she recognized the slender form of Gillian Ellenberg. The girl, dressed in black jeans and a black long-sleeved polo, darted over to the car before Lydia could open her door.

"Mrs. Krause—Lydia, I need to talk to you!"

"Of course, dear. Come inside."

"Nicole's in trouble. It's really bad." The words spilled from her mouth as she followed Lydia into the kitchen. Lydia gestured to the table and Gillian hurled herself into a chair.

"Has she come home?"

Gillian shook her head from side to side. Tears filled her blue eyes and she scrubbed them away. "She called me on my cell when that creep Ringo fell asleep. He's guarding her like a hawk."

"Why didn't she leave when she had the chance? Want something to eat?"

Gillian turned her gaze on Lydia. Behind the girl's spiky hair and black lipstick shone her great beauty. "Yes, please. I'm starving. I haven't eaten since this morning."

Lydia put a bagel in the toaster and slices of turkey and cheese on a plate. She brought out containers of salads and eating utensils. Gillian scooped a mound of coleslaw onto her plate and devoured it as though she were starving

"Sorry," she apologized when she came up for air. "I have a fast metabolism. I have to eat pretty much all the time."

Lydia smiled. "I'm delighted to feed someone with a hearty appetite."

When Gillian's plate was empty and she showed no sign of refilling it, Lydia brought out the pastries she'd bought at the gourmet shop. Two of them disappeared quickly.

"Milk, tea, or coffee?" Lydia inquired.

"Milk would be great."

Lydia filled a glass, then sat down to listen to the rest of Gillian's story.

"Nicky's afraid to come home. I begged her to, but she said there was no point. He'd come after her and get her."

"Ringo? But why?" Lydia's eyes widened with fear. "Don't tell me she's in an abusive relationship."

Gillian raked her hand through her short hair. "I don't know. She's terrified, and I'm not sure it's of Ringo. She claims she saw something, but she won't tell me what. The only thing I got out of her was where she and Ringo are staying. She told me after I swore up and down I wouldn't call our parents or the police."

She clutched at Lydia's hand. "My boyfriend's out of town, and there's no one I can turn to. So I thought you'd help me." She gave a little smile. "Grandpa said you were a whiz when it came to solving problems."

Lydia winced, remembering how little she'd done to help Daniel before someone murdered him. "What do you want me to do, Gillian? I'm afraid I'm not the person to break down the door and rescue your sister. I think we should leave it to the police."

"No! If Nicole said not to, there's a reason." She cast Lydia a baleful glare. "I'll go myself!"

She flung herself from her chair and made a beeline for the door.

"Wait, I'll come with you!" Lydia called after her.

Gillian ignored her but had difficulty undoing the lock. When Lydia put a hand on her shoulder, she flinched.

"I said I'd go with you."

"If you want," Gillian said. "We'll take my car. Yours would stick out where we're going."

The cottage was in a rundown residential area two towns east. Gillian parked in the rutted driveway, behind a rusted pickup truck missing a tire. The place looked deserted. No light shone from any of the windows.

"I don't think anyone's here," Lydia said.

"The electricity's been cut off," Gillian answered without breaking stride as she headed for the back door. All in black, she was barely visible amid the scraggly bushes, and it dawned on Lydia that Gillian had dressed for the occasion.

"Nicky, are you there?" Gillian called as she rapped on the glass panel of the warped door.

Lydia wondered at her temerity. Ringo was a drug addict. For all she knew, he had a gun, which he'd pull on whomever came to his home or hideout or whatever the vernacular was. As much as she wanted Nicole to appear and leave with them, Lydia was relieved when the silence continued.

"Maybe they went out," she suggested, ready to return to the car and the safety of her home.

"I doubt it." Gillian slipped a charge card from her pocket and edged it along the crack between the door and the frame. A moment later, she turned the handle and a damp, fetid odor assailed Lydia's nostrils.

"Nicky," Gillian called softly, switching on a flashlight that cast a narrow but potent shaft of light on the grungy kitchen. Lydia trailed behind as Gillian walked down the narrow passageway, beaming the flashlight on the empty space that must have been the living room. She stopped at the bedroom. Lydia peered over her shoulder. A mattress covered by a garish-colored quilt filled half the room. Gillian zoomed in on the knapsack in the corner and rummaged through it.

"This is Nicole's. Some of her clothes are here. No sign of her cell phone. I hope she has it with her."

"Do you think she ran away from Ringo, or with him?" Lydia asked.

"I don't know. Ringo has a beat-up, old jalopy, but it wasn't parked outside. Nicole and I share our car, so she doesn't have her own wheels. But Mom said she withdrew a large sum of money from the bank, so maybe she can call a cab."

If her boyfriend didn't help himself to it all. Lydia knew Gillian was disappointed not to have found her sister. Hearing negative comments would only make her feel worse.

They climbed back into the car and Gillian retraced their route. At the first red light, she turned to Lydia. "Thanks for coming with me. My mom would kill me if she found out I'd gone alone."

"I'm sorry we couldn't bring Nicole home," Lydia replied. "I think it's time to call in the police."

"Nicky's terrified. She believes the police won't be able to protect her."

"Why don't you try calling her now?"

Gillian pulled into a strip mall and reached for her cell phone. "Hello?"

In the streetlight, Lydia saw her eyes flash with anger. "Damn you, put my sister on! Hello! Hello!"

Gillian tossed the phone onto the back seat of the car. "Ringo answered then hung up when he heard my voice."

"Gillian, this is serious. We have to call Detective Molina and tell him the situation."

The girl's eyes filled with terror. "He's a homicide detective! My sister's not dead." She whispered the last word.

Lydia placed a hand on the girl's trembling shoulder. "Of course she's not," she said, hoping this was true, "but he was in charge of your grandfather's case. He'll know whom to contact."

"I—I don't know," Gillian said, looking down at her lap. "I have no idea what to do now. I thought I'd go there and talk to Nicole, at least. Find out what's going on."

"You did your best for your sister," Lydia said gently. "I think you came to me because you knew I'd suggest bringing in the authorities."

Gillian nodded without lifting her head. "I guess," she whispered.

"Would you like me to drive?" Lydia asked.

"No, I'll be okay in a minute."

When they reached Lydia's house, Gillian refused to come inside. "You call him," she said. "I trust you to tell him everything. I'll be at home if he wants to talk to me."

"All right, Gillian. I'm sorry I couldn't be of more help."

Sol called Lydia back half an hour later, and listened without comment as she told him of her outing with Gillian. When she'd finished, he asked, "Are you up to grabbing a bite and catching an action movie?"

"Sure, but don't you want to check out the cottage?"

He sighed. "Not really. Your report was pretty damn complete. Do you remember my colleague I brought along for the drug bust at Evelyn's house? Jack Delaney?"

"Of course."

"If you'll remember, Jack's in narcotics. I'll give him a ring, tell him what you've discovered, and let him take it from there. Ringo's a druggie, not a murderer."

"What about Nicole? Her family's frantic."

"I'll send a few men to scout out the area and talk to neighbors, though people in that part of town claim not to know anything. Can you be ready in half an hour?"

Lydia frowned as she hung up the phone. Sol's response wasn't what she'd hoped it would be. Why hadn't he offered to go there himself? Take more of an interest? After all, this was Daniel's granddaughter. Maybe Nicole's disappearance had something to do his murder. Maybe Nicole—Lydia refused to finish that sentence, even in her mind. She had to believe that Nicole, while terrified and with her grubby boyfriend, was alive and well.

A furry head butted against her legs, jolting her from her musings. She filled Reggie's plate and had no sooner set it on the floor when the phone rang. It was Evelyn.

"Lydia, I'm flying home tomorrow evening. Do you think you could pick me up at MacArthur at seven thirty?"

"Of course, I can, but why are you cutting your visit short?"

"I need to be in my own home. And now that they've caught Daniel's murderer and my attacker, I can rest assured I'll be safe." Evelyn tsk-tsked into the phone. "It just goes to show how you never know what lurks in a person's heart. I never would have dreamed Stefano would harm either Daniel or me."

Lydia bit back her doubts about Stefano being the murderer. Instead, she said, "And supposedly he committed atrocities during the Serbian-Bosnian fighting."

"I suppose Denise put him up to it. Have they charged her yet?"

"I think they're questioning her at this point," Lydia said. "The police haven't found any evidence to prove her complicity."

"They'll find it," Evelyn said with fervor. "It's just a matter of time. Have you spoken to Polly? She's frantic with worry about Nicole's taking off like that."

"I really must call her," Lydia said.

"That's about it, dear. I have to go change my outfit. Gayle and Roger are taking me out for a farewell dinner, and I don't want to keep them waiting."

"One more thing," Lydia said quickly. "Did Allen Holtstein happen to borrow money from Daniel?"

Evelyn let out a cynical laugh. "Several times, as I told the police. When Allen and Rochelle took me out for dinner, I told them I forgave him his debt. You never saw a happier fellow!"

"That was kind of you," Lydia said.

"Actually, I was being realistic. I figured Allen would cry poverty and wouldn't have repaid the loan, anyway. Besides," Evelyn lowered her voice, "I feel sorry for them. Rochelle's in the early stages of Alzheimer's. She says the most outrageous things."

Lydia hung up, relieved that the Holtsteins had no reason to kill Daniel. Then it dawned on her—Evelyn forgave Allen's debt after she'd been struck on the head. It didn't put him in the clear, but if it had been Allen, at least he wouldn't come after her now.

Time for her to change outfits, too. Lydia slipped into black silk pants, a slinky top with a deep V neckline, and black strappy heels. She freshened her makeup in the bathroom, then stood back to admire her handiwork. Pretty sexy for a grandmother going on fifty-nine!

The phone rang and a male voice she didn't recognize asked to speak to her.

"This is Lydia Krause," she answered, puzzled. "What can I do for you?"

"Lydia, Tom Coltrane here. Of New Horizons Enterprises."

She gave a start. New Horizon Enterprises owned Carrington House and several other catering establishments.

"Hello, Mr. Coltrane," she responded with more warmth than she felt.

"It's Tom, Lydia. I apologize for calling you on a Sunday evening when you're probably dining with family, but we've a committee meeting Tuesday morning, and we need your answer by then as to whether or not you'll take the position of overseeing the Carrington Suites."

"Right," she said slowly. "Tuesday's the fifteenth." How could she have forgotten? "I apologize for not getting back to you with my response. I've been deluged with—" She paused to think of a euphemism for her sleuthing. "Family issues," she finished lamely.

"I'll make no secret of the fact that we want you for the position. With your background and Len's rousing commendation, you're the woman to run the new Suites. Provided you want it, of course."

And he was hoping she'd say yes then and there. Lydia frowned. It wasn't like her to sit on the fence for this length of time, but she still hadn't made up her mind. She plunged ahead.

"I'm still in the middle of a crisis here, but it should be resolved by Monday evening. Can I call you then with my answer?"

Tom Coltrane exhaled noisily. "You drive a hard bargain, Lydia, but I'll abide by your answer." He rattled off his cell phone number.

"I'll call you tomorrow night," she promised, and hung up.

Chapter Twenty-One

I n the car, Sol told her that police officers were checking out the cottage and others were following up every lead in hopes of locating Nicole and Ringo.

"Now relax and enjoy the evening with me. For once I'm not in the middle of a case."

"I intend to," Lydia said, deciding that tonight wasn't the time to mention the Holtsteins. "Where are we going?"

"I'm taking you to my favorite restaurant. I hope you like Thai cuisine."

"I love it," Lydia said, surprised by his choice. She'd assumed Sol was a meat and potatoes man.

"Thought you would." Sol gave her a dazzling smile. "Everything's freshly made. Their pad Thai's outstanding, but I can't resist their panang duck. Order it every time."

They chatted about casual topics during the ten-minute ride. The restaurant was in a shopping center. It's glamorous decor—golden masks, jadite figurines, and elephant-sequined wall hangings against a softly lit red wall—was a treat to her eyes.

The hostess, dressed in elegant Thai costume, greeted Sol by his first name.

"Lily, this is my good friend Lydia."

Lily smiled. "Welcome to Thai Palace."

She seated them at a corner table and brought a pair of chopsticks for Sol. "Would you like to eat with chopsticks, too?" she asked Lydia.

"Yes, please."

When she looked up from the extensive menu, Lydia found Sol watching her with a bemused smile. "Admit you're surprised."

"What do you mean?" she demurred.

"That I like Thai food. Can eat with chopsticks. I also enjoy hockey games, the occasional Broadway show." He gave her an impish grin. "I even read a hefty biography on occasion."

Lydia felt her ears redden. "Well, we do seem to spend a good deal of time talking about homicide cases."

"I love my work, but I'm more than a homicide detective, Lydia. Did you know I almost became a college professor?"

"You're kidding!"

"I'd just started my PhD in history when I got the devastating news that one of my best friends had been murdered. I was angry, upset. I stopped going to classes. My parents finally sat me down— told me I wasn't helping Charlie by ruining my own career. I realized I wanted to find the guy who killed Charlie, not talk about international trade agreements and wars, so I quit school and joined the force."

Lydia nodded. "Did they ever find your friend's killer?"

"One of them. The other disappeared inside Mexico. A two-bit thug. I hope he got what he deserved in a bar fight or somewhere."

Their appetizers arrived, and Lydia bit into a dumpling. It was heaven, as was the rest of the meal. Don, the chef-owner and Lily's husband, emerged from the kitchen to meet Lydia and to ask if they'd enjoyed their food.

When they left, Lily hugged them both and said to come again soon.

"I feel like I've just met your family," Lydia said once they were outside.

Sol laughed. "We'll leave my mother and my brother and his family for another day."

The movie theatre showing the action film was more than half empty. Lydia wasn't surprised, as the film had come out two months before. But Sol probably didn't have many opportunities to take time off to go to the movies.

They chose seats in the middle of a row towards the rear. Sol tossed their jackets on an empty chair then reached for her hand. Lydia suddenly felt like a demur girl of sixteen out with her new boyfriend. Sol squeezed her fingers. "I hope you like this film."

She giggled. "So do I."

"You get to choose next time."

"Sounds fair to me."

They watched the coming attractions. When the announcements not to talk, litter, or use cell phones came on, Lydia reached into her pocketbook to turn hers off.

"I have to leave mine on," Sol said. "Just in case."

"Don't you ever get a minute entirely to yourself?"

"Only when I leave the country, which hasn't been for seven years."

The main feature appeared on the screen, and Lydia relaxed into her high-back seat to lose herself in fantasy. It was a story of a heist gone wrong, with a fair amount of humor and male bonding. Not what she would have chosen, but she enjoyed the plot's twists and turns, and the lead actors were great to look at.

"Don't you get enough of this stuff?" she whispered to Sol.

"It's different when you're not doing the chasing," he answered, kissing her neck.

It was a peck, not meant to be erotic, but it sent chills and thrills to every part of her body. Lydia closed her eyes and smiled, anticipating how they'd be spending the last part of the evening. It was fun being in an adult man-woman relationship instead of having to endure the dating rituals she could barely remember from so many years before.

They drove back to Twin Lakes, laughing over silly things. As Sol pulled into her driveway, Lydia asked, "Are you coming in for a while?"

"Of course."

They kissed deeply and passionately in the kitchen.

"Would you like something—coffee? Wine?"

"I want you," Sol said, pulling her closer.

Lydia took his hand and led him to the bedroom. They undressed quickly and fell onto the bed, limbs entwined.

"I more than like you, Lydia Krause," Sol murmured as he ran his hands down her body.

The phone rang. Beneath him, Lydia froze then stretched out her arm.

His lips on her ear whispered, "Leave it. Please."

"I can't. People only call this late when something's wrong." She scooted from beneath him and lifted the receiver. "Hello?"

"Lydia? It's Gillian. I hope I didn't wake you."

"You didn't. What's the matter?"

"Nicole called. She got away from Ringo and ran to the mall on Veteran's Highway. I'd pick her up, but Mom's watching me like a hawk. Nicole made me swear I wouldn't tell her, so I can't leave the house. And no police. She was emphatic about that."

"I'll get Nicole." Lydia stood, ready to hang up.

"Thanks, Lydia."

"Of course. Give me an hour, then call me on my cell phone." She gave Gillian her number.

"Thanks so much, Lydia. I'll tell Nicole you're on your way."

Lydia leaped from the bed and began dressing. Sol let out a gruff burst of laughter.

"I thought I was the cop here, who gets called out in the middle of the night."

Beneath his joking tone, Lydia detected puzzlement and hurt. She hooked her bra, then met his gaze.

"Nicole managed to get away from Ringo. She called Gillian but doesn't want her parents involved. I'm going to get her."

When he pulled his cell phone from his pants' pocket, Lydia covered his hand. "Nicole doesn't want the police brought in, but I'd like you to come with me."

Sol opened his mouth in amazement. "Who's calling the shots here?"

Lydia ran to her closet and pulled out her favorite jeans instead of stepping back into her good silk trousers.

"Nicole is. I'm the babysitter and taxi service. Are you coming with me?"

"You're damn right I am!"

"Good! Then I hope you'll drive. My night vision isn't that great."

Sol dressed quickly in silence. Lydia knew he was pissed, but she squelched her automatic response to assuage his ego with an apology. She had nothing to apologize for. But one slipped out anyway.

"I'm sorry for the interruption," she said.

"Me, too," Sol said, and she felt somewhat better when he bussed her cheek.

She stepped into her loafers, and threw a sweater over her shoulders, her mind rushing ahead to Nicole, hoping she was all right. *She's fine! All we have to do is pick her up at the mall and bring her home to her distraught family.* Lydia told herself it was a good thing she didn't work on Mondays or she'd be calling in for another personal day. Some personal day! All these events had nothing to do with her personally.

"Damn!" she muttered aloud.

"What now?" Sol asked, strapping on his holster.

"Tomorrow I have to let them know if I'll take the position with Carrington Suites, and I haven't the foggiest idea what to do."

"What position with what Suites?"

Lydia's hand covered her gaping mouth. "Don't tell me I never mentioned it."

"No, you never mentioned it."

Sol strode through the front door and along the path to the driveway, clicking open the locks on his car as he went. Lydia climbed into the passenger seat, and he started the motor. As they exited Twin Lakes, she said, "To tell the truth, I've been too busy to give it much thought—which is why I haven't been able to give Tom Coltrane an answer. I still don't know what I'll say tomorrow night."

"You've been too busy playing Miss Marple."

"Excuse me?!" Lydia glared at his profile in the dim light.

"You heard me."

"I am not playing at anything," she said, fighting to keep a civil tone, wondering how they'd gotten to this point. "Gillian called me to help her sister."

"You should have told Gillian to call the police."

"I did, but Nicole doesn't want the police on the scene. I don't know why, but she must have a good reason."

Sol patted her knee. "You get off on this cops and robbers stuff, Lydia. Don't lie and say you don't."

"I—" She stopped. While she liked detecting and being in on the chase, her involvement always came about because of her relationships with people.

"You resent my connection to Daniel's family and friends, that they turn to me for old-fashioned friendship and comfort." She squirmed. "All right, I don't mind picking up a clue or two."

"Except there's no murder case now, Lydia. Daniel's murder's been solved. Case closed."

"If you say so."

They drove the rest of the way in silence, until Sol asked her to tell him the exact spot where Nicole would be waiting. They turned into the mall. Though many of the stores blazed with lights, they were all locked up for the night.

"What a place to have to wait for someone to pick you up," Lydia murmured.

Sol made no comment.

"There's the pizza parlor," Lydia pointed. "But I don't see Nicole."

He drove across parking spots, and swung around in front of the pizza parlor. "Where the hell did she go?" he muttered.

"I should have called Nicole to say we were on our way, though Gillian must have told her."

"She probably realized it wasn't smart to stand in front of a lighted store, which might give a passing rapist ideas. I'll drive slowly. Keep watch."

"I will," Lydia said, glad that Sol had come with her.

They drove from one end of the mall and back again. Sol frowned. "I'll check out back. If she's not there, I'm calling in the troops."

Lydia nodded. Her stomach felt queasy. Something terrible had happened to Nicole. Maybe Ringo had come after her, furious because she'd run off. Maybe he—but she shook her head before she could complete her thought.

They found her lying on her side in a fetal position beside an overflowing dumpster. Sol bent down to feel her pulse. Lydia cringed at the sight of blood oozing from the cruel blow to the side of her head.

"She's alive. Pulse weak," Sol said. He called for an ambulance while Lydia called Gillian to relate the bad news

.

Chapter Twenty-Two

All eyes were fixed on the young doctor conferring with Matt and Polly in the corner of the waiting room. After he left, Polly burst into tears and buried her face in Matt's chest.

Matt patted her back. "Pol, the doctor wants me to fill out forms and answer some questions. I'll return in five minutes."

"I need you here with me."

Gently, Matt disengaged himself. "Polly, honey, I promise to come back as soon as I can."

"Don't leave me!"

Matt cast a frantic eye around the room. Denise and Arnold responded as a team, positioning themselves on either side of Polly—*like parents walking their daughter down the aisle*, Lydia thought. They sat her down on a plastic seat between them, freeing Matt to take care of hospital paperwork.

"He says her vital signs are good, but she's still unconscious," Polly sobbed.

"Whoever did it struck her from the side," Matt said as he left the room.

"The way Evelyn was struck," Lydia murmured to Sol.

"Very possibly," he agreed, looking grim.

"Do they know who attacked Nicky?" Bennett asked.

"Like she can tell them," Gillian answered sarcastically. "Use your brains, Bennett. Nicole's been zonked and she's out for the count."

"Don't talk like that, Gillian!" her uncle ordered. "You're upsetting your mother."

"My poor baby," Polly moaned.

Daniel's three children and two of his grandchildren had come together on this Sunday night—united, for once, Lydia thought—by the brutal attack on Nicole. Polly must have called Denise, who must have asked Bennett to drive her to the hospital. Had one of Arnold's sisters implored him to keep vigil at a Long Island hospital close to midnight on a Sunday night? Or was he already on Long Island because he'd been the person who had attacked Nicole?

But for what reason? And how would Arnold know where to find Nicole when no one but Ringo had known her whereabouts for the past week?

A police officer entered the waiting room looking for Sol. They spoke in low tones and, strain as she might, Lydia couldn't make heads or tails of their conversation. When Sol returned, he took Gillian to the far end of the room to ask several questions. When he was done, he tapped Lydia on the shoulder. "Ready to go home?"

Lydia approached Polly, who was being comforted by Gillian. "I'm so sorry, Polly. Please call if I can do anything."

Polly grasped Lydia's hand. "I just want Nicole to be all right."

Denise, with whom Lydia hadn't exchanged one word, glared at Lydia and Sol as they left the room.

"Denise is angry at both of us," Lydia commented as they started down the long, florescent-lit corridor.

Sol let out a humorless laugh. "You, by association. She blames me for her boyfriend's murder, and was outraged when we questioned her regarding her father's homicide."

"There's no reason why Stefano would kill Daniel if Denise wasn't part of it."

"Not true, Lydia," he answered brusquely. "Tadic might have done it on his own, if he planned to marry Denise for her inheritance."

"Maybe Stefano didn't kill Daniel," Lydia said.

"Maybe he didn't."

She turned to stare at him. "Are you saying the case is still open? Which reminds me, I have to tell you something about Rochelle Holtstein."

"Rochelle Holtstein? Not her husband, Allen?"

"Well, maybe both of them, but Rochelle—"

Sol threw back his head and roared with laughter.

"What's so funny?" Lydia demanded.

"Your playing detective. Tossing out half-baked ideas based on intuition, with no evidence, no proof to back them up."

Then I won't tell you, if that's how you're going to be.

They walked the rest of the way in silence. When they reached Sol's car, he unlocked the doors and they slid into their seats.

"You're not going to tell me Rochelle Holtstein attacked Nicole tonight, are you?" he said.

"Of course not."

Sol turned on the ignition "Good! Because we've reason to believe the same person who struck Evelyn attacked Nicole."

"Nicole's boyfriend?"

"Could be. He's an addict. He could have gone after them for different reasons. Or maybe it was someone else. At any rate, I'm stationing an officer outside Nicole's hospital room. In case he comes back to finish the job."

Lydia thought a minute. "But Evelyn's valuables were found at Stefano's place. Do you think Ringo and Stefano were working together?"

"Maybe. Or could be the jewelry was planted."

Excited, she asked, "Does that mean you've opened the case again?"

He turned to face her. "You know, Lydia, that's precisely the kind of information I'm not at liberty to share—with you or anyone else."

"Oh!" Rebuffed, she clamped her lips shut, determined not to speak again for the rest of the drive home.

Sol said nothing to break the silence. To Lydia, the fifteen-minute trip seemed like an hour. Questions raged in her head, questions she longed to ask Sol but wouldn't. Were the cops looking for Ringo or did they have other suspects? And why was Sol suddenly acting so awful, refusing to tell her anything about the case? She was still smarting from the way he'd laughed at her when she'd mentioned Rochelle Holtstein, and hadn't let her finish her sentence. He had no right to be so—so condescending, especially when he didn't have all the answers.

He slowed down as they approached her house. Lydia leaped from the car in record time.

"Good night," she said.

"Good night."

So much for his concern about their relationship. She punched in her garage door code, wishing the sound of his car driving off didn't make her feel forlorn and sad.

Despite a restless night, Lydia awoke early the following morning. She ran a few washes and straightened up the kitchen cupboards, all the while debating her big decision.

Should she take the managerial position? She recognized the need for structure in her life. The fact that murder had cropped up in Twin Lakes for the second time in a year had to be a fluke. A rare coincidence. Her energy level required her to make the most of her administrative abilities and intellect, and take on a healthy amount of responsibility. She was perfectly suited for the position they were offering. After the initial hectic period, it would be a nine to five job, no weekends. She would have an assistant. Lydia grinned, thinking maybe she'd take Jessica with her. She doubted Jessica would leave Len, but she'd make the offer.

Or should she continue to work at Carrington House? It filled enough hours of the week, leaving her time to spend with her granddaughters, go out with friends, and sit by the pool during the summer months. She'd have that this summer, anyway, because construction on the Suites was just beginning. The rooms wouldn't be ready until the fall.

She still couldn't make up her mind, and was relieved that she didn't have to give her decision—at least for the present.

The day yawned before her. Lydia called the hospital to find out how Nicole was doing. When asked if she was a relative, she answered that she was an aunt, and received the information that Nicole was still unconscious.

"Damn," she muttered as she put down the phone. She waited until a quarter to nine to call Barbara. Her friend practically sang out her greeting.

"And how are you, Lydia dear?"

"I've been better." She told Barbara about Nicole.

"How awful! Who does Sol think did this?"

"He won't say. Only that the Nicole and Evelyn were probably attacked by the same person."

"But why? It doesn't make any sense."

"I've no idea, but I'm getting the feeling they're no longer certain that Stefano killed Daniel. Or if he acted alone. Nicole's boyfriend, Ringo, might be involved. I don't know anything. Sol's as quiet as a clam."

"Are you two fighting?"

"Of course, not! What makes you think that?"

"The way you spit out his name."

Lydia paused, then said, "Things are kind of cool between us. Gillian called last night and interrupted us at a delicate time. It infuriates him that I'm involved in what he considers his case. I can't help it if I'm friendly with Daniel's family."

"And that you insist on checking out facts for yourself."

"That, too," she admitted.

"Did you tell Sol about Rochelle Holtstein?"

"I started to, and he laughed at me."

"Lyddie, I'm sorry. What that woman told us could very well be a confession of murder."

"Or the Alzheimer's spinning a tale. Either way, it will have to wait. More importantly, I don't believe Stefano killed Daniel. And though Sol won't admit it, I doubt the police do, either. I have an idea who might be behind all this. Are you free today?"

Barbara sighed. "Sorry, I'm not. Andrew and I are going out east for lunch and a meandering kind of day. He's picking me up soon."

"I'm glad things are going well for you and Andrew. You deserve to be happy."

"Thanks, Lyddie. I wish things were better between you and Sol."

"So do I," Lydia said wryly. "Either they'll improve, or they'll come to an end. Talk to you later."

Next, Lydia dialed Ron's number. Bella answered and went to get her husband.

"Ron, do you think you and Mick could meet me in an hour?"

Ron sounded excited. "You have news, Lydia!"

"Kind of," she hedged, not wanting to go into everything.

"Great! I'll call Mick. Where shall we meet? The Starbucks on Main Street?"

"Why not? Can you be there at ten?"

"I'll call back if we can't make it."

Lydia arrived early and staked out a table at the far end of the room. When Ron and Mick walked in, avidly conversing as always, she felt a smile forming on her face. She'd grown very fond of the two old buzzards, and was grateful for their interest in finding the person who had murdered Daniel and attacked Evelyn and Nicole. As sure as she had two granddaughters,

Lydia knew the same assailant, who was still very much alive, had struck all three victims.

"What's up, Lydia?" Mick asked.

"I want to share some information with both of you and get your take on another."

"All right," Ron said. "What's everyone having?"

Once he had their orders straight, he wandered off to the counter. After Ron returned and they all had a chance to sip and to dunk at least one bite of biscotti, Lydia told them about the attack on Nicole.

"How awful!" Ron said. "I hope Nicole comes out of this without any brain damage."

"Does Sol think Nicole's boyfriend attacked her?" Mick asked.

Lydia looked from one earnest face to the other. "It might be him. To be perfectly honest, I doubt that Sol intends to tell me anything else about this case."

"That's too bad," Mick commiserated. "It sounds like you and your detective are having your ups and downs."

Lydia shrugged, not wanting to go into her personal life.

"I asked you to meet me because I don't think Stefano killed Daniel." She felt she was betraying Sol's confidentiality, but given his behavior she ignored the pang of guilt and went on. "When I told him Evelyn intended to come home in the next few days, he looked perturbed. I think the same person who struck Nicole also attacked Evelyn and killed Daniel."

Ron and Mick thought it over.

"I don't know," Mick finally said. "Both women were hit on the head and both of them survived. But Daniel was another story. That was planned and carried out."

"I think it's safe to assume the assailant's a man," Ron said. "Maybe this Ringo fellow. He sounds like a bad one."

"What about a relative?" Lydia paused, then continued. "Arnold showed up at the hospital last night. Interesting that he was on Long Island the same night his niece was attacked. For that matter, how did he know she'd been attacked and had been taken to the hospital?"

"That's easy enough," Ron said. "Weren't the police questioning Denise, assuming she was part of the plot to kill her father?"

"Yes. Sol and his team spent hours questioning Denise."

"Then it's only logical that Arnold came to give her moral support, and he happened to be on Long Island when Denise got the call that Nicole had been attacked."

Lydia nodded. "Then there's Bennett. Working where he does, he had access to digitalis. And probably to needles to inject the digitalis into the candy. And he could have struck Evelyn and his cousin."

Ron frowned. "Let's say the kid's capable of killing his own grandfather to get at his mother's inheritance, that he's willing to kill Evelyn when he realizes the money goes to her first. But why would he go after his cousin?"

A young couple sat down at the next table. Their conversation included a good deal of loud laughter. Lydia threw Mick and Ron a warning glance. The men finished up their coffee and pastries.

"The weather's great. Let's go for a walk," Mick suggested. The others followed him out of the coffee shop.

They made their way to the bench, where weeks earlier Ron had related the sad tale of Timmy John. *I must convince them to tell Sol how the poor boy died. It's the right thing to do—for Timmy John's memory and for the sake of any living relatives.*

Mick sank onto the bench as though he'd walked miles instead of half a block. He was exhausted, Lydia realized, and looking extremely pale. But his blue eyes gleamed with vitality.

"Where were we?" he asked, turning from Lydia to Ron.

"We were talking about Bennett," Lydia said, wrinkling her nose. "An unsavory character, from what I've seen and heard about him. He hated that his mother was dating Stefano."

"So Bennett killed Stefano, too?" Mick asked. "Come on, Lydia. That's a bit far-fetched."

She thought a bit. "Unless Bennett, Stefano, and Nicole's boyfriend were involved in drugs together."

"How can we find out?" Ron asked.

Mick frowned. "I doubt I can find out that kind of information. Too bad your boyfriend shut you out of the loop, Lydia."

Too bad is right.

They tossed around a few more possibilities, but nothing worth pursuing.

"I could offer Denise condolences for Stefano's death, and throw in a few questions about his dealing drugs," Lydia said. "Of course she'll lie, but I'll get a sense of whether or not she or Bennett are involved."

Mick glared at her. "Don't you dare go anywhere near Denise. If she has a hand in all this, she'll know you're on to her."

"And tell Bennett. He'll come after you in a flash," Ron added.

Lydia shrugged, feeling foolish. "I suppose that's it then. Thanks for meeting me."

"Our pleasure," Mick said, struggling to his feet.

They stood outside Starbucks before heading for their cars.

"Let's face it, we're fresh out of ideas," Ron said, sounding morose. "We'll leave the investigating to the police, since there's nothing more we can do."

Lydia nodded in agreement and kissed them good-bye.

Chapter Twenty-Three

For the first time in as long as she could remember, Lydia had nothing to do. Time spread before her like the blank screen of a computer. After ten minutes of driving aimlessly around, she decided to head for Carrington House to offer Len and Jessica a few hours of her time. As she wended her way along the narrow road leading to the mansion, she had an impulse to look over the site where the Suites were to be constructed.

She cut to the right, onto the rutted path, and decided to go the rest of the way on foot. The area had been cleared of trees and underbrush, and a dozer was leveling the land. Lydia imagined the two Victorian-style houses to be built, each containing twelve suites, with a manmade pond between them.

"As artificial as our two lakes," she murmured. But the results would be beautiful: restful rooms amid a bucolic setting. Nothing to scoff at. On the contrary, she had a healthy admiration for elegant playgrounds and vacation havens for the wealthy. They deserved it, she figured, after working hard to earn their money. While most of the people who stayed at the Suites would be attending weddings and bar mitzvahs at Carrington House, the company hoped to also lure guests yearning for a pampered escape from home. There were plans to build tennis courts and a swimming pool. Arrangements would be made for anyone opting for a game of golf at one of the local courses.

If she took the position, she'd have a big say in choosing the décor of the suites. That would be fun, Lydia thought. And a hell of a lot more interesting than picking out furniture for Twin Lakes' new clubhouse.

She entered Len's office and nearly laughed when he stared up at her bug-eyed. "Lydia, what are you doing here on a Monday?"

She shrugged. "I had some spare time, so I came by to see if you wanted me to put in some hours."

He grinned. "I can always use extra Lydia-hours."

It turned out he had a situation that required immediate attention. A wedding scheduled for Saturday had to be postponed because the bride was in the hospital with pneumonia. Her mother called early that morning from New Hampshire, pleading with Jessica to notify the guests, the photographer, and the orchestra, as she knew nothing about the arrangements and wasn't on speaking terms with the groom and his family or the maid of honor. Jessica tried to explain that notifying all those people wasn't the responsibility of Carrington House, but after announcing she wouldn't be paying for the affair and shouting out the maid of honor's phone number, the woman hung up.

"What did the maid of honor say?"

"That she and the groom had discovered they were mad for each other and were going away for the weekend." Len handed her sheets of paper. "She faxed us the guest list, the numbers of the photographer and the orchestra, and said if we didn't call, nobody would."

"Nice friend," Lydia said.

Jessica popped in, a wide grin on her face. "Rosalinda's terrific. I explain something to her once, and she's got it down in her head. As soon as I'm done going over the basics, we'll help with the guest list."

"All three hundred of them," Lydia said, scanning the sheets of names.

"And they'd rented the biggest two rooms," Len said sadly.

Jessica winked at him. "You forgot to tell Lydia the smaller of the two rooms has been rented for Saturday night."

"Len likes us to feel sorry for him," Lydia tossed over her shoulder as she exited his office. "He thinks we won't work hard if anything positive happens."

She spent the next few hours working her way down the guest list, informing everyone she called that the wedding had been canceled. More than half of the people weren't home, so she left the messages on tape, glad that she didn't have to offer the pneumonia story and feign ignorance of a future wedding date. At one o'clock, Jessica stuck her head in the door and asked if Lydia wanted to go out for lunch with her and Rosalinda. Lydia asked her to bring back a tuna fish sandwich, then called the hospital to inquire about Nicole's condition. She was still unconscious, a nurse informed her. Lydia thanked her and hung up. She called home to pick up phone messages. No one had called.

Damn him! She slammed down the phone. Was Sol angry because their lovemaking had been interrupted, or because she'd gotten involved in his case? Was he afraid she was going to find Daniel's murderer before he did? Fat chance. She had no idea if the guilty party was Arnold, Denise, Ringo, or Bennett. Or any combination of the above.

Jessica and Rosalinda returned from lunch chatting like old friends.

"We'll help you call the rest of the wedding guests," Jessica said.

Lydia handed them each a list of names. She was pleased that Rosalinda accepted hers with a smile of good humor. No doubt about it, Jessica had found the perfect office worker.

She left Carrington House at four-thirty and, still reluctant to go home, drove to her daughter's house.

"Grammy!" Brittany and little Greta shouted in welcome when their mother opened the front door.

"Mom, what are you doing here?" Meredith asked while her daughters hugged Lydia.

"I haven't seen you guys in such a long time," Lydia explained. She noticed the car keys in Meredith's hand. "Are you going out?"

"Actually, we are. I have a few errands to run, then we're meeting friends for pizza." She paused. "Want to come along?"

"I'd love to. That is, if it won't be any trouble."

Meredith grinned. "Are you kidding? I can always use another pair of hands."

Lydia climbed into the passenger seat of her daughter's car, taking pleasure in the ongoing banter between Meredith and the girls. Despite her hectic life now that she was teaching again,

Meredith seemed relaxed as she listed the four stops they were about to make, and told Brittany no, they couldn't stop for ice cream on the way.

The small hand shaking Lydia's shoulder made her flinch.

"Grammy, you didn't answer me!"

"Sorry, Greta." Lydia turned around to her three-year-old granddaughter.

"I want to know when I can play mini-a-ture golf," Greta repeated.

"In a few weeks, sweetie. Just as soon as they put down the sod."

"Greta's too young to play miniature golf," Brittany said. "Isn't she, Grammy?"

"I am not!"

"Are, too."

"Brittany!" Meredith warned. "Stop tormenting your sister."

"I'm not tormenting her. I'm telling her the truth."

Tears welled up in Greta's grey eyes. "I can so play. Grammy said."

"Yes, I did," Lydia said, wondering why Brittany, usually so patient with her younger sister, was acting this way.

Meredith pulled over to the side of the road. She unhooked her seat belt and turned to face her daughters. "If I hear another word from either of you, we come straight home from errands and I make you scrambled eggs for dinner."

"I don't—" Brittany began, then covered her mouth. "Sorry."

Silence reigned as Meredith pulled back into traffic, and they continued on their way.

"I'm impressed," Lydia murmured.

"They know I mean it," Meredith answered, but from her smile Lydia knew the praise had pleased her. "What's new, Mom?"

Lydia glanced back at Brittany and Greta, who were now engrossed in a silly game, their past spat forgotten. In low tones, Lydia told her about Nicole. "She still hasn't regained consciousness. I hope there's no brain damage."

Merry shook her head. "I'm so sorry. Poor Polly's been through so much this past month. Do the police have any idea who attacked Nicole?"

"Maybe her boyfriend."

"He looked pretty scruffy to me." She glanced over at her mother. "Well, at least they've caught Daniel's murderer."

If only they had, Lydia thought, not wanting to upset Meredith.

Dashing from the cleaners to the supermarket, then eating dinner with four active little girls and their mothers in a noisy pizza parlor gave Lydia no opportunity to worry about Nicole, or to dwell on the unraveling of her relationship with Sol Molina. The one time her mind drifted, two small hands fixed on either side of her face.

"Isn't that right, Grammy?" Greta demanded.

"Absolutely!" she agreed, and was rewarded with a garlicky hug.

Meredith, often moody in the past, exhibited good parenting and good humor throughout dinner. She allowed the girls to sit with their friends in a separate booth, and to order another soda—something she didn't bring into the house—but stopped them from table-hopping with friends at the far end of the restaurant. When she realized Lydia was growing tired and wanted to leave, Merry brought the outing to an end.

To Lydia's further surprise, neither Brittany nor Greta made a fuss about having to leave their friends. They simply put on their sweaters, said their good-byes, and walked out to the car ahead of their mother and grandmother.

"You've done a wonderful job with the girls," Lydia said.

Meredith beamed with pride. "Thanks, Mom. Somehow it works better for me when I'm teaching."

"Does it now?" Lydia asked, half teasing, half chiding because Meredith had resisted returning to her job.

Instead of taking offense as she would have months earlier, Meredith hugged Lydia. "I'm glad you came out with us tonight."

"I am, too," Lydia agreed.

She drove home in the twilight, feeling her fatigue slipping away and being replaced by the worst case of the fidgets she'd had in years. It was seven o'clock, and she hadn't the slightest desire to go home to an empty house. What for? To watch TV and hope that Sol would call?

The balmy early summer breeze drifted into her open window, stirring up memories of June evenings when she and Izzy had first met. A yearning for something romantic or exotic overcame her, and for a moment she debated driving the long trek into Manhattan.

Instead, she settled on watching a foreign film in Huntington, forty minutes away. Lydia rarely went to the movies alone, but she felt at home in the art theatre, with its cozy snack bar and three auditoriums. The movie she chose, an edgy German film, came on shortly after she arrived. Close to twenty people made up the audience, many of them singletons like her. *See*, she told herself as though she were lecturing a recalcitrant child, *plenty of people go to the movies alone.* Though she enjoyed the film, she would have preferred to go with someone to discuss the story afterwards. But Barbara was out somewhere with Andrew. And Sol? God knew what Sol was up to.

As she drove home, she told herself she had no reason to feel gloomy and sad. She was a woman of means, with a lovely home and a possible new job in the wings. She had two wonderful daughters—both married—and two lovely granddaughters. She had friends, and she enjoyed good health. True, her significant romantic relationship—if that still existed—was problematic. Her lover was sexy, virile, and exciting. He was also pigheaded, macho, and resentful of what he considered her interference in his work.

Lydia felt a stab of guilt as she thought of Nicole lying unconscious in a hospital bed. She'd been so intent on filling up her day, she hadn't bothered to check on the poor girl's condition.

She'd remedy that right now! The hospital was no more than a ten-minute ride from her present location. Lydia glanced at the clock on the dashboard. Nine thirty-five. Visiting hours were probably over. If that was the case, at least she could find out how Nicole was doing.

Chapter Twenty-Four

Lydia stopped at a supermarket to buy a basket of flowers and a "get well" card. She scribbled a note wishing Nicole a quick recovery as she waited to pay the cashier. That accomplished, she climbed back into her car and headed for the hospital.

The central hall was dimly lit, with only a handful of visitors mulling around. The rest appeared to be leaving. Visiting hours must be over. From years of experience, Lydia knew no one was likely to stop her if she walked briskly past the hospitality desk on her way to the bank of elevators. She remembered that Nicole was on the sixth floor. What was her room number? Six twenty-two! Down the right-hand corridor, on the left-hand side.

She was in luck. The one nurse manning the circular nurses' station was facing the other way as she laughed at whatever her telephone friend was saying. Lydia stepped adroitly out of the path of the middle-aged couple exiting a room, their heads turned back to the patient whom they were reassuring looked marvelous and would be up and about in no time.

She glanced into the rooms as she passed. Some of the patients were already asleep. In one room, a nurse was adjusting a patient's bedding. Lydia hurried past, not wanting to be stopped.

Nicole's room was at the far end of the corridor. Unlike the other rooms, the door was shut, and an empty chair was placed beside it. Lydia turned the handle and peered inside. The patient in the bed closest to the door was snoring, no doubt in a medically induced deep sleep. She tiptoed into the room and stopped at the curtain drawn around the other bed—Nicole's bed. The hairs on the back of her neck rose. Something was terribly wrong.

Over the humming of monitoring machines came the rasping sound of someone struggling to breathe. Lydia ripped aside the curtain and gasped. On the far side of the bed, Bennett was yanking a tube from Nicole's mouth.

"Stop that! What do you think you're doing?"

Bennett disappeared from view. Lydia turned to run. She had to get the hell out of there to save Nicole and herself.

She grabbed the door handle, about to shout for help, when a hand clapped over her mouth.

"Shut up, you interfering bitch!"

Bennett's other hand gripped her upper arm. Lydia tried to elbow him in the gut and was rewarded with a knee to the kidneys.

"Ouch!"

"Keep your mouth shut and do as you're told. We're taking the stairs once the coast is clear."

He opened the door wide enough to peer into the corridor, then pushed her toward the door under the Exit sign. Lydia balked and was rewarded with a punch to the ribs.

"Stop that!" she mumbled into his hand.

"Don't give me a hard time, or I'll kill you right here."

Her mind churned as they struggled down the steps. Bennett was strong and almost half her age, but if he had no weapon, she'd better make a run for it—the sooner the better.

She must have paused, giving him a sense of what she was thinking, because he shoved her hard against the wall. Lydia straightened up, ignoring the pain in her side, and descended as slowly as she dared.

They walked down one flight and then another. "Why were you trying to kill Nicole?" she asked now that his hand no longer covered her mouth.

"Shut up! I have a knife and I won't hesitate to use it."

"I don't believe you!" Whatever had possessed her to say that?

"Oh, yeah?" His laugh sent chills down her back. "Want to see it?"

Lydia shivered. "You didn't use it on Nicole."

"Of course not!" Bennett sounded offended. "She's my cousin."

"Then why were you pulling out her tubes?"

They reached a landing. Lydia couldn't suppress a tremor as they started down what she figured was the last set of stairs before the parking lot.

"I'll never figure why Nicky took up with that creep. I send some business Ringo's way, but he's not fit to clean her shoes. Anyway, I had to take care of something and Nicky saw it go down. She went crazy. I can't trust her to keep her mouth shut."

Lydia's voice quivered. "And so you tried to kill her?"

"She's done for. She can't make it without oxygen. I managed to pull that before you stuck your nose in."

"Oh, no!" Lydia moaned, earning herself another poke in the ribs. "But the cops had someone guarding the door."

He laughed. "Even cops have to pee."

They'd reached the short hallway that led to the parking area. Lydia looked around the dim florescent-lit hallway. Shadows played on the vomit-green walls. Their footsteps sounded hollow in the emptiness. Where was everyone? Sure, it was after visiting hours, but this was a hospital, for God's sake.

Bennett opened the door, and demanded to know where she'd parked her car.

Lydia didn't answer. If she was going to run, it had to be now. Once he got her inside her car, it was only a matter of time before he killed her.

"See this?" He reached inside his baseball jacket and pulled out a hunting knife in a leather sheath. "In case you think I'm lying. Now, for the second and last time—where did you park your car?"

Trembling, she pointed. "Two aisles over."

"Good girl." He patted her shoulder. "We'll get in your car and you'll drive where I tell you. Won't you?"

Lydia nodded.

"Move!"

She tried to obey, but her limbs remained rooted to the spot.

He prodded her. "Go on!"

Reluctantly, she set one foot in front of the other until she reached her car. Her mind clanged with fear and the frustration that she had no escape plan. Every move she made brought her closer to death.

Lydia pressed the remote button that unlocked the car doors. Her fingers shook so badly she had difficulty inserting the key into the ignition.

He pointed. "Exit over there."

She did as he instructed, her mind churning furiously, seeking a way to escape with her life. She waited at the red light as cars sped past on either side of the four-lane road.

"Turn left and head for Robinson Avenue."

"Where are we going?"

"You ask too many damn questions."

He couldn't hurt her while she was driving. The thought emboldened her. "What do you plan to do with me?"

Bennett eyed her thoughtfully. "That depends on your cooperation. Now I want you to pick someone up."

He turned on the radio and started pushing buttons. The opening bars of a popular song filled the car. Lydia gave a start, and the car swerved into the right lane. Bennett reached out to steady the steering wheel and set the car back on its course.

"What the hell are you doing? You'll get us killed." He switched off the radio and took out his cell phone. "Hi," he said, his voice neutral.

He listened a minute, then said, "Sorry I'm late. I ran into something. Wait for me outside. I'm in a hurry."

Lydia heard what sounded like someone complaining, though she couldn't make out any words. Bennett frowned. "It's not cold. For once, just do as I ask, okay?"

The person on the other end continued. Bennett shifted the phone to his other ear. "I love you, too. Bye, Mom. Gotta go."

Mom? "That was your mother!" Lydia yelped. "You mean to tell me Denise is involved in all this?"

"All what?"

"Killing her own father. And Stefano."

Too late, she realized her mistake. She nearly lost control of the wheel again, when he stuck his face close to hers. "My mother had nothing to do with anything. You got that? And when we pick her up, you keep your mouth shut." He grinned maniacally, and she forced herself not to wrinkle her nose at the foul odor of his breath. "One word about Nicole or anyone else and I'll slice you up like London broil. You'll be begging me to put you out of your misery."

Lydia nodded. She was certain Bennett intended to kill her as soon as he had the opportunity. But if he didn't want Denise to know what he was up to, she was safe for the next ten minutes. She'd risk asking questions. The more she knew, the better equipped she'd be.

"If your mother's not involved, why am I picking her up?"

"Why not?" he asked belligerently.

"It's kind of strange, don't you think?"

"I'll tell her you were visiting Nicky. There's no problem—as long as you remember what I said and keep your mouth shut."

"All right." Lydia stopped at a red light, figuring he had no intention of answering her question.

A minute later, he surprised her. "My mom and I always look after each other. I drove her to an AA meeting and it's over. Ended ten minutes ago."

"Oh," she said, though his words made her skin crawl. He'd planned to kill Nicole and then drive Denise home from her meeting all along. He had the sensitivity of a snake. Lydia drew a deep breath, and asked, "Does she know you killed Daniel and Stefano?"

Bennett shrugged. "She'd never ask, and I'd never tell her, but sometimes she looks at me in a way that makes me think she suspects." He gave a little laugh. "Not that it matters. In the end, she forgives whatever I do."

A wave of desolation engulfed Lydia. She could expect no help from Denise. She forced herself to speak calmly and not reveal her desperation. "That must be wonderful, having a parent who accepts whatever you do."

"It's great."

The light changed, and Lydia drove slowly on. She drew a breath, then asked, "But why did you kill your grandfather? And strike Evelyn? And Nicole?"

His laugh was harsh. "Why do you think? The old man was a rich son-of-a-bitch, but he never gave my mother enough money for us to live on. He deserved to die. And Evelyn stood in the way of my mother's rightful inheritance. Still does, for that matter."

Lydia shivered to think of his trying to hurt Evelyn again. She had to get free. "What did Stefano have to do with any of that?"

Bennett scowled. "We had some business together, and he thought he could short me."

"You didn't like him going out with your mother."

"You're damn right about that! She's too good for him. I finished him off just as Nicky came by his place for some smack. I told Ringo to stay with her until she calmed down and saw reason, but she took off. Turn left here!"

Lydia drove past car repair shops locked up for the night and stopped before the small brown church, a light bulb shining over the front door. Beyond the parking lot, which appeared to be empty, were three houses. There was no sign of Denise. Bennett swore as he stuck his head out the window.

"Damn it, I told her to wait for me outside. Honk the horn, will you?"

Lydia pressed down and released a blast of noise until Bennett yanked her hand away. "What the hell do you think you're doing?" He slapped her head.

Denise, dressed in a short-sleeved blouse and pants, ran hugging herself against the evening chill.

"I told her to bring a sweater," he muttered, then he stuck his head out the window again. "Hey, Mom! Get in the back seat."

Denise looked at him. "Where's your car?"

"I had a bit of trouble and ran into Lydia. She's giving us a lift."

Denise peered into the car and offered Lydia a smile. "Hi, Lydia. Thanks for the ride."

Lydia made no response, but Denise didn't seem to notice. She climbed into the back seat, chattering about her meeting, how everyone had to rush home and felt bad about leaving her on her own.

"But I told them you'd be along any minute, and here you are," she said brightly, lighting up a cigarette.

"Please don't smoke in the car," Lydia said.

Bennett glared at her but said nothing. Denise quickly extinguished her cigarette in the ashtray.

"I keep forgetting how most people can't stand smoke, when, for me, it's the lesser of two evils." She giggled. "Three, actually."

"Where to?" Lydia asked.

"Drive my mother home." Bennett reeled off the address.

Lydia crawled down the block, stalling for time. In the rearview window she watched Denise stretch her arms overhead and yawn. "I'd say let's go out for a bite to eat, but I'm exhausted. Tonight we talked about facing the bald truths in our lives." She sighed. "It was heavy going."

Having a bite with Bennett and Denise was the last thing Lydia wanted to do. No, next to the last thing. Mother and son began discussing the AA meeting. Lydia felt as though she were an actress in a bizarre movie. Bizarre or not, she cleared her throat, about to change the subject of the conversation.

"Denise," she began.

"Yes, Lydia."

"Do you know what Bennett was doing when I met him in the hospital?"

"The hospital? Oh, you went to visit Nicky. That was sweet, Bennett."

"Shut up, Lydia!"

Lydia looked at Bennett. "Your son was pulling out Nicole's tubes. She's probably dead right now, as dead as your father and Stefano. Bennett killed them all."

A wail rose from the back seat. "Benny, how could you?"

"Mom, don't listen to her! She's making it up."

"Tell her how you killed Daniel for her inheritance and Stefano for drug-related business."

"It's a lie!"

Denise's sobs filled the car. "You swore to me you changed."

"I did, Mom. I swear to you, I did! Only—"

Denise appeared not to have heard him. "You promised to lead a respectable life. Instead, you murdered the people I love."

"Mom—"

"When Stefano said someone took his truck that morning, I figured it was you. Who else knew where he was? Where to find his keys? I drank to stop myself from working out the rest, but I knew. I knew! The police had the right idea, only I told them they were crazy. My Benny would never murder his grandfather or the man I loved. Oh, Benny, how could you?"

Bennett turned to face Denise, his tone seductive. "I did it for you, Mom. So we can have a good life together, the one we always planned."

Denise's laughter was a hideous sound. "Is that what you tell yourself?"

"You promised we'd stand by each other, no matter what."

"I talked about you tonight, Benny. I told the group how you threw that line back in my face again and again—so I'd accept things I knew were wrong."

"You shouldn't have talked about me, Mom." Bennett sounded scared.

"You were a terrified seven-year-old when I said those words to you. Your father had just slammed out of the house, taking my last twenty dollars, leaving us six months behind in the rent."

They were caught up in their past, oblivious to Lydia. More vehicles joined the flow of traffic as they approached the main street of a town. Lydia slowed down. Time to unbuckle her seat belt and exit the car. Bennett wasn't wearing his, she noticed.

"Haven't I taken care of you?" Bennett demanded. "Got you what you needed?"

Denise's tone turned derisive. "Such a devoted son. You were the only kid who supported his mother's habit. Well, I'm clean now and I don't need your 'help.'"

"Mom—"

"You killed my father for the money and tried to do the same to Evelyn. Why Stefano? And why poor Nicky? What did she ever do?"

"It turned out to be necessary."

"Necessary? You're a monster, Bennett! I gave birth to an unspeakable monster!"

Bennett's voice rose like that of a child's. "You don't mean that, Mommy. Tell me you don't mean it!"

Denise sniffed. "But I do."

Bennett rounded on Lydia, shoving his bugged-eyed face into her line of vision. "I told you to keep your mouth shut, but you didn't listen. You'll pay for turning my mother against me! Starting now!"

He pulled the knife from his jacket and pressed it against her throat. Denise screamed. Lydia gasped. Terror surged through her body. But his accusation that she was to blame for his mother's rejection rankled enough for her to retort, "It's your doing, Bennett."

Venting spurred her on. She accelerated and passed the car in front of her, earning an angry honk from the driver.

"Hey!" Bennett shouted. "Slow down!" He lowered the knife.

Denise leaned over the front seat and thrust her hand between Lydia and Bennett. "Give me that!" she demanded.

"I will not. Sit back and be quiet!"

Hope blossomed in Lydia's breast, now that she had Denise's sympathy. She turned to her. "Your son's planning to kill me, aren't you, Bennett?"

"The sooner the better."

Not while I'm moving, you won't! Lydia maneuvered the Lexus into the gap between two cars in the left lane. A horn blasted. Her only chance was to continuously change lanes and keep Bennett off balance.

"Turn right here!"

Lydia swerved back into the right-hand lane but passed the turn.

"Damn it, I said to turn!"

She drove faster than usual and feared she was losing control. But she still wore her seat belt, and had a better chance of surviving a car crash than a stabbing.

"Bitch!" he shouted. Lydia blinked as the point of the knife waved inches from her right eye.

"Are you crazy?" Denise screamed. "Put down the knife!"

"Keep out of this, Mom! Lydia, make a U-turn and go where I tell you to go, or I'll kill you here and now!"

Lydia felt a sting on her upper arm. She glanced over and saw blood dripping onto the seat.

"Benny, don't hurt her!" Denise reached over the front seat to shove his hand away.

"I'll show her!"

Bennett held the blade against her neck. He meant to wreak serious harm! Lydia floored the accelerator and veered into the left lane. Back into the right lane. The car shook, thrusting him against the passenger door. She had to keep moving! Without slowing down, she waited till a pickup truck passed on her left, then darted behind it.

From the corner of her eye, she watched Bennett draw back his arm, the knife gripped in his fist. She shuddered, dreading what was coming.

"Don't!" Denise threw herself forward, jamming into the space between the front bucket seats as her son struck.

A dreadful cry filled the car. Bennett began to wail. Lydia glanced at the body slumped beside her, separating her from Bennett.

"Mommy, get up! I know you can if you try."

Lydia moaned as Denise's arm fell against her. She feared the woman was dead, but she was afraid to stop driving. Bennett would kill her once she stopped. Her foot felt glued to the gas pedal as she pumped harder and harder. She shot through a red light. A siren sounded in the distance. Lydia turned her head, past the hump that was Bennett rubbing his mother's back and saw red lights flashing.

The police!

She drew in a jagged breath as she lifted her foot from the accelerator and eased over to the side of the road.

Chapter Twenty-Five

Lydia and Sol stepped out into the evening air. She locked her front door and offered him a half smile.

"Are you sure you're up to a dinner party?" he asked.

"Of course, I am!" she said with more enthusiasm than she felt. "It's been almost three weeks since that ride from hell."

Because his hands were laden with packages, he gestured at the garage with his chin. "Have you driven your new car yet?"

"No, but I'm driving to the library tomorrow. Barbara said she'll come with me."

"Good idea."

She squeezed his arm. "Thanks for not pointing out that this was the second time a car of mine to be involved in a murder."

He bent over to kiss her temple. "Not your fault."

They'd walked five yards when Lydia suddenly stopped. "Oh, my God, I forgot the wine!"

"One bottle of chardonnay," Sol said, holding it up.

She glanced down at the plastic bag in her hand. "I have the strawberries."

"I've got the ice cream. One gallon of chocolate peanut butter."

"And freshly whipped cream," Lydia said as they crossed the road. "Evelyn's going to kill us when she sees everything we're bringing. She called twice this afternoon to say she has everything under control."

Sol gave her a pained look. "Lydia, I wish you wouldn't use that expression."

"'Under control?'" she asked in feigned innocence as they started up Evelyn's driveway.

"I mean 'going to kill us.'"

Lydia pressed the bell. "What's the problem? Daniel's murderer's in custody. Everything's under control." She cast him a dirty look. "For real this time."

Sol groaned. "I said another drug dealer killed Stefano. That much was true."

"You also insisted you were satisfied that Stefano killed Daniel. Case closed."

He sighed, exasperated. "For the fourth time, I admit that I lied. I couldn't let you in on the fact that we were closing in on Bennett, now could I?"

"Sorry," she whispered, and reached up to kiss his cheek. She didn't mean to be argumentative tonight, the first time Sol would be attending a party with her friends.

Evelyn greeted them in a chef's apron. She kissed them both then started to scold. "Why did you bring all this? I've enough food for an army."

Lydia followed her into the kitchen, drinking in the aroma of baked chicken and mushrooms. Evelyn stored the whipped cream, wine, and strawberries in the refrigerator and the ice cream in the freezer. Then she turned to give Lydia her full attention.

"How are you, my dear?"

Feeling Evelyn's keen eyes studying her, Lydia opted for the truth.

"I'm okay most of the time, though I get these bouts of nerves. The worst is when I wake up in the middle of the night, my heart pounding so hard I'm afraid it will burst out of my chest."

Evelyn rubbed her arm. "It will pass."

"The table looks lovely," Lydia said, admiring the fine china and crystal settings in the dining room.

"We'll be nine," Evelyn said. "Polly and Matt might stop by for dessert."

"How's Nicky doing?" Lydia asked.

"She's alert and beginning to speak. Asking lots of questions, which the doctor says is a good sign."

"Thank God! I was so afraid he'd succeeded."

"I know. Good thing the nurse heard the scuffle and came in immediately to reconnect the tubes."

"And had the sense to dial 911." Suddenly dizzy, Lydia leaned against the wall. She was grateful when Sol appeared and wrapped an arm around her waist.

"I'm fine," she insisted, but didn't resist when he walked her into the living room, where he set her down on the sofa as carefully as if she were a porcelain doll. *I'm fine.* She took a deep breath as she sank back against the cushion. Her harrowing ride with Bennett had knocked the stuffing out of her, and there were moments when she wasn't quite herself. The doctor said they would pass. She certainly hoped so, as she intended to return to work on Tuesday.

The doorbell rang, and Evelyn went to welcome Ron, Bella, Mick, and his wife. Hearing a woman's Irish lilt among the voices, it occurred to Lydia that she'd yet to meet Mrs. Diminio.

The sight of Mick in a wheelchair brought the sting of tears to her eyes. She blinked them away as he wheeled toward her, a broad smile on his pale face. Lydia kissed his cheek. Mick gave her the once over.

"You're feeling better these days." It was a statement, not a question.

"I am."

Mick winked. "I must say, Ms. Krause, you look absolutely fetching tonight." He cast Sol a meaningful glance. "I hope your lad appreciates all of your attributes."

"Let's say I appreciate most of them," Sol said.

Mick reached out, and his wife took his hand. She was petite and birdlike, with white hair and bright blue eyes that lit up her face. "This is my Caitlin," he said. "Caitlin, meet Lydia and her swain, Sol Molina. Detective Lieutenant Molina."

Caitlin offered Lydia an impish smile. "I finally get to meet Mick's Wonder Woman."

Wonder Woman! Lydia blushed at the compliment as Caitlin extended her hand to Sol. "And it's a pleasure meeting you, too, lieutenant."

"My pleasure," Sol said.

He and Caitlin drifted away as Ron approached. He patted Mick's back and enveloped Lydia in a hug, then sat down beside her.

"Feeling better?"

"Much."

"Glad to hear it."

Lydia glanced from Ron to Mick. They were bursting with news. "Okay. Spill it."

Mick said, "Tell her, Ronnie."

Ron cleared his throat. "Mick and I took a ride down to the police station and told them our tale. We got a tongue lashing, and then the captain disappeared. He was gone for a good half an hour. We were worried. Pictured ourselves behind bars. But it looks like we're getting off."

"With a slap on the wrist," Mick said. "For the sake of a dying legislator."

"An eighty-five-year-old legislator who served his county well," Ron added, not missing a beat.

Mick wanted no sympathy, and not turning soppy was the least Lydia could do for her friend. "Does Sol know?"

"Of course," Ron said. "We had our little chat three days ago. Station house news spreads even faster than it does in Twin Lakes."

"Sol never mentioned it," Lydia murmured.

"Better that he doesn't," Mick offered. "And don't bring it up, or he might ask some questions you won't care to answer."

The doorbell rang. Ron turned around and whispered, "It's Allen and Rochelle."

Mick tugged her arm. Lydia leaned toward him so he could whisper in her ear. "Turns out he didn't kill his boss. The police figured it was the guy's estranged wife and her boyfriend who did the deed, but they didn't have enough evidence to go to trial."

"I'm glad Allen didn't do it," she whispered back. "Or Rochelle."

As though by tacit agreement, they separated and moved in three different directions as the others came into the living room. Lydia greeted Bella, Allen, and Rochelle, then linked arms with Sol.

"Your debriefing session finished?" he asked as he kissed her cheek.

She nodded, feeling her ears burn. *He knows everything and has chosen to be amused instead of angry.*

Evelyn called them to the dining room, and they took their places around the elegantly set table. There was little conversation as her guests served themselves from the two enormous salad bowls and proceeded to eat their first course.

Rochelle turned to Sol. "Did you know all along that Bennett was the person you were after?"

Lydia cringed. She'd brought Sol into a social situation where people felt free to ask him about the murders, but he seemed unperturbed by the question.

"We had our suspicions from the start. Bennett had a record for dealing drugs. At work, he had access to legal drugs."

"Did he kill Stefano for dating his mother?" Mick asked.

"We can't factor that out. Denise and Bennett had one weird relationship. Also, we figured Stefano was killed by the guy he worked for, and that turned out to be Bennett." Sol looked at Lydia. "Bennett took Stefano's red pickup truck the morning you drove Evelyn to the airport. It was his way of showing Stefano that he could have him thrown into jail if he wanted, and he'd better stop stealing from him. Stefano ignored the warning, so Bennett killed him."

Evelyn sighed. "It would have pained Daniel so to know the depth of his grandson's depravity."

For a moment, silence reigned. Determined to change the subject, Lydia said, "I've a bit of news I'd like to share with you." She waited until everyone's attention was focused on her, then said, "I've decided to take the position of executive manager of the Carrington House Suites."

Cries of congratulations filled the room. Ron raised his glass. "To Lydia. A woman of the twenty-first century."

"I'll drink to that," Sol seconded, and downed the rest of his wine.

Later, as they walked back to her place, Sol asked, "Does this mean you'll be working nine to five, five days a week?"

Lydia shook her head. "Only at first. I made it clear I'd set everything up, hire the right people, then step back and make it a part-time job."

"I hope you can get some time off this summer."

Lydia looked at him. In the darkness, she couldn't read his expression. "I suppose that can be arranged. Why do you ask?"

"I thought we'd take a trip somewhere."

Lydia stared at him. "Really?"

"Really. Time rushes by and I don't want to waste any of it."

Lydia grinned. "That doesn't sound like 'let's-go-slow Moli na.'"

He grabbed her and held her close. "The fear of losing you shoved the other fear out the window." He stepped back to gaze into her eyes. "Besides, I need a break from work." He took her in his arms again and kissed her, slowly and deliberately.

When she could speak, Lydia said, "Let's go to a place where people are kind to each other, and homicide is something they read about in books."

CHECK OUT THESE OTHER GREAT READS FROM ROWAN PROSE

A former Spanish teacher, Marilyn Levinson writes mysteries, romantic suspense, and novels for young readers. Her Golden Age of Mystery Book Club series was a King Rivers Life Magazine's "Best of 2014," and on Book Town's 2014 Summer Mystery Reading List. She's an Agatha nominee, a Library Journal "Pick of the Month," on Goodreads's list of the 200 "Most Popular Books Published in 2017," a Suspense Magazine Best Indie, and was on Book Town's Summer (and) Fall Reading Lists. She also writes under Allison Brook. Marilyn loves traveling, reading, knitting, doing Sudoku, and visiting with her grandchildren. She is co-founder and past president of the Long Island chapter of Sisters in Crime. She resides in New York with her family. www.marilynlevinson.com